Emergency Contact

MARY H.K. CHOI

SIMON & SCHUSTER BFYR

NEW YORK   LONDON   TORONTO   SYDNEY   NEW DELHI

SIMON & SCHUSTER BFYR

An imprint of Simon & Schuster Children's Publishing Division
1230 Avenue of the Americas, New York, New York 10020

For information about special discounts for bulk purchases, please
contact Simon & Schuster Special Sales at 1-866-506-1949 or
business@simonandschuster.com.
The Simon & Schuster Speakers Bureau can bring authors to your live
event. For more information or to book an event, contact the Simon
& Schuster Speakers Bureau at 1-866-248-3049 or visit our
website at www.simonspeakers.com.
Also available in a SIMON & SCHUSTER BFYR hardcover edition
Interior design by Brad Mead
Jacket design by Lizzy Bromley
The text for this book was set in Dante MT Std.
Manufactured in the United States of America
This SIMON & SCHUSTER BFYR export paperback edition March 2018
10 9 8 7 6 5 4 3 2
Library of Congress Cataloging-in-Publication Data
Names: Choi, Mary H. K., author.
Title: Emergency contact / Mary H. K. Choi.
Description: First edition. | New York : Simon & Schuster Books for
Young Readers, 2018. | Summary: "After a chance encounter, Penny
and Sam become each other's emergency contacts and find themselves
falling in love digitally, without the humiliating weirdness of having
to see each other"— Provided by publisher.
Identifiers: LCCN 2017048139 (print) | LCCN 2017059681 (ebook) |
ISBN 9781534408982 (Ebook) | ISBN 9781534408968 (hardback)
Subjects: | CYAC: Text messages (Cell phone systems)—Fiction. |
Dating (Social customs)—Fiction. | Colleges and universities—Fiction.
Classification: LCC PZ7.1.C5316 (ebook) | LCC PZ7.1.C5316 Eme 2018
(print) | DDC [Fic]—dc23
LC record available at https://lccn.loc.gov/2017048139
ISBN 9781534425934 (export paperback edition)

For Mom

PENNY.

"Tell me something, Penny . . ."

Penny knew that whatever Madison Chandler was going to say, she wasn't going to enjoy it. Madison Chandler leaned in close, mouth smiling, beady eyes narrowed. Penny held her breath.

"Why is your mom such a *slut*?"

The taller of the two girls glared pointedly at Penny's mom, who was chatting with Madison's father a few feet away.

Blood pounded in Penny's ears.

Possible reactions to Madison Chandler calling your mom a slut:
1. Punch her in the face.
2. Punch her disgusto, knuckle-dragging, pervert father in the face.
3. Do nothing. Rage-cry later in the privacy of

your bedroom while listening to The Smiths.
You are a dignified pacifist. Namaste.
4. Unleash the pyrokinetic abilities bequeathed
    to you upon birth, scorching the shopping
    mall with the fire of a trillion suns.

Penny scanned her opponent's green-flecked blue eyes.
Why was this happening? And at the Apple Store no less? This
was a safe space. A haven. Penny was almost out of this stifling
town for good. She was *so close*.

"I asked you a question." Madison sucked her teeth. She
had those clear braces that fooled no one.

Punching her would be therapeutic.

"Hello? Is anyone in there?"

So therapeutic.

Christ, who was Penny kidding? It was option three. It was
always option three. At this stage of the game there was no need
to be a hero. Especially at 5'1", with a "cute" right hook and
reaction times that were sluggish at best.

Whatever. In four days Penny would be off to college and
the opinions of these micro-regionally famous people would
no longer matter.

Just as Madison drew back, to glare at her from a different, arguably more menacing angle, Penny's assigned Apple
Genius materialized with her brand-new phone.

Deus ex-MacStore dude.

Penny clutched the smooth box. It gleamed with promise and felt expensively heavy in her hands. She glanced over
by the laptops where "Maddy's Daddy," as he'd introduced

himself (barf), was doing a looming-leering thing at her mom, Celeste. Penny sighed. She'd been campaigning for a new phone since Christmas, and this was not at all going down how she'd planned. Penny had envisioned more fanfare. At least some help picking out a case.

"Seriously, what's with your mom's geisha whore outfit?"

Okay, Madison Chandler may have gotten a Chanel caviar purse at fourteen (it was a hand-me-down) and a Jeep Wrangler at sixteen, but wow, there were sandwiches smarter than this girl.

First off, geishas weren't prostitutes. Common mistake. Typically made by the willfully ignorant and intellectually incurious. Some geishas beguiled their clients with dance and artful conversation like in *Memoirs of a Geisha*, a novel Penny adored until she discovered some rando white guy had written it. Second, as anyone with even the most cursory observational skills can tell you, the kimono offers exemplary coverage. It was burka-adjacent or perhaps chador-ish, since kimonos didn't have the hair and face covering bit.

Still, Penny wished, not for the first time, that her mom would stop wearing crop tops. Especially with leggings. It was positively gynecological. Penny, of course, was dressed in her customary shapeless black garb that was appropriate both day and night for being ignored by everyone.

"We're Korean," whispered Penny. Madison's lip twitched in confusion, as if she'd been informed that Africa wasn't a country. "Geishas are Japanese," she finished. If you're going to be racist you should try to be less ignorant, although maybe that was a contradiction. . . .

Mr. Chandler roared with laughter at something Celeste said, who, for the record, was hot but not that funny.

"Daddy," whined Madison, making her way toward him.

Daddy? Yuck.

Penny bet they were the type of family that mouth kissed. Penny walked over too.

"If you want, you can come by my office and I can take a look at your portfolio," continued Mr. Chandler. He was at least six foot five and Penny could see straight up to his nose hair.

"As I tell all my clients, it's the early bird who gets the retirement worm. Especially with an empty nest." He nodded at Penny.

"Dang it," he said, patting his pockets with a practiced air. "I don't have a card, but if you want to . . ." Mr. Chandler held his phone out and mimed typing into it with a toothy grin.

Penny shut it down.

"Mom." Penny grabbed her by the wrist. "We have to go."

• • •

Everything about the way Penny's mom interacted with Mr. Chandler with his gleaming wedding ring and his hot-pink polo shirt infuriated her. It was the same old tale with Celeste and guys. You'd think she'd give it a rest and pay some attention to her *only daughter* the week before she left for college, but no, she was too busy flapping her lash extensions to some fake-tanned creep.

In the car, Celeste rearranged her boobs in her gray striped top and latched her seat belt. Having a MILF for a mom was garbage.

Celeste pulled out of the parking lot as the uneasy silence thickened.

On the highway, the Japanese cat mounted on her mother's dashboard rattled. Penny stared at it. It was the size of a dinner roll, with a detached, spring-loaded head and blank cartoon eyes. This one, a recent addition, had usurped plastic Hello Kitty when Kitty's features got bleached off by the sun. Celeste insisted on accessorizing everything. It was pathological. It reminded Penny of the rich bitches in the "Super Six," Maddy and Rachel Dumas and Allie Reed and the three other glossy-haired sadists who wore a ton of rings and bracelets and had a new, sparkly phone case every week. You could hear them walking down the hall since the jangling crap attached to their book bags made such a racket. Thing is, if Celeste had gone to Ranier High, she probably would have been friends with them.

Penny longed for a crew. She was on "Oh, hey" status with a bunch of kids, but her closest school friend, Angie Salazar, transferred to Sojourner Truth High the summer before junior year, leaving Penny socially unmoored. If there were a sub-basement level with a trapdoor below utter invisibility, Penny would have found a way to fall to it. Her social standing was nonexistent.

The cat continued to rattle. If it carried on in this way, it would be toast before they hit the freeway. It was trinket Darwinism. A fragile animal had no business being mounted in a fast-moving vehicle. Certainly not a fast-moving vehicle commandeered by her mother, who had no right to commandeer anything in the whole wide . . .

"Why do you do that?" Penny exploded. She wanted to

punch a hole in the window and fling the cat out. Possibly hurl herself after it. Today was meant to be different. Penny'd let herself get excited about it for weeks. Her mom had taken the afternoon off, and it hurt Penny's feelings that Celeste would ditch her as soon as she saw the Chandlers. Not that Penny would admit what was really bothering her. Pathetic outcasts had standards too.

"What?" Celeste rolled her eyes. The teen-like gesture coming from her mom set her off even more. Penny wanted to shake Celeste until her fillings came loose.

"Why do you flirt with everyone all the time?" Celeste was the mom equivalent of a feather boa. Or human glitter. "It's getting old, you know."

"Who are you talking about?"

"Oh, you know exactly who . . ."

"Matt Chandler?"

"Yeah, gross, nasty 'Maddy's Daddy,' who, incidentally, is married!"

"I know he's married." Celeste huffed. "Who was flirting? I was being polite, which, by the way, wouldn't kill you. With your eye-rolling and scowls. Do you know how embarrassing . . . ?"

"Embarrassing? *Me*? Embarrassing *you*?" Penny balked. "That's rich." Penny crossed her arms prissily. "Mom, he was a creep and you're there oozing your smiley, ridiculous . . ."

The car cat clattered as if nodding.

"How is he a creep? Because he wanted to give me investment advice?"

Penny couldn't believe how dense her mother could be. It was clear to everyone that "Matt" wanted to give her a lot more than investment advice. Christ, even Madison knew what was up.

"How is it possible that you're this stupid?"

Celeste's mouth opened then shut. A pained expression flashed across her face. Even the curls on her head appeared to deflate.

Penny had never said anything as explicitly, deliberately mean to her mom before. She felt bad about it as soon as it flew out of her mouth, and while her mother wasn't dumb, she was frequently mistaken for being, well, a little airheaded. Celeste ran regional operations for a multinational events-planning agency, spoke in hashtags, and was frequently dressed as if attending a boy-band concert. That was her way.

Penny was constantly running defense for her. The neighborhood men circled Celeste like sharks, conveniently underfoot to help with high supermarket shelves or offer unsolicited mansplainage on any number of topics. The way they lingered by Celeste's car, eyes glittering like seeds, as if waiting for something, sketched Penny out. It didn't help that Celeste was invariably welcoming.

Just one example: Last Valentine's Day, Mr. Hemphill, their ancient mailman, presented Celeste with a tiny box of drugstore chocolates. It was the size of a mouse coffin, with four oxidized bonbons inside, and he kept mentioning the Vietnam War as though they had something in common. It was clear that he wanted to wear their skin and as far as Penny was concerned, *this* was the last guy you wanted knowing where you lived. Celeste wouldn't hear of it.

Penny gazed out the window. Fighting with her mother had

become routine. But now that Penny was leaving, Celeste *had to* get better at navigating the world. Steering clear of unrepentant scumbags was a start. Penny was exhausted. Of worrying about Celeste. Of resenting her. The flitting fast-food restaurants and gas stations blurred in her vision. She blotted the hot stray tears with a sleeve so her mom wouldn't see.

• • •

Later that day Penny's boyfriend came by. Not that Penny ever publicly referred to Mark as her "boyfriend." He functioned more as a stopgap for complete isolation when Angie moved away, which was a totally awful way to think about it. Especially since empirically Mark was out of her league. At least physically. Which wasn't everything, except in high school maybe it was. Most of the time Penny couldn't believe they were dating. When Mark first showed interest, Penny thought he was defective or else messing with her, and when he didn't seem to be doing that, her suspicion only grew. Penny was nothing if not aware of what she looked like and what she looked like was exactly the same as she did when she was in first grade. Smallish eyes with a snub nose and humongous lips that her mother promised she'd grow into but she never did. She and Mark *looked* confusing together. It didn't help that Penny had learned that relationships often seemed to mean the opposite of what you called them. You could have over a hundred "friends" on social media and still have nobody to talk to. Just as Angie (that Brutus) had dubbed Penny her *best* friend until she ghosted completely. And while Mark referred to Penny as "bae," which just made her deeply uncomfortable because: gross, he *also* described pizza as not only "bae" but "bae AF." Which, yeah, obviously, but that was the problem. They both liked pizza way more than their *person*.

"So, did you get it?"

Penny desperately wished she hadn't.

Penny knew part of her lukewarm disposition toward Mark was that he was the type of guy Celeste would've picked out for her. He had dirty-blond hair and the preppy good looks of a Hollister model. Not on the billboard but easily in a catalog group shot. Toward the front since he was short.

Mark was also younger by a year, which was clutch when you were sorta-kinda-not-really-but-maybe dating since that meant he had a different lunch period. His crew qualified as popular since it included moderately popular soccer kids despite the rest of the squad being burnouts. Mark smoked a lot of weed and had a brain like a sieve. Which was unfortunate. Even the cute things that would have made good inside jokes were forgotten, like how autocorrect on his phone kept changing "goddammit" to "god donut," so when Penny sent the donut emoji as an expletive he only ever thought she was hungry.

Mark was unwavering.

Penny blinked first.

"Do you want a snack or something?" She opened the fridge, grabbed a pitcher of sweet tea, and poured them both glasses. It was the only thing Celeste knew how to "cook."

Penny thought back to the first day Mark talked to her after fifth period. Thing was, he *was* defective in a sense. Everybody knew he had "yellow fever." His ex was this smoking-hot Vietnamese girl Audrey, whose dad was transferred to Germany with the air force, and in middle school he'd briefly dated Emily, who was half Thai.

"Well?" Mark wouldn't be deterred. "*Did* you get it?" He grinned winsomely.

Penny drew her tea to her mouth with such force that she hit the glass with her teeth.

"Baby," he said. Behind "bae," Penny despised "baby" as a thing for a grown adult woman to be called. It was so prescriptive. Like dressing sexy for Halloween.

Mark sat on a stool on the other side of the kitchen island and gestured alluringly for her to come over. His hair fell over his right eye.

God, he was handsome.

Mark opened his arms and she walked into them.

"We may as well get used to communicating like this," Mark whispered, breath tickling her ear. "We both hate talking on the phone, and you know what they say about pictures, Penny." He paused for effect, Penny couldn't believe he was going to continue. "They're worth a thousand words."

Wow.

Penny hitched her chin onto his shoulders. Mark smelled mildewy. It was comforting in a sense. Mark often smelled as if he hadn't done laundry in a while. She weighed her options.

Possible gambits to mount a distraction for a boyfriend who's prone to distraction:

1.   Break up with him. A long-distance

relationship based on cataclysmic levels of
meh was soul-eating.
2.   Have sex with him to change the subject.
3.   Burst into tears and explain nothing.

"Yes." Penny sighed. "I did get it." Then she added, "Thank
you." She tried to sound sincere.

Technically "it" was a "they" and "they" were nudes. Penny
recalled the twin pepperoni constituting her boyfriend's nipples
and inwardly shuddered. Mark thought sexts were an appropriate and fun way to christen a new phone. Penny thought
vehemently otherwise.

Okay, so they weren't full-on frontal—bless. Mark was still
sixteen, and Penny didn't need the FBI landing at her college
dorm for kiddie porn. They were risqué, though. Each went
slightly beyond the treasure trail. With a few different filters.
Penny was even sure he'd Facetuned at least one, which was a
quality she simply could not respect in a man. She knew that
the proper, more sporting response was to reciprocate. A boob
(hint of nip tops) would suffice. But she didn't want to. At all.
All she wanted to do was delete them, pretend none of this
ever happened, and leave.

She'd be off the hook then. At least technically. The statute
for follow-up nudes couldn't extend beyond the city limits surely.
Even so, Penny should have considered going out of state.

SAM.

Sam enjoyed an odd commute. A single staircase and about nine yards of hallway. On one hand, he could rely on experiencing zero traffic. On the other, he felt like he was always at work. House Coffee, where Sam was manager, was an Austin institution. It was a small, gray Craftsman with a gabled roof and a wraparound porch with a big white swing out front. It was, for lack of a better word, homey, and the first-floor café boasted creaky wood floors, large windows, built-in bookcases, and ratty sofas with mismatched chairs.

The upstairs contained four rooms, two baths, and resembled the domicile of some wackadoo hoarder. When Sam first moved in he'd snooped for hidden treasures that might fetch a fortune at auction. The actual findings were less *Antiques Roadshow* and more those TV specials where once the twin brothers die—both crushed under an avalanche of VHS tapes—they find forty-six dollars' worth of stamps and thousands of empty Chef Boyardee cans where the changing labels denote the passage of time. Every room but one was overrun with boxes of files, books, clothes, and whatever else Al Petridis, the proprietor of House, couldn't fit in his own house. In the smallest room, farthest from the stairs, there was a mattress on the floor.

That's where Sam slept.

Like some orphan. Which he technically wasn't, though he may as well have been.

Sam lay in bed and collected his thoughts. It was dark out. Still. Another restless night meant another grim day of functioning as if underwater.

He glanced at his jail-broken iPhone. Four forty-three a.m. He'd gone to sleep sometime before two. He remembered a time when you couldn't kick him out of bed before noon. Salad days.

GUH.

At least there was coffee. Reliable, delicious, life-giving coffee. He padded downstairs.

An hour later, the aroma of freshly ground beans commingled with the smell of carbs frying in grease.

"Christ, Sammy. Donuts?" Al Petridis, Sam's boss and landlord, loomed over him. At a head taller than Sam and a hundred and fifty pounds heavier, Al was an enormous Greek with forearms the size of barrels. He reminded Sam a little of Donkey Kong, but Sam didn't think it was the sort of thing you told another man. Al was first to sample any of Sam's baked creations. And the burly benefactor unfailingly called it "trying." Even if he'd had a muffin a thousand times, he'd say, "Sammy, can I try a muffin?" As if he didn't know exactly what the experience would be. As if there was any doubt that he would want the whole thing.

Spoiler: Al always wanted the muffin.

That was fine by Sam. Al didn't charge Sam rent. Not a red cent. Ever. His boss went so far as to pay Sam a few dollars over minimum wage, and for that Sam would bake, cook, clean, and shave crop circles in the man's back if he'd ask.

"What is that, nuts?" Al poked a freshly glazed pastry with a meaty forefinger.

Ever since he was a kid, Sam loved to cook and bake, whipping up increasingly complicated dishes, making substitutions wherever necessary, which was often, since his mom rarely bought groceries and he was alone a lot. At twelve he discovered you could make a somewhat convincing facsimile of Thai food with peanut butter and jarred salsa. At least according to the palette of a preteen Texan of German descent who at the time hadn't tasted real Thai food.

Al had given Sam free rein of the kitchen more than a year ago, ever since Sam had silently handed his boss a lemon chiffon cake for his wife's birthday (her favorite) with a Post-it note on the top: "For Mrs. Petridis." She'd declared it the best she'd ever tasted, and although Al knew better than to make a big deal of it, his better half insisted on passing Sam pamphlets for culinary school. For Sam's birthday they bought him a small stack of hardcover cookbooks and the gesture moved Sam so profoundly that he couldn't make eye contact with Al for a week. At the Petridises' urging, Sam secured his food handler's permit and now created the weekly menu of sandwiches, soups, and salads, as well as the pastries. He got up at five a.m. to prep, while Finley, his ace, his number two at House, a dark-skinned, lanky Mexican kid with a big hipster beard and a Scottish name, came in at eight to man the register and bus tables.

"That one's pistachio," Sam told Al. "And vanilla-hibiscus, espresso, and salted dark chocolate." Sam had gotten the recipe from a food blogger, who said they were irresistible to women and wrote candidly about her exploits that testified to it.

"Want?" Sam handed over the tray as a matter of course.

"Yeah, I'll try a donut." Al's round face halved the smaller circle with a single bite. "Namazinnn, Sammy!" he said with his mouth full. Al's shadow hovered ever closer to sample the other flavors. Other than his mom, Al was the only person allowed to call him Sammy.

Al cocked his head. "Say, Sammy, you all right?" Al was also the only one to regularly inquire about his mood.

The thing about Sam was that he had a tell. Well, two. They weren't an exact science, but they gave you a sense. One was his hair. He had a great head of hair. Dark and longer on top, his ex-girlfriend—who came up as "Liar" on his phone now—had referred to it as *irresponsible* hair.

If it was relaxed and tucked behind his ears, Sam was chill. If it was slicked back, he was spoiling for a fight. If it was fluffy—a very rare treat—it meant he completely trusted whoever was around at the time. Sam's hair hadn't been fluffy in a while.

Today it was tucked back yet also, kinda, done. With the telltale sheen of product. It was inscrutable.

Avid Sam observers, especially if they were monitoring him in his own habitat, could check for his next tell. Sam's happiness was somehow tied to his desire to bake. When you walked into House and there in the display case was a cold lone scone and an anemic trio of store-bought Danish, you were better to keep a wide berth. You should treat him as you would a man with a scab where his eye had been and the words "NOT TODAY, SATAN" branded in giant letters across his forehead—with caution.

While House bought their bread from Easy Tiger, pastries typically were Sam's domain. If the case and cake stands were resplendent with crunchy fresh-baked coffee cake, whoopie pies, or caramelized banana bread pudding pots with cream cheese frosting, it meant that Sam was liable to make out with you if you walked in. Plus, you'd enjoy it. Sam was a dynamite maker-outer. Today he'd whipped together a dozen hand pies and the donuts and nothing else—and that could mean anything.

"Yeah, Al. Doing great." Sam carefully face-planted the largest O into a shallow dish of vanilla-hibiscus glaze and set it carefully on a wire rack. The smile may have been the most unnerving part. Sometimes Sam appeared a touch unhinged on the rare occasions he did it. As if his face were out of practice. Not that he frowned either—that betrayed too much information. Mostly he stared straight through you.

"Okay, then," said Al, glancing over at Sam as he left. Just to make sure.

Sam dipped another donut in glaze. His hands were bony and veiny and moved quickly. His arms, lean, tanned, and blanketed in tattoos, would have looked at home on a Russian convict. Sam had a lot of tattoos. All over his chest, back, and calves.

He wiped up a bright fuchsia dribble of icing with his left hand and continued dipping the remaining three donuts with his right. He was pleased with the results.

Some guys wouldn't call baking or the ability to make a Pikachu foam cappuccino topper particularly manly pursuits, but Sam wasn't just any guy. He didn't concern himself with how fist-pumping frat dudes with crippling masculinity issues and no necks spent their time.

Fin came in and immediately eyed the racks. There were six trays with four immaculate donuts cooling on each.

"What are these, limited-edition?" he asked. "We'll sell out these shits in an hour."

"Nah, they're off-menu. I'm making these for someone," Sam said. Fin huffed the sweet donut steam.

"You can't bake for these girls out the gate, Sam. You've got to manage expectations."

Sam smiled his wonky smile.

Fin studied him warily.

"Dude. Please." Fin's shoulders slumped. "Come on, tell me these aren't . . . Please tell me you're not dating lyin'-ass Liar again," said Fin, hands up in a defense pose. "Yo, I get it. She's hot—no disrespect—but the last time y'all broke up, I didn't know if *I* was going to make it."

Sam ignored any mention of the Great Love of His Life.

"Seriously, Sam, you were in a bad place for so long," said Fin. "Monster-ass chem trails coming out of your ears, man."

"They're not for her," Sam said.

Fin hung up his backpack, threw on an apron, and glanced at the rack that held bloopers. "Can I kill these?" Sam nodded, and Fin took down a misshapen glazed in a single bite. "Mmmm," he said, cramming another half into his mouth. "These are way too good for her anyway."

PENNY.

It was the big day. Penny considered feeling sad. It was supposed to be bittersweet, wasn't it? Leaving home and going off to college was A Thing. She blinked for moisture—no dice. Along the lines of having a sneeze you can't find or an itch that lives too deep under the skin, college felt surreal, conceptually out of reach. Even the application process felt like it was happening to someone else. It was unimaginable that there would be any consequences to filling out the forms and writing the essay. She applied to only one place—the University of Texas at Austin—and got in. By law. Everyone in the top ten percent of their Texas high school did.

Penny's new phone chimed next to her on the bed. It was Mark.

> *Good luck baby!*
> *Text me when you get there!*

Penny rolled onto her back and smiled. She considered what to write back. The screen beneath her thumbs was so shiny. God, her phone was beautiful. Rose gold, in a black rubber case that read, *Whatever, Whatever, Whatever,* it was easily nicer than anything she'd ever owned. She wiped down a smudge with her T-shirt. It was way too pretty to be desecrated with nudes. Especially with a 2436-by-1125-pixel resolution at 458ppi. Penny sent a generic smile emoji back.

She went downstairs. While Penny's walls were bare, every other surface in Celeste's home, much like her car or her desk at work, was covered with keepsakes.

According to Penny, her mom wasn't very mom-like, much less Asian-mom-like. It wasn't solely that she dressed like a fashion blogger and was younger than other moms. Celeste didn't monitor Penny's homework or insist on piano lessons. Okay, so maybe Penny's idea of an Asian mom came from the movies, but she hadn't grown up with a lot of Asians in her life. Let alone Koreans specifically. Penny had a Korean name and it was bogus. It was "Penny"—not even Penelope—spelled out phonetically in Korean characters so it didn't actually mean anything.

When she was three they'd visited her grandparents in Seoul, but she'd been too little to remember anything and they'd never gone back. Celeste did, however, dedicate a Korean corner in her home. An altar of sorts. It included a miniature Korean flag and a framed poster of the 1988 Olympics with the cartoon tiger mascot. There was also a small laminated picture of the pop star Rain in a white suit from years before he went into the military for mandatory service. The first time Penny's friend Angie came over, she asked her if it was a photo of her brother.

Elsewhere in the house there were snow globes galore, Eiffel Towers of varying sizes and framed pictures of World-Famous Art—two renditions of Van Gogh's *Starry Night* (one on a tea towel), Monet's water lilies, and several of Degas's blurry ballerinas. Penny called the whole lot "fridge magnet art." Stuff you'd seen enough times that you could imagine the factory workers in China rolling their eyes about having to keep churning it out.

The only memento Penny prized was a framed picture of her parents. She'd carefully wrapped it in a T-shirt and stowed it in her backpack to bring to school. It was the only photo she had of them, possibly the only one in existence, and Penny treasured it. It was the source of 50 percent of the material in her "dad" dossier. Other information included:

1. Penny's mom and dad had met, of all places, in a bowling alley on dates with other people.
2. Her dad had a cute butt (Celeste's words) because he played baseball in high school.
3. They were inseparable. Until, of course, they weren't.
4. He was Korean too!
5. His name was Daniel Lee and as far as Penny knew he lived in Oregon or Oklahoma. It could have been Ohio. In any case, it started with an O.
6. In those three states combined there were 315 Daniel Lees. Some were probably white. Or perhaps black.

In the picture, Penny's parents are at the beach at Port Aransas. They're kids. Celeste hasn't visibly changed over the years (Asian don't raisin) except her face was rounder then, fuller in the cheeks and lips. They're sitting on a black and yellow Batman beach towel. Daniel Lee has a straw cowboy hat perched on his head but no shirt. Celeste's wearing a trucker hat that says PORN STAR, a bright red bikini, legs crisscrossed, and she's grinning behind huge white sunglasses while holding an ICEE. Celeste swears the ICEE must have been a pregnancy craving since blue raspberry usually makes her gag. To Penny, it's cosmically unfair that her mom's tummy can be that flat while she's pregnant, but then it's hardly fair that her dark-eyed father would skip town two months before Penny was born either.

"He was the funniest guy I'd ever met," Celeste said when Penny unwrapped the parcel on her eighth birthday. "He asked the best questions." Penny had been asking a lot of questions for a genealogy assignment. She wanted to know everything (mostly as it related to her)—whether he asked about Penny, if he had another family with brothers and sisters for her to play with, when she could see him. But Penny could tell Celeste hated talking about him. She became withdrawn and went to her room with a headache. So Penny shoved the questions to the back of her brain and never brought him up again. The photo, she kept in a drawer.

Downstairs, Celeste was sniffling in the kitchen, as she'd been when Penny went to bed. Penny suspected a performative aspect to her mom's crying. Comparable to YouTubers sobbing during heavily edited confessional vlogs, Celeste bawled lustily during the semifinals of reality singing competitions and any movie involving animals. Penny would rather eat a pound of hair than reveal her true emotions. Not to mention how Penny wasn't sure she'd be able to stop once she got going.

"Mom?"

Celeste glanced up from the wadded tissues in her hands. Her eyes were puffy as if she actually *had* been crying all night.

"Hi, baby." She smiled before crumpling again. "Can I *please* come with you? I could buy you lunch. Help you decorate?"

"I can buy my own lunch," Penny said. "Plus, you'd have to trail me in your car and drive all the way back by yourself. *I'd* have to get back in *my* car and follow you to make sure you got home safe. A vicious cycle."

Celeste swallowed. "You know, I didn't know it would hurt this bad?" She seemed genuinely surprised. Celeste's narrow shoulders quivered like an agitated Chihuahua. Penny sighed and hugged her. She was going to miss her.

Oh, shit. Am I going to cry?

She squeezed her eyes tighter for any reciprocal condensation.

Nope.

"Well, I'm proud of you," Celeste said, pulling away and smiling bravely.

Penny peered down at her. Celeste seemed small. Feeble really. And damp. In the afternoon light, in jeans and a faded T-shirt that read SLAY HUNTY, Celeste resembled an incoming freshman as much as Penny did.

It was sad that things had gotten so bad between them.

When Penny was in grade school, they'd been thick as thieves. Back when the greatest excitement Penny could imagine was having a Starbucks salted caramel mocha for breakfast, Penny thought she was so lucky to have her mom as her best friend. She could stay up late, wear makeup, borrow her mom's clothes, and dye her hair any color of the rainbow—life was a riot—a never-ending slumber party. In middle school Penny started to see things differently. She no longer texted her mother a thousand times a day for outfit approval or advice. Celeste and Penny became a study in contrasts. Celeste was proud of her well-mannered, studious daughter, teaching her how to forge her name on letters from school and getting Penny her own credit card for "fashion emergencies." Celeste encouraged Penny to get her hardship driver's license at fifteen, not because they needed her to but because Celeste thought it would bolster Penny's popularity to drive her friends around. The harder Celeste tried, the more Penny pulled away. If anything, Penny resented that Celeste had decided somewhere along the way that her daughter could parent herself.

Penny walked to the driveway with her mom trailing her. She turned for a one-armed hug. Imagining herself as part of an animal control unit lassoing a python in a studio apartment, she held Celeste's gaze with her own the whole time. Then— with no sudden movements—she deftly popped the car door open with her free hand and slid in.

Seat belt fastened, Penny eased out of the driveway and into freedom. Part of her dreaded going to college alone. In the Instagram Stories version, her dad would haul her boxed-up belongings in a big truck. They'd argue about what to play on the way there and he'd give up the aux cord, since he'd miss her so much. As he left, he'd get choked up, handing her fifty dollars while mumbling something about making good time, and Penny would know deep in her heart how much he loved her.

"I love you, baby!" wailed Celeste, jolting Penny from her thoughts.

Penny rolled down her window. "I love you too, Mommy. I'll call you later. I promise."

This time Penny did feel a pang. Her nose got that stinging, chlorine feeling you get right when you're about to cry. She checked her rearview to see her already small mom getting smaller, waving big.

• • •

An hour and a half later, Penny pulled into the curved driveway at Kincaid.

"Jesus," she whispered, clutching her steering wheel to gaze up at the building. Kincaid was among the oldest dorms at UT, and it was hideous. Penny wondered if you could *feel* the ugliness from the inside. Boasting eight floors painted in alternating blue and salmon layers, it resembled a Miami hotel from the 1970s more than a dorm. Eighty units of eyesore that were the tackiest part of the campus skyline. The lurid hues reminded Penny of kicky animal-print scrubs favored by pediatric oncologists. It was the upbeatness that made the whole thing depressing.

Throngs of anxious parents and freshmen huddled around SUVs carting enormous plastic bins, laundry baskets, and floor lamps. Just as Penny rolled down her window to scope the scene, a freckly brunette stuck her face into her car until they were nose-to-nose. Her eyes were bulbous, glinting with a helpfulness that bordered on menacing.

"Name?" yawped the girl. Penny smelled Fritos on her breath.

"Lee," she supplied. "Penelope."

"Hmm . . . Lee?" She drew her finger down her clipboard and then tapped it. "Ah," she said triumphantly. "There you are, sweetie."

Ugh. *Sweetie.* This chick was nineteen tops.

The girl's eyes flickered over Penny's red lipstick. Penny had found it with a note to "smile more!" in her backpack pocket. Celeste had a habit of tucking cosmetics or clipped-out articles about the effects of positive thinking among Penny's things. Sneak-attack gifts that felt like criticism.

"Sweetie?" Penny sang back. "Can you back up a smidge? You're practically inside of my face with your face?" She said it exactly how she imagined the girl would, with everything going up in a question.

There was no way Little Miss Texas Corn Chip was going to "sweetie" her into submission.

The girl swiftly withdrew her head.

"Oh my God?" she chirped, bleached teeth gleaming. "So many of the parents literally can't hear me? I've been yelling for hours?" The girl inspected Penny's lipstick again. "Wait. I'm obsessed with how matte that is. What is it?"

"Isn't it fabulous?" Penny enthused, reaching for the tube in her bag. "Too Thot to Trot?" she read off the sticker on the bottom. Christ, she felt as if saying makeup names out loud set women's rights back several decades.

"Ugh! I knew it! I *love* Staxx lip kits? You know T-T-T-T's sold out everywhere, right? Why are the good reds always quickstrike?"

"Ugh, right?!" exclaimed Penny, who had no idea what she was talking about. "It's the worst?" The girl rolled her eyes theatrically in agreement.

"Okay, so you're in 4F," she said, drumming her shellacked nails on her clipboard. "Elevators are toward the back. And you can unload anywhere you can see a blue sign. Buuuuuuuut . . ."

She placed a purple laminated pass on her dash. "*This* buys you parking for the rest of the day. Just return it to the front desk when you're done."

"Thank you?" said Penny brightly. "You're a lifesaver?"

The girl beamed. "I know?"

Penny's face strained from the false cheer. It was frankly impressive that Celeste's addiction to trendy makeup and some doofus imprinting on her like a baby farm animal could land her parking privileges. More yakking and some thigh-slapping laughter at dad-jokes scored Penny a hand truck from her neighbor down the hall. Rules for friendliness were a racket. In no time, college Penny would be as adored as Celeste. Granted, she'd have to get a lobotomy to keep it up, but maybe the exchange rate was worth it.

When Penny swung her door open, she noticed the following: Her room smelled of Febreze with a top note of musty carpet. It was discouragingly small to be shared with another person. Plus, it was already inhabited by a dark-haired girl sitting on the bed by the window. A girl who was not her roommate. Penny and Jude Lange had Skyped twice over the summer, and this chick with indoor sunglasses and a wide-brim Coachella hat was not her. The girl neglected to glance up from her phone.

"Hello?" Penny began lugging her stuff in.

The girl silently continued typing.

Penny cleared her throat.

Finally, the girl removed her oversized bedazzled sunglasses to get a glimpse of Penny. She had famous-people eyebrows and wore a tan suede vest with foot-long tassels.

"Where's Jude?" the girl asked in a manner that suggested Penny worked there.

"Uh, I don't know."

The girl rolled her eyes and returned to her phone.

Penny glared and once again wished her hostility could incinerate people.

Possible responses to a possible home invader who was possibly a maniac and possibly has a switchblade under her hat:
1. Fight her.
2. Start screaming and pull your own hair to signal that you're even crazier and not to be trifled with.
3. Introduce yourself and find out more information.
4. Ignore her.

Unsurprisingly, Penny chose the path of least resistance. She grabbed her toiletry bag out of her suitcase and made a beeline for the bathroom. It was the size of a closet. You could've washed your hair while sitting on the toilet by leaning into the shower stall. Penny placed her bag on the toilet tank, figured it was perilously close to potential pee splash-back and set it on the side of the sink.

From another stash bag, she pulled out a roll of toilet paper, a microbe-free shower curtain, a toothbrush holder that didn't have a well on the bottom where water could collect, a brand-new shower mat, and towels. Penny arranged everything exactly the way that made sense. TP was hung in the correct direction ("over" obviously; "under" was for murderers).

When she was done, she marched back out and went for option three. "Penelope Lee, Penny," she said, extending her hand to the girl.

The girl stood up and considered Penny's paw with distaste until Penny was forced to lower it. Penny's eyeline was to her boob (option one would not have been cute). "Mallory Sloane Kidder," she said, still typing on her phone. "Though I'm in the process of changing my name to Mallory Sloane. Professionally."

Mallory had symmetrically winged eyeliner, thick hips, and pointy metallic nails. Penny didn't know what "professionally" implied.

"Actor," Mallory Sloane (formerly Kidder) said briskly. She sat back down and crossed her legs. Her nails tap-danced furiously as she texted. "I've done off-off-off-Broadway."

Penny wondered about the jurisdiction of off-off-off-Broadway. It probably had nothing to do with actual Broadway in New York. With enough imagination, hyphens, and prepositions, the corner of East César Chávez and Chicon could probably qualify as off-Broadway.

"Uh, rad," Penny said.

Mallory held up a finger to indicate for her to wait.

"It's Jude," she said, typing into her phone. "Your roommate."

"Cool."

"She's my best friend, you know."

Tappedy, tappedy tap.

"Since we were six."

Penny rolled her eyes. Quickly so she wouldn't get her ass beat by this giant.

"Is everything okay?"

Mallory held up her finger again. Penny wondered how much force it would require to break it in three places.

"She wants us to meet her at a coffee shop on the Drag."

There had to be some rule against moving to a second location with a stranger. For all Penny knew, her new roommate and this obnoxious broad could be "best friends" from a fetish message board that specialized in cutting up Asian girls for hot dogs. It was all so typical. Penny was at college ten minutes and she was already the third wheel.

"Let's go." Mallory set about collecting her things and then looked at a dawdling Penny as if she were stupid.

"Look, they have donuts."

Penny grabbed her backpack.

Mallory Sloane Kidder might have been an asshole, but her argument was airtight.

SAM.

Jude smiled at Sam.

Sam smiled at Jude.

Jude's smile was better than Sam's.

Sam remembered the first time she'd smiled at him. It was Christmas Day a decade ago and Sam was ornery when he opened the door. Bad enough he was forced to wear itchy pants that bunched at the crotch, but to add insult to injury, his mom, Brandi Rose, made him put on a tie.

"Put on a tie," she'd said. Just like that. She had curlers in her hair and smelled of the perfume that had appeared mysteriously in a glass teardrop on the bathroom counter.

"Hurry up." She swatted his arm as she squeezed past in their comically snug hall. Sam studied her as she shambled into the kitchen and tried to see her as a man would, as a woman. She looked haggard. The broken blood vessels around her nose had been covered with a thick powder that aged her.

"What tie?" he shot back. At no point in his eleven years of existence had anyone thought to buy him a tie. She huffily pulled one from his dad's stuff that was collected in Walgreens bags in the hall closet and threw it at him. It was green and maroon with musical notes at the bottom.

"Do you even know how to tie a tie?" she shouted, switching on the vacuum.

"Obviously," he yelled back.

He YouTubed it.

It used to be that Sam's mother spent her days off from the hotel in her room, dead to the world. But these past few weeks had been ominously different. She'd spent days baking, cleaning, and buying holiday decorations they couldn't afford. Her nervous energy made Sam watchful, though it had been oddly reassuring to see the kolaches arranged on cookie sheets—prune and apricot. There were also spiced stars, *Zimstern* in German, that made the air fragrant with cinnamon, reminding Sam of happier times. Like the one Christmas they'd spent as a family with a shitty plastic tree and a few of his dad's vinyl records wrapped in newspaper for Sam underneath.

They hadn't celebrated the holidays for years, and he could tell from Brandi Rose's short temper and the tremble in her hands that she was at least sober for once.

Sam loosened his tie as he answered the door. Brandi Rose wasn't big on communication, and other than the barb about the tie and instructions to look nice, Sam didn't know what she had planned. He hadn't been expecting company. And certainly not a kid. Let alone a smiling blond, seven-year-old girl in a blue velvet dress and a ponytail. The kid had the same horse face as the stern, brown-haired guy next to her. His eyes were dark, as cold as holes, and behind them was Brandi Rose's new boyfriend, Mr. Lange. He held a red satin bag aloft with a bottle of champagne peeking out of the top. His smile faltered only for a second when he saw that it was Sam.

"Merry Christmas, kiddo," bellowed Mr. Lange.

"Hey," said Sam.

Mr. Lange was sixty-nine years young. It's how he'd described himself to Sam when they'd first met, grinning and waggling his eyebrows at the mention of "sixty-nine." He was Brandi Rose's fiancé as of a month ago. Sam had met him exactly once during their alarmingly short courtship. They'd gone out for steak dinners at Texas Land & Cattle, and the crypt keeper kept touching his mom's knee. Sam wondered if his hand felt like twigs and dry leaves, especially since Mr. Lange had wiry white hair on his knuckles.

"She's a spitfire this one," he told Sam, stroking his mother again on the thigh. They'd met at the front desk of the Marriott, where Brandi Rose worked and Mr. Lange often stayed. "Old-fashioned, too. Wouldn't give me the time of day until she saw I was serious." He'd lifted her hand for Sam to see. A teardrop-shaped emerald sparkled on her ring finger. Her birthstone. Brandi Rose giggled, a foreign, hollow sound that horrified Sam.

"This is Drew, my son," Mr. Lange said, patting the other man on the shoulder. "And my granddaughter Jude." Sam nodded evenly.

"Oh," sputtered Brandi Rose, appearing behind him. Her voice was strangled, higher pitched than usual. "You said you were picking us up . . ." She evidently hadn't expected company either.

"You're not Sam," interrupted the kid. Apparently he and his mother were in the presence of three generations of geniuses. The men wore suits. Sam pulled on his tie again.

"It's my fault," said Drew, shooting his hand out to Brandi Rose by way of a greeting. "I insisted."

She took it and Sam instinctively stepped toward Drew to buffer his mom.

"We were having Christmas lunch at the Driskill," Drew explained, casually pointing out that Sam and his mother hadn't been invited to the fancy hotel restaurant. "And as you can imagine, the notion of a complete stranger marrying my father just didn't sit right with me. I had to see what his new lady was about." He said this in an affable manner that belied its implication. That he suspected Brandi Rose was a gold digger.

"Oh," said Brandi Rose again. Sam fought the urge to slam the door.

"You're way too little to be my uncle," whispered Jude.

It was trippy how memories worked. Sam couldn't dredge up a solitary detail from Thanksgiving Day two years ago, or what he'd done this past New Year's, yet he remembered everything about when he and Jude met.

The little kid wouldn't shut up. Mr. Lange and Brandi Rose made short work of the champagne, and Drew parked Jude in Sam's room with a plate of cookies while the "grown-ups talked."

Jude's family was loaded. At seven she had her own iPad

and phone, as well a bag of "travel-size games." And as much as Sam wanted to ignore her, she wouldn't stop yammering.

"Do you know how to play backgammon?" She set up the pieces on his bed. Sam cranked up the music in his shitty headphones and turned his back in response. Until the yelling really got going. That's the thing about mobile homes. The walls were wafer thin. Jude's eyes widened.

Sam sighed, plugged his headphones into Jude's iPad, and put them on her. He showed her a few videos. Heavy hitters like corgis waddling on a trampoline and baby pandas squirming to a medley of dancehall music. There was a supercut of a cockatoo that played piano with its feet, and once Jude settled into an instructional of a woman making cupcakes resembling acid-washed jeans, Sam checked on his mom.

Through the crack of his door he could see Brandi Rose at the sink alone, drinking a tall glass of orange juice that likely contained as much vodka. The men were out of sight though not out of earshot. For the next hour Sam and Jude watched videos. By the end of the afternoon Sam could tell a kind of resolution had gone down. He hoped the wedding was called off. That Mr. Lange's impetuous proposal had been the handiwork of a senile man and his jerk son had in fact saved the day. They weren't quite so lucky. The happy couple married a few weeks later, with a five-day honeymoon cruise on the Mayan Riviera. Despite the joyous nuptials and the infinite promises, Brandi Rose's husband failed to move them out of their trailer home; nor did he ever spend a night in her bed.

When it came time for the Langes to leave, Jude's dad collected her, took out his wallet, removed four twenty-dollar bills, and tossed them on Sam's bed, not once looking directly at him.

He shut the door without a word.

• • •

"Uncle Sam!" trilled Jude.

Five years of extensive orthodontia and a contraption known as reverse-pull headgear had corrected the more equine aspects of Jude's face.

"Hey, Jude," he said. It was unsettling to see her again. They'd had coffee a month ago, when she was in town for orientation, yet at no point in the following weeks did Sam believe she'd leave California to study six blocks away.

Jude was now five ten to Sam's six foot (okay, five eleven and a half), but whereas Sam was scrawny, Jude was solid. She reeked of health in that sun-kissed West Coast way. Sam bet she could bench-press him if she wanted. He felt both strangely protective of her in a mammalian way—like how he imagined people in normal families felt toward each other—and deeply uncomfortable that she'd be hanging around.

"YAY!" Jude squealed, engulfing him. "It's Uncle Sam!" She'd taken to calling him that on the flurry of texts signaling her arrival. She thought it was hysterical since Sam wasn't exactly the "USA! USA!" type. Nor was he her uncle anymore. Brandi Rose and Mr. Lange's doomed union lasted just under two years. A month before he'd owe alimony, he proposed to a twenty-five-year-old server from a Cracker Barrel in Buda. He was a class act through and through.

The pressure of Jude's tanned arms encircling him was

pleasant, a relief. It had been several months since Sam had been embraced with uncomplicated affection, and his ex-niece was like a gigantic golden retriever that loved you on sight.

"You hungry?" he asked, squirming out of the hug. "How was the flight? Are your folks here? How's it feel to be a freshman?"

Then a beat. "Do you *love* questions?"

Sam awkwardly fixed his hair and took a slug of coffee to have something to do with his hands.

"Caffeine's a helluva a drug," she said, eyeing his cup.

He laughed.

"To your first question: I'm starving," said Jude. "Flight was good. Parents couldn't agree on who should bring me down, so we settled on nobody. They're splitting up."

"I'm sorry."

Sam had met Jude's mother only once—she was tanned and wore yoga clothes to dinner—and Sam had never warmed to her dad.

"It's fine," she said, and gave him a crooked smile. "They were miserable. By the way, they say hi."

"No they don't," Sam said.

Jude laughed.

"Well, my mom does," she admitted. "But my dad did ask about you. Whether or not you had plans to go back to school."

Sam shrugged. "We'll see," he said. Sam *was* going back, just not to UT.

"Well." She grabbed his forearm. "At least he won't be visiting. He may have been born in Dallas but he still thinks Austin is for drug addicts and trust-fund hippies."

Sam smiled dryly.

"Oh," Jude continued. "And I don't know how it feels to be a freshman, I love questions, and my first order of business was coming to see you to say hi." She served up another of her trillion-watt grins and waved right in his face.

"Hiiiii!" She was such a cartoon.

"Hi back," Sam said, and busied himself with a plate of pastries. "I made these for you."

"Whoa, for me?"

"Donuts and cherry hand pies," he said.

"Wait, you made these?"

He nodded.

"Jeez, I'm going to be over here all the time," she said. "I can't believe you bake."

"Well, they're fried," he said. Sam wondered what constituted "all the time."

"Even better." Jude pulled out her phone. "I'm going to tell my friends to come by."

Sam nodded.

Jude was good about that sort of thing. Sharing and sometimes oversharing. They'd been thrown together at family functions a few more times and he'd eventually grown to enjoy her consistent stream of conversation. It was a nice respite from the rancor of the grown-ups, and even after the split, Jude never allowed Sam to lose touch. And he'd tried. Jude remembered birthdays and sent silly messages at the holidays with unsolicited updates from her life. Her congeniality was unflappable. Sam meanwhile had no idea when her birthday was ever since he deleted all his social media accounts.

"Do you want a coffee or something?" he asked.

"Iced please."

"Milk and sugar?" Another fact he didn't know about her.

"Tons," she said, beaming.

•   •   •

"Yaassssssssssssss!!!!!"

A tall brown-haired girl dressed as if she were attending a desert festival galloped in, trailed by someone bearing an uncanny resemblance to the tiny Asian girl from the Japanese horror movie *The Grudge*.

"Yasssssss!!!" shrieked Jude back, hugging the brunette as the tassels on her shirt jangled.

"Bitch, finally!" yelled the taller girl. Their long knobby limbs reminded Sam of king crabs clasped in an embrace.

The Asian girl smiled at him for a second, then changed her mind. He responded with a grimace.

Jude untangled her tanned arms and lunged for the shorter girl.

"Hiiiiiiiiii," sang Jude into her hair, practically lifting her off the floor. "Yay, it's Penny."

The girl patted his niece's back twice—*pat, pat*—and locked eyes with him helplessly.

"This is my best friend, Mallory," Jude said. "And my roommate, Penny."

"So, you're Uncle Sam," said Mallory, reaching for his hand. She had a firm handshake. The sort that quickly became a contest.

"I'm Mallory Sloane," said Mallory Sloane.

"Pleasure," he said, refusing to acknowledge her grip. She bit her lower lip in a seductive manner. Sam smiled and quickly said hi to the other one. She waved at a spot slightly left of his ear.

"So, what can I do for you ladies today?"

"Can you make me a flat white?" asked Mallory, who kept her sunglasses on inside.

Sam loathed the arbitrary taxonomy of fiddly coffee drinks and had long since learned them all out of spite.

"Sure," he said, grinding beans for a short shot.

"Do you know what that is?" she challenged.

"Yep," he said. "Latte with a modified espresso to milk ratio. With microfoam."

"Nice try, Mal," said Jude.

"What are you having," he asked. "Penny was it?"

Sam followed Penny's sight line to her shoes. Which, coincidentally, were exactly his shoes though smaller.

"Great taste," he said, nodding at her feet.

Penny's mouth made the shape of an "O," but no sound escaped.

Dorm lotteries made for the funniest groupings. Sam's old freshman roommate, Kirin Mehta, used to sleepwalk and sleep-pee in a corner of their living room every weekend. Sam hoped that these two girls—the mute and the sexpot—got along for Jude's sake.

"Let me guess," he said to Penny. "You want a bone-dry half-caff cappuccino with a caramel drizzle?"

Penny cleared her throat and nodded.

"What are the odds?" he asked her, fairly certain that it wasn't at all what she wanted.

Sam studied Penny out of the corner of his eye. Her messy

hair lent her an air of zaniness. She looked like a scribbled-in-graphite drawing.

"Actually, may I have an iced coffee?" she piped up.

"Of course you *may*," he said pointedly.

"Oh, Uncle Sam?"

He swiveled to see Mallory leaning toward him, elbows hooked on the bar. Her not-insignificant boobs were hoisted to where they almost hit her chin. She lowered her sunglasses with a silver-painted talon. Clearly, too much time had elapsed since Mallory was paid attention to.

"What's up?"

"Is it true that you bake?" she asked.

He nodded.

"Maybe someday you'll bake something for me," she said, suggestively tilting her head.

He tilted his head to mirror hers.

"No maybes about it, Mallory," he said. "Eat off Jude's plate right now and I'll have baked that for you. Happy trails."

"You're funny," she tittered, sashaying off to follow her friend.

Sam shook his head. There was no way he was going to mix it up with a freshman. Let alone a friend of Jude's. Even he wasn't that dumb.

PENNY.

The three girls sat on a floral couch toward the back with Jude in the middle. They set down their drinks, and Penny noted that Jude's femur was almost twice as long as hers.

"So." Mallory leaned to address Penny. "Jude mentioned you were an only child too."

"Mm-hmm."

"I have two little sisters," Mallory continued, sipping her coffee. "Whereas Jude hasn't had to share anything in her life, let alone a room."

Jude jabbed her friend in the ribs and grabbed another donut.

"What Mal's so subtly trying to tell you is that I'm a slob." Jude took a bite, spraying crumbs in her lap to prove her point. "Look, I'm way too busy living life to mull over something as dull as cleaning. Besides, everyone knows geniuses are messy."

Mallory plowed on.

"It's just that I happened to notice earlier that you were highly organized," she said. "It's going to make things interesting. I live in Twombly, but you should expect me around a lot."

Ah, Twombly. Rich-bitch housing.

Penny wondered why Jude couldn't just visit Mallory at Twombly. They had a Pilates studio in the basement and a screening room that showed movies that were still in theaters.

Sam met them with an espresso and set it down on the coffee table.

"Can you visit more with us?" Jude asked him.

"In a bit," he said. "I'll be right back."

The girls watched him go.

"Whoa," said Penny, realizing what should have been obvious. "It's not just the shoes," she whispered.

"What?" asked Mallory in an outside voice. Penny huddled closer.

"Me and your uncle are wearing the same *outfit*."

Jude and Mallory craned their necks. It was true; they were both wearing black T-shirts with three-quarter-length sleeves, black belts with burnished silver buckles, and skinny black jeans with holes at both knees and black high-top Chucks.

"Oh my God," said Jude. "He was such a skater when we were kids. I didn't realize he'd crossed over to the dark side."

Mallory snorted.

"Remember in sixth grade when you had the wallet chain and those enormous, disgusting khakis?" asked Mallory. "God, you were obsessed with Uncle Sam. Watch, Jude's going to start dressing in mourning garb now."

Sam was arranging dirty mugs on a tray. He had a cowlick on his head. An unruly little curlicue that rose off his otherwise *very cool* hair. He probably hated it. Penny loved when that happened. When a single detail rebelled against the package. She wanted to touch it. Penny looked away before she got caught staring.

Mallory bit into one of the donuts. "Ack," she said, sticking her tongue out like a baby. "I hate pistachio." She removed the offending clump from her mouth with her fingernails and set the damp mass on the table.

Penny silent-screamed.

"Then why pick the one that is clearly pistachio?" asked Jude. "It literally has visible pistachio pieces on it. Mal, it's green!"

Jude picked up the offending pile of mash *with her bare hands* and looked for somewhere to deposit it.

Penny silent-screamed harder.

In a flash, Penny removed a package of wet wipes from her backpack and handed one to Jude. Then she squirted hand sanitizer in her hands since she couldn't bleach her brain. Best friends were one thing, but this was perverse. Who touches someone's half-chewed food? And who spits out half-chewed food in public in the first place?

"Thanks," said Jude, bundling the lump into the wipe. "How's the pie?"

"Good." Penny passed the rest off and took another half a donut before Mallory tainted the rest.

"Shit." Jude bolted upright. A lurid red dollop of filling toppled onto her white shirt.

With her free hand, Penny offered Jude another wet wipe and a stain stick.

"Seriously?" Mallory grabbed Penny's kit from her lap before she could protest. "Clown car much? Are you going to pull out a ladder and a Volkswagen bus next?"

Penny wanted to ask who in the hell would put a bus in a car but was distracted by whether or not she'd packed anything mortifying in her go bag.

"Good Lord, it's like doomsday prepping in here." Mallory pawed through the pouch. "Band-Aids, ChapStick, tampons . . . I've heard of teen moms, but you're a teen grandma or something. Let me guess—you have little packets of Sweet'n Low and coupons too? How adorable."

"So adorable," repeated Jude, smearing the stain stick onto her shirt.

Penny despised the word "adorable." It was trivializing.

Mallory continued laying out the contents of Penny's emergency crap bag onto the coffee table as if they were surgical instruments. Hand sanitizer, ear plugs, thumb drive, Advil, Q-tips, bobby pins, sewing kit, tiny IKEA pencil . . .

"Ooooh, and a single condom." Mallory held the foil square between her thumb and forefinger.

That was it.

Penny snatched back the condom and the bag, gathering her things off the table.

"Mal," Jude admonished, sweeping the rest of the items together. "Don't be a dick."

"I can't be inquisitive?" Mallory objected. "Besides, I'm saying nice things." She leaned back with smug satisfaction and regarded Penny. "You're so organized. I bet you're a math genius or something. Let me guess—you're an overachieving Asian kid who skipped ten grades? Are you secretly twelve years old and a freshman in college?"

Penny glared.

"Come on, you can tell me," said Mallory.

Reasonable responses to a mildly racist verbal attack that was also somewhat complimentary:

1. Slap the ever-living shit out of her with the other half of the pistachio donut.
2. Calmly tell her that you *are* a genius *and* a witch and that your binding spells had the added effect of rendering your enemies bald. Especially the asshole racist ones.
3. Scream at Jude, ban Mallory from their room. Slap everyone.

"Come on, Penny," said Mallory after a while. "I was just teasing."

"You know what?" Penny turned to Mallory. "I'm only being nice to you as a courtesy," she said. "You don't get to be bitchy for no reason, and you don't get to be racist to me. And certainly not in such a lazy, derivative way."

Penny felt the familiar prickle of moisture at her eyes. She rarely cried at sad things, mostly mad ones. It was a fun and easy way to lose arguments. She took a deep breath and exhaled slowly.

"Racist?" said Mallory. "Who the hell are you calling a racist? That's such an offensive thing to say to . . ."

"Jesus, Mal," said Jude. "Stand down."

"I'm a lot of things," huffed Mallory. "But I'm not racist."

"Said every racist ever," spat Penny. She rolled her eyes so hard she saw brain.

The three girls finished their coffees. Penny wondered if her entire college experience would be this much fun. It was like high school except that it followed you into your bedroom. Great.

Finally, Mallory broke the silence.

"My boyfriend got a new truck."

The comment was met with more silence.

"This is my attempt at changing the subject," Mallory said after a while.

Penny relented. "What kind of truck?"

"A Nissan."

"Mallory's boyfriend is Benjamin Westerly," said Jude meaningfully.

"Who the hell is Benjamin Westerly?"

"He's huge in Australia," said Mallory.

"I have no idea what that means," said Penny.

Jude chortled.

"Ben's in a band," Mallory explained. "He's famous to roughly a hundred thousand people who absolutely worship him. His fan army's very passionate. Plus, he's twenty-one. Australia is incredibly progressive. They had a woman prime minister."

To Penny, Australians felt like off-brand, bizarro British

people. But then again, Penny didn't personally know any Australians. Though it said something shady that every other place on Planet Earth went placental for their animals while Australians held on to marsupials. Wow, maybe Penny was racist too.

"That's cool," she said after a while.

"What did I miss?" Sam joined them, setting another espresso down next to his old one. Penny regarded the twin cups.

"Tepid," he explained, finally taking a seat on the chair next to her. Penny loved that word. It was the most perfect way to describe the temperature. The word "pith" was the same. Everything about it recalled the spongy stuff in oranges.

Sam reached over her to grab a packet of sugar. "Pardon my reach."

Penny held her breath and leaned back so she wouldn't creepily fog up his cheek. She caught a part of the tattoo where the sleeve of his T-shirt rode up. It was either a hand or a set of hands. It easily ranked within the top three most erotic sights of her life.

"Everything was delicious, Sam," purred Mallory.

Sam's armchair was set slightly higher than them on the sofa and he crossed his legs elegantly. His right knee brushed Penny's left and she almost passed out. With the comically small espresso cup in his thin hands, Penny wondered for a second if he was gay. Not that it was any of her business.

"So what classes are you taking, J?"

"We're calling me 'J' now?" asked Jude. She was visibly pleased by this.

Sam laughed. "I'm trying it out."

He rubbed his bicep to reveal a shadow of another tattoo

under his other sleeve. It was some kind of animal. Penny's knee felt warm where he had touched it, and she flushed. Penny wondered what the tattoo was. Potentially a horse head. A chess piece maybe. A black knight.

Penny would probably get a bishop tattoo if she were to get anything off a chessboard. They were discreet and effective. Total stealth movers. Mallory and Jude would get queens. So would Penny's mother for that matter.

Uncle Sam.

Sam could have been in a band. A dreamy, brooding band. Penny thought cigarettes were pointless and smelled awful, but she imagined that Sam smoked and that he looked cool doing it.

God, she would totally smoke a cigarette if he offered her one. They'd be a striking pair in their identical outfits leaned up against a wall and smoking all cool.

As cool as glaucoma and lung cancer.

Penny had never had a cigarette in her life, and if they did smoke together Penny would probably have a coughing fit that lasted forever and ended on an audible fart.

Jesus, pull it together.

Seriously, what was happening to her? Besides, she had a boyfriend. She tried to conjure Mark's face and got as far as the general slope of his nose plus his hair. Mark who'd gotten white-kid cornrows in fifth grade and wore the same navy-blue fleece all winter without washing it.

Sam was different. Sleek. Brooding and angular. An Egon Schiele portrait. Schiele if she remembered correctly had been a protégé of Gustav Klimt and had a propensity for drawing himself in the nude.

Nude.

"So," Sam said, leaning back and crossing his arms. "What are y'all majoring in?"

Schiele probably didn't say "y'all" though.

"Media studies," said Mallory, fluffing her hair. "I want to be talent."

"Marketing," said Jude. "It was the least boring major Dad was willing to pay for. . . ."

Sam up-nodded, volleying the query to Penny. Penny hated this question. Her answer came off as pretentious.

"What was your major?" Penny deflected.

"Film," he said.

"Oh, the film program at UT is excellent," she said in a voice a full octave higher than her normal register. "I mean, it's the birthplace of mumblecore, the Duplass brothers, Luke and Owen Wilson, Wes Anderson . . ." She couldn't stop the word-vomit.

"Wes Anderson was a philosophy major," Sam interrupted.

She blushed harder.

Kill me now.

Sam smiled disarmingly.

"I don't know why I know that," he said.

"Why film?" Penny squeaked. On some level she knew whatever you picked in college didn't matter in the real world. People rarely pursued a career in accordance with their major, though it was a decent Rorschach test for self-perception. It said everything about how you saw yourself.

"I wanted to be a documentary filmmaker," he said. Penny wondered about the past tense. "There are so many unbelievable stories going on in the world, just quietly happening around you. There's this Hitchcock quote about how in regular movies the director is God and how in documentaries God is the director. I always loved that."

He stacked his espresso cups.

Penny knew emoji hearts were flying out of her eyes. She was smitten mitten kittens. She'd never heard anyone her age talk about the work they wanted to do. Not that Sam was her age exactly. Penny swallowed the rest of her questions: whether he felt like a ghost trolling the living, mining their existence for ideas; whether or not he got lonely watching other people the way Penny did.

"Jesus, you're emo," observed Mallory, scrolling through her phone.

Sam chuckled. "I dropped out anyway. Couldn't afford it."

"Well, I think college is a sham." Mallory shrugged. "I'm here as Jude's plus one and to shut my mother up. We're better off trying to invent an app or something."

The four of them sat in silence considering the depressing reality.

"Just don't invent an app that invents apps," Penny piped up. "The job market's bad enough without you taking robot jobs from the robots."

Sam laughed.

Sam had resting bitch face until he laughed. Penny had never wanted anything as bad as to make him do it again.

"God, the app singularity is the worst thing I can imagine," he said after a moment.

Penny was thrilled—Sam either read science fiction or knew

enough about it to know what to call it when computers got smarter than humans and started to phase them out.

"Social media would be a mess," she said, smiling. "Who's catfishing the catfisher?"

"Do Android phones dream of electric sheep?" he asked.

They both groaned, but a dad joke with a Philip K. Dick reference was Penny's sweet spot. Dad jokes were Penny's favorite. (You didn't need to be Freud to figure that one out.) His hotness was making eye contact unbearable, and her cheeks tingled pleasurably.

"Anyway," sang Mallory impatiently.

Penny cleared her throat.

Sam cracked his knuckles in a super-attractive, kinda menacing way. With his arms in front of his chest, she could see more hints of tattoos at his throat. The French word for throat is *"gorge."* And, Christ, his was indeed.

Mallory said something dumb about empathy and the value of the human spirit. Penny wasn't listening.

Sam had somehow found the Perfect Shirt with the Perfect Collar, which was stretched out *just enough* to create this enticing peekaboo effect.

Penny thought again about Mark. Mark, who wore polo shirts on dates and only read self-help books that you could buy at the airport, from *The 7 Habits of Highly Successful People* to *Who Moved My Cheese?* And the old standby *The 4-Hour Workweek.*

Good Mark.

Uncomplicated Mark.

Mark whose calls she'd sent to voicemail twice today.

Sam absentmindedly patted his cowlick down, showing a flash of white above his armpit.

Even Sam's armpit was hot.

"Do you want to have dinner with us?" Jude asked him.

"Can't," he said, and stood up suddenly. "Work."

Jude nodded, her disappointment apparent. "Maybe next time?"

"Sure," he said distractedly as he excused himself.

•   •   •

"Daaaaaamn," whispered Mallory, ogling Sam as he left.

Daaaaaamn, thought Penny.

"I didn't know Uncle Sam was such an intellectual," Mallory breathed, fanning herself dramatically with her hand.

"Ew, stop." Jude swatted her best friend's leg. "That's literally my father's brother."

"Former stepbrother, by marriage, for, like, five minutes," corrected Mallory. "And he's not old."

"He's twenty-one," said Jude.

"First cousins marry," said Mallory.

"Wow . . . ," said Jude, shaking her head.

"What?" shot Mallory. "Seriously, what's the deal? He's so hot. Dark, but hot. And you." Mallory turned to Penny. "What's with your awkward bullshit and then pulling out your flirtation A game?"

"Yeah, you guys seemed to get along," said Jude. Both pairs of eyes studied Penny with new interest.

"I'm being neighborly," Penny demurred. She turned to

Mallory. "I can be friendly as long as strangers don't go rummaging through my personal effects."

"Ha," Mallory said. "Whatever, what's his type?"

"Mal," warned Jude.

"What?" Mallory blinked innocently.

"Mallory, you are not allowed to go for my uncle," said Jude.

"*Allowed?*" said Mallory. "But what if he goes for me? Uncles love me."

"Don't." Jude turned to face her friend. "I mean it. You know I don't need any more drama with my family right now. I'm invoking an ironclad friendship ask."

"Family?" retorted Mallory. "I'm about as related to Sam as you are at this point."

"You know the rules. Ironclad asks don't have to make sense," said Jude, waving her hand dismissively. Her mouth was a firm thin line. Penny knew that face. It was when you were so mad you had to train everything to keep still or you'd cry.

"Whoa," said Mallory. "Jude Louisa Lange. Do you have sexual feelings for your former uncle by marriage?"

"Stop!" hissed Jude back.

"It's the only explanation," countered Mallory.

"Ew. No. That's not it at all. . . ." Jude sucked down the last of her coffee. "Friends hooking up with family makes things awkward and complicated. So can you not?"

"Aw, babe," said Mallory, finally wrapping her arms around Jude. "Okay. Ironclad friendship ask invoked. You can't fault a girl for wanting to be your best friend *and* your aunt."

Jude laughed.

Penny eyed the two girls. Either Jude did have a crush on

Sam and wasn't admitting it, or something was up with her family for real. She couldn't imagine Mallory backing down easily otherwise. Penny recorded the information in a new folder in her head.

"Besides," continued Jude. "I think he had a rough summer too."

"Why?" asked Mallory.

"Well, he didn't exactly tell me and he's impossible to spy on most of the time, but . . ." Jude opened Instagram on her phone. "Look . . ." She searched and found the page of a MzLolaXO and kept scrolling.

"I think he has girl trouble . . . ," said Jude.

Penny wondered why "girl trouble" meant some dude had dating drama and that "women's trouble" was about periods.

"Oooh, she's super hot," said Mallory.

MzLolaXO *was* hot.

In fact, Lola's look was psychological warfare. She was pretty, by scientific and mathematical standards. The kind of attractive that compelled cornballs to come out with flouncy terms like "ravishing" or "exquisite" to describe women. They also almost always referred to them as "creatures" and definitely "females." Lola was long and thin in the way that certain beautiful people "forgot" to eat or else only nibbled on aesthetically pleasing morsels like Ladurée macarons or sliced kiwi.

But it was also the way she dressed—incidentally—as if her destroyed denim skirt were placed to protect the modesty of a prudish audience. She was Instagram famous in the way that some girls just are. As if they were designed to indiscriminately detonate insecurities in other women. Basically, she was the perfect stylistic match for Sam. No wonder Sam dodged Jude's offer for dinner. He probably had way better things to do than hang out with them.

Jude kept swiping, a terrorizing merry-go-round of Lola doing things while looking attractive.

"But who even has this many selfies?" said Mallory, wrinkling her nose. "Other than a total narcissist."

Penny was willing to bet Mallory had more than this many selfies. They admired Lola stretching in a crop top to where the dagger tattoos on her rib cage showed.

"See," said Jude. "Sam's in literally every fifth picture from here. . . ." She continued scrolling up. "All the way to here."

"That's years," said Mallory, impressed.

"That's what I'm saying," said Jude. "He was in this perfect relationship and now he's not, and honestly, I've been talking to Dr. Greene about it and she thinks he's depressed."

"Dr. Greene is Jude's therapist," said Mallory.

If that were true, depression suited Sam.

"So, don't confuse him, Mallory," she finished. "He's very vulnerable."

Penny thought about the types of girls who loved vulnerable guys. Or else misunderstood ones. They were generally the types to marry serial killers on death row.

"Fine," Mal relented. "I have a boyfriend anyway."

"Thank you," said Jude. "You, too." She nodded at Penny, smiling broadly. "Please don't date my uncle."

"Pfft," scoffed Mallory.

Jude reached over and tucked a tangled strand of Penny's hair behind her ear and patted her cheek.

SAM.

Knowing that your only computer was about to crap out on you despite not having nearly enough money to replace it can only be described as horror. Horror and terror. *Torror.*

Sam drummed impotently on the trackpad a few times and pounded hard. The pinwheel of death persisted.

Shit.

He calmly closed the sticker-covered laptop, briefly considering rolling into a ball and ugly-crying for the rest of the day.

The ancient machine—his trusted steed since junior year of high school—already didn't qualify as a laptop because it had to be plugged in or it would die. Plus, the colors bled together on-screen so you felt as though you were on hallucinogens no matter what site you were on.

But if a computer was at a virtual standstill on the information superhighway, it had to be taken out back and shot.

Sam breathed deeply and raggedly counted to ten.

By his tabulations, he didn't have enough in his checking account to get money out of it. An ATM wouldn't dignify you with a response unless you had the minimum of twenty bucks and Sam had seventeen dollars. Minus the two bucks for the ATM fee.

The catch-22 was demoralizing. He needed the laptop to take an online film class through Alamo Community College so he could learn what he couldn't from YouTube tutorials—how to block a shot like Roger Deakins, the best cinematographer in the world. Or to light in the style of Gordon Willis, who'd DP'd *The Godfather*. Okay, so he knew he wouldn't learn *exactly* that in a sixteen-week course, but forking over the $476.00 for class and access to supplies was cheaper than camera and gear rentals for four months. Only now he couldn't torrent any of the required watching.

Sam flexed the toes on his right foot. The sole of his black sneaker was split where it met canvas. He grabbed black gaffer's tape out of his backpack, tore off a piece, and taped the hole shut. The sticky electrical tape solved most issues— except fried motherboards. Maybe he'd stop going outside altogether. He'd shuffle shoelessly from his bedroom to House and back again—a correspondence-course-taking Sisyphus.

He checked the clock above the door: two forty-five. That glorious lull between the lunch rush and the four p.m. caffeine fix. The only customer was a short guy with a ridiculously coiffed pointy beard working on his gleaming thirteen-inch MacBook Air, complete with portable laptop stand and extra keyboard. Sam briefly considered mugging him. Even if it was possibly the dumbest idea to rob someone where you not only worked but also lived.

He listlessly thumbed through the discarded copy of the city's alt-paper of record, the *Austin Chronicle*, on the coffee table closest to him. Ever since he'd moved in upstairs, his world had become tiny. He wondered if he still possessed the necessary antibodies to venture outside. Maybe he'd get some ancient disease that we thought we were done with, like polio or smallpox. Did people get smallpox anymore? He needed to read a book once in a while. Isn't that what people in recovery did? Get a hobby? Christ, "recovery" was so dramatic.

Sam could have killed a beer right now. Hell, he could tear through a six-pack lickety-split. He thought about the yeasty bite of a Shiner Bock, his mother's favorite and the first beer he'd ever tasted at six years old, and how it had been months since he'd held a cold one to his mouth.

Instead he took a long pull from a glass of water and cleaned. He needed something to do with his hands while his thoughts churned. Sam fluffed pillows, bused tables, wiped down counters, recycled the papers, twisted the group handles from the espresso machine, dumped their filter baskets with a series of satisfying snaps, and rinsed everything out with scalding water. He was reassured by the way his knuckles felt tight and parched afterward.

Sam imagined his rough hands entwined with Lorraine's. Liar Lorraine. His ex. She'd had beautiful hands. "Hand-model hands" her friends had called them. Long, articulate fingers with slender nail beds. But Sam worshipped her feet.

Stubby-toed and flat, she hid them as a policy, refusing to wear sandals in the summer, which only served to make them more desirable. They were hilarious, full of personality. Clever feet that picked pens up from the floor when they thought no one was watching.

The rest of Lorraine had consistently been too cool for him. As aloof as a black-and-white photo of a French girl. Sam knew from the second they met that he had to ask her out. He had to.

He was seventeen to her nineteen. She was DJing at a tiny club with no sign called Bassment, wearing a white silky slip dress. Her hair was pale pink and shoulder-length, dyed ultramarine at the tips. Huge swoops of black encircled her shimmering hazel eyes. She was unmistakably sexy. Sexy. Sam hated that word the way other people hated "moist" or "panty," but there was no other way to describe her. The Great Love of His Life was plain sexy. And terrifying.

Not that Sam was all the way innocent when they met. From the time he was eleven, he hung out with a ragtag assemblage of derelicts who thought it was hilarious that this little kid had no curfew and drank as much booze as they did. "Little Sam" had a smart mouth and the ladies loved him. He was selfie bait for older drunk chicks.

There wasn't a bar that the kid couldn't get into—he knew everyone, or at least his dad did and he was the spit-and-image of his old man—though precocious as he was, he'd never been in love. That was until he saw Lorraine up there on the dais, neon green headphones, ignoring him. Sam was a goner. Sucker-punched and clobbered.

He waited an hour to talk to her. Then another. Another two passed.

At three a.m., when the lights came on, he nodded and asked, "So, where we going?"

"Food," she said, tossing her bag at him.

They drove to a diner, where she devoured a heaping plate of migas. Sam ordered coffee, and when they were finished and walking out into the street, without warning she hoisted herself into his arms, wrapped her legs around him, and kissed him. Sam was stoked—stoked that it was happening and stoked that he'd grown three inches over the summer and could lift her. Her breath tasted of green peppers and cigarettes and her confidence was mind-blowing. His mother used to say you shouldn't marry anyone you wouldn't want to divorce, and he understood that now. Lorraine was the emotional equivalent of a hollow-point round; the exit wound was a shit show.

Sam restocked the almond milk, consolidated the baked goods into a single cake stand, and switched out the bar mops. The new ones smelled good, bleach-clean. He held them under his nose. Sobriety meant a low-level boredom all the time. Taking pleasure in small, repetitive tasks was the big show of the whole day. Sure there weren't dazzling, dizzying highs anymore, no careening around town with the most enigmatic and emotionally toxic woman he'd ever met. There would be no screwing each other's brains out in a dazed, compulsive panic, but at least there were clean bar mops. He admired the neatly folded squares of cotton and rearranged one so the blue stripe lined up in the stack.

Right then, as if she begrudged him this tiny victory, Liar texted him.

Call me.

Shit.

Sam's hands got clammy when his fight-or-flight response was triggered. Under the right light you could actually see the sheen of moisture appear on his palms. He'd made a time-lapse video of it once.

He felt equal parts sick and excited when he heard from her after an absence. The last time they spoke was twenty-seven days ago. Just one day more and he would've kicked the habit for good. At least that's what the books on substance abuse told him. He thought he'd turned over a new leaf. In fact, he'd even begun jogging. Okay, so he'd hopped around the block twice in his busted shoes, but he'd cut back to three cigarettes a day, which for him was the same as completing a half marathon.

He thought about the pressure of her lips on his. The lemony scent of her hair. He closed his eyes and considered their last meeting and the bad ideas that followed. She'd stormed his newly small life and disappeared in a mushroom cloud of devastation. Again.

After that last run-in, he'd sent three unanswered texts before he'd been sufficiently humiliated. The first because he told himself he wasn't the type of guy who slept with someone and ghosted. The next two because his stupid brain was gobsmacked and running on a flustered delay. Now boom: Liar on line one.

This is what she did. It was as if she knew the moment he was able to wake up without wanting to die and couldn't abide by it.

Sam stared at the text.

Call me.

Three more hours of work to go before he could stew in the dark in his room.

What the hell was "Call me"?

Only sadists left that message.

Sadists and bullies. She might as well have written: "Gnaw off your hand."

Sam knew he was on the right side of history. Let the record show that she was the cheater. He was the spurned lover, the cuckold, the humiliated, the victim.

GTFO with your Call Me's!

Not that he wasn't tempted.

Sam sighed. Maybe if he called she'd tell him where she'd buried his balls and his heart.

People cheated on people every second of every day all over the world. It's just that Sam couldn't believe it had happened to him. By Lorraine no less. *His* Lorraine.

Jesus.

He'd entombed the event of their actual breakup so deep it'd been effectively redacted from memory. Sam leaned on the counter and retrieved the original file from 103 days ago.

That fateful morning she'd told him she wanted to go to the breakfast taco spot before work. The not-that-good spot on Manor that charged extra for pico de gallo.

Sam wondered if ordering a michelada with his eggs would be distasteful. He needed something to take the edge off after the night they'd had. They'd doubled-down on martinis after a week of fighting about money and Lorraine's crazy work schedule. And while they both knew going out was a doomed enterprise, compounded by Sam's desire to swing by his mom's, they didn't care.

That morning Lorraine's hair was pulled into a bun. She appeared admirably refreshed, and Sam was grateful that no matter how much dysfunction there was at home, he could rely on his girlfriend to be there for him. He reached under the table to touch her knee when the chips arrived. He'd shoved a few in his mouth before she told him about some guy named Paul from her work.

It hadn't meant anything.

Though it had been building up for some time.

It had happened more than once.

Sam reacted by yelling loud enough that parents eating nearby with their young children gave him the stink-eye.

Lorraine sat there stone-faced.

"Do you love him?"

"Do you love me?"

"Is it something I did?"

"What the hell's the matter with you?"

"Did it feel good?"

"Better than me?!!!"

She wouldn't tell him his last name. Or where he lived.

"I don't love him," she said.

"Why, then?" Sam implored. He was sobbing. Inconsolable.

Lorraine, on the other hand, rarely ever cried, and turned cold whenever he did. Her expression hardened, as if his outpouring of emotion slaked any desire for her to feel anything.

In hindsight he was glad it wasn't the good taco spot because it would have been ruined forever. Anyplace that charged seventy-five cents for condiments could burn in hell. On principle.

"This," she whispered through clenched teeth. "This is the problem. Why does it have to be this way with us? Someone having a meltdown. Paul was . . . He was a distraction. I needed to get out of this. Us."

"No," he said. As if that would make the moment less real. Sam shook his head, mind stalled out at the denial stage of grief. "No. We love each other. We'll always love each other. You're a part of me." He searched her face, uncomprehending. It felt crazy to him that she was even another person. Her arm may as well have been his arm. That his arm had the power to turn against the rest of his body and walk away made no sense. Sam felt something in his chest crack.

"We're addicted to each other," she said. "It's not healthy. Paul's boring—don't get me wrong—but he has stability."

Stability. Sam knew what that meant. Stability meant rich. Paul must have been rich. Rich in the same way she was. Rich like he'd never been and never would be. Sam reached for her just as she stood up, hesitated, and then walked out.

After that morning, he'd moved into House and they'd gone months without speaking or running into each other. Sam had made sure of it. He avoided their old haunts, telling no one where he lived, and he worked as many hours as Al had for him. It was while on a toothpaste run at Walgreens that she called his name from down the aisle. Sam couldn't believe how companionable they still felt as they hung back in the parking lot. They made small talk, and no one brought up Paul. When she suggested they run to Polvo's for a margarita, it seemed like a great idea. A pitcher of House Ritas later, it seemed an even better idea to take their trip down memory lane all the way back to her apartment. He hadn't drunk a drop since. Twenty-seven days. Each one a feat.

When she disappeared again she became "LIAR" in his phone, and he tried to forget.

But with a text, a single directive, he felt the pinprick of the tiniest portal open in his heart. She had such beautiful skin. Especially her clavicles. Christ, and her elbows. He loved tracing his fingertips across the crest of bone on any part of her body.

No, he told himself.

He wanted to reconfigure his brain. Why couldn't he control when he thought about her? Why couldn't he control when she thought about him?

When they first broke up he'd watched *Eternal Sunshine of a Spotless Mind* and *High Fidelity* on a loop. He stopped sleeping. One morning Fin, sensing a need, reached out and hugged him. The two of them stood there for well over ten minutes while Sam cried so hard he got the hiccups.

Nope. Never. Again.

He deleted the text.

· · ·

For the next two hours, he tidied obsessively. Jude texted again, and Sam nearly had a heart attack thinking it was Lorraine. It was another invitation to dinner, but again he begged off, citing work. He felt equal parts guilty and annoyed. He considered telling Jude he would be busy for the foreseeable future but decided it wasn't worth the trouble. His lower back hurt and Sam wondered if the customers could detect the crazy in his eyes.

When his shift ended, he was spent. Sam settled the register and yawned. He could hear Fin in the back, hauling trash. Fin unfailingly let the screen door slam, which drove Sam nuts, but this time he was too tired to bitch. The only good thing about getting up at the absolute asscrack of dawn was that he was closed by eight and in bed sometimes by eight fifteen. Even if all he did under the covers was blink and not drink.

Earlier that year, Al had installed an impenetrable security system that amounted to a fake video camera affixed above the door and an automated gate that was already no longer automated. Sam walked outside to pull it closed. It took both hands and his full body weight.

"Put your back into it, *flaco!*" Fin yelled over his shoulder.

Sam laughed. "Your mom," he said. Fin cackled and cracked open a beer.

Your mom? God, he *was* tired.

Sam's nickname in high school had been AIDS because kids are jerks and because he was so emaciated. He hated his concave body with his visible veins and the individual, stringy muscles that you could watch move under his skin when he worked. Yet somewhere along the line, girls started seeing something in him other than the skinniness, and by then he stopped caring.

Still, there were times when he wished he were a big, hulking, ham-fisted dude who could slam the stupid gate shut in one go.

"Sam," called a voice from the shadows.

Sam jumped and made a high-pitched "wooot" that he immediately regretted.

He knew who it was instantly. And she'd for sure heard his sapless, startled *woooot*.

"I texted you," Lorraine said. He could detect flint in her tone.

Sam was surprised that it had taken only one afternoon for Lorraine, a.k.a. LIAR, to materialize. Patience wasn't her thing, though dropping by after a disappearance was bold even for her.

"What do you want, Lorraine?" Sam shot back.

"We have to talk," she said.

Original, he thought.

"What could there possibly be left to discuss?" He finished locking up. "I mean, if anything, your *silence* for the past month suggests there's nothing on the docket."

He wished he could subtly sniff his pits to see how he smelled. Why was he only ever running into her when he was completely unprepared? Of course, she was buttoned up for work and wearing a blazer. Liar was the worst.

"Seriously, Lorraine," he continued. "You made it clear. We're ancient history. The Paleozoic era. Older even. Whatever comes before the Paleozoic era. The Anthropocene . . . No, wait, that's now. . . ." He shoved his sweaty hands into his pockets.

"Stop talking," she said.

He scowled at her.

"Please."

Lorraine stepped into the light. She was pale. Paler than usual, which was already poet blouses and Oh-My-Goth levels of pallor.

Sam walked toward the porch steps and sat down. She followed. The sunset smeared pink across the sky as they stared out to the street.

"What is it?" His hand twitched for the cigarettes he didn't want to smoke in front of her.

"Sam," she said. "I'm late."

No joke, he thought for the split second before the full weight of her words hit him.

He took a deep breath and ran his hands through his hair. They felt numb.

Of course she was late. It made sense. In fact, it was the only news it could have been. It's not as if anything ever went the way he thought it would. Lorraine, for that matter, was not returning to his life after a spell of soul-searching to tell him she still loved him.

Christ.

Late.

They'd done it this time.

The dreadful rush of adrenaline was so immediate that he clapped his hands. Just once. Some lizard-brain Texas hardwiring kicked in to where all he knew was to act out the caricature of a high school football coach in times of crisis.

"Okay," he said in a purposeful tone. "How late?"

Clear eyes, full heart.

"I don't know," she said.

"What?" Sam squawked. "Aren't girls supposed to, you know, keep track?" Sam understood that the female reproductive system was a mysterious universe, but this seemed far-fetched. Then he thought about the teen moms on TV who accidentally had their babies on the toilet.

"Did you take a pregnancy test?"

Lorraine rolled her eyes. "Yeah, Sam."

"And?"

"Positive."

Shitshitshit.

"How many?"

"Four," she said. "No, three."

Now, Sam wasn't an ob-gyn or anything, but this seemed an irrationally small number of sticks to pee on before any thinking human could declare themselves in or out of the unwanted-pregnancy woods. In fact, Sam couldn't believe she hadn't taken at least twenty, and even still Lorraine should go to the doctor for a blood test to be completely positive. Positively positive.

Shitshitshit.

"Okay," he said, placing his hands on her shoulders. "You have to take a bunch more. I'll take you. We'll go right now."

He almost pounded her back in high-strung jocular cheer.

"Sam, you're freaking me out."

"No, don't freak," he shrieked. Sam smiled with all his teeth displayed. "It'll be fine. You should go to a doctor, a specialist, eliminate any doubt. For peace of mind."

"A specialist?" she said. "You sound insane."

Sam wiped his palms on the tops of his thighs.

"What about your regular doctor? Don't you go to some fancy guy?"

"I can't go to Dr. Wisham," she said, rolling her eyes. "He's my pediatrician."

Why was she still going to a pediatrician?

"Why are you still going to a pediatrician? It doesn't matter," he recovered. "I'll pay for it." Sam wondered about the going rate for plasma donation and how much a slightly underweight human male could spare before he keeled over and died. Maybe he could donate a toe to science.

Sam cleared his throat. He rubbed his chin. Most of the time they'd been good about condoms. Most of the time.

"I have an appointment with Planned Parenthood on Thursday," she said.

It was Friday. Thursday was way too many nights away.

"I can't miss work," she explained.

"I'm sure they'd understand if—"

"I can't," she interrupted. "It's a big deal. I'm the only entry-level team member, and I'm running production on three tent-pole activations for a client. Some random can't cover for me because I'm . . . 'worried.'" Lorraine rolled her eyes. Sam found the rest of the word salad more offensive than "worried," though he bit his tongue. "It's not as if I work in fast food or anything." She peered at him guiltily. "No offense."

First of all, managing an artisanal coffee purveyor was not working in fast food. Second of all . . .

"You're in advertising," he said. "You're not exactly saving lives. *No offense.*"

Shit. Tact. He needed to chill. Sam took another deep breath. She glared at him.

"I'm sorry," he said. "I'm still processing. So next week, do you need me to come with you?"

Sam considered the logistics. Maybe he could borrow Fin's car.

"No," she said.

Paul was probably driving her. Every time Sam thought about faceless, rich-ass Paul, he felt rage collect in the pit of his stomach in blistering pea-size sores.

"How late are you?"

"Three weeks?"

Jesus.

Three weeks was an eternity in the life cycle of late periods. Or so it seemed from everything he knew about periods. Which wasn't much.

They stood in silence. Sam pulled out his cigarettes. Then he imagined pink, teeny-tiny, microscopic baby lungs coughing. He put them away.

"I wanted to take a morning-after pill," she said. "But then I didn't, and . . ."

Sam thought about how careless they'd both been.

"Why didn't you tell me you were worried?"

Sam's stomach lurched guiltily at the prospect of Liar dealing with this herself.

"I thought about it."

"You waited three weeks to text me."

"I figured it was only a little late."

"Well, now it's kinda very incredibly late," finished Sam.

"I'm worried," Lorraine said, not meeting his eyes.

Wow. Was she going to cry? As screwed up as the circumstance was, was this when Sam would get to see Lorraine cry?

"Well." Sam held her and she let him. It made him feel strong and capable. "We'll figure it out."

"How?"

"Just that I'm here for you. I support you. I mean, it is mine, right?"

She pushed him away. Hard.

"Are you serious?"

"Well, Jesus, Lorr, it could be Paul's!" His anger swelled red-hot and righteous.

"I haven't been with Paul since before you!" she yelled.

Sam smiled before he caught himself.

Ha. Suck it, Paul.

Sam studied Lorraine then. Shit. He was in way over his head. Still, he couldn't help focusing on how she was mad at him and how he was stupidly elated that he was capable of making her this mad. It was all quite possibly the most idiotic circumstance to bring a baby into. A blameless, chubby nugget of person caught in the middle of two selfish screw-ups. Sam could feel his anxiety thrum in the back of his chest.

"If you are pregnant," he said slowly, "what do you want to do?"

He thought about the A word.

A-B-O-R-T-I-O-N

AH BORSH SHUNN

BORSCHT

As in the beet-red soup with soft bits in it.

Borscht. Borscht. Borscht.

"I don't know if I could terminate," she said.

TERMINATE.

Sam's mind glommed on to the glimmering red light in the Terminator's eye at the end of the movie, when the cyborg refused to die.

"I'm not a child, Sam," she said. "I'm not some knocked-up fifteen-year-old. I'm twenty-three. That's old enough to know better. My mom had me at twenty-four. . . . I can't."

He stared at her. Just drank her in. Blond hair. Small hands. Blue blouse. Black slacks.

It was a fair response.

It seemed exactly the sort of thing you'd know about yourself. Except Sam didn't know anything anymore.

PENNY.

When Penny was in ninth grade, two events of great portent occurred. One, she read Art Spiegelman's graphic novel *Maus*. Two, she figured out that she wouldn't be popular until she was a grown-up and that was fine because life was a long con.

Penny had Amber Friedman's birthday party to thank for this wisdom. Amber Friedman was a girl from French class who famously woke up at five forty-five every morning to straighten her curly hair only to set it in differently shaped curls. Everybody figured she was well off since her dad was a music journalist for *Rolling Stone*. And while life was tough for Penny as the daughter of a MILF, having a dad with more Instagram followers than God was also a monumental suck. Amber's dad cast a long shadow. It didn't help that his daughter wasn't cute. Not that she was ugly. She simply had one of those faces where the features were crowded into the middle like a too-big room with tiny furniture.

Then there was her personality. Amber loved butting in to finish other people's sentences—even with teachers—and sneezed with a high-pitched "tssst" at least a half-dozen times. To Penny it seemed a bid for the wrong kind of attention. Anyway, Penny hadn't been properly invited to the get-together. Amber's mom and Penny's mom were friendly from an Ethiopian cooking class they'd taken years ago and happened to run into each other at the market.

"But, Pen, Amber's going to be so disappointed," said Celeste, adding, "I got you both the new nail gel kits from Sephora." Celeste dangled two shiny black bags.

Penny was more susceptible to bribery then. She rode her bike over and figured there'd at least be snacks and cake and enough people that she could bail inconspicuously.

When she arrived, six pairs of eyes bored into her from the living room of the pokey ranch house. It smelled as if cat pee had been doused liberally with Pine-Sol, and Penny couldn't help thinking about how if you could smell anything it was because you were breathing particles of it into your body. Penny encouraged her face not to betray her thoughts as she said hi to Melissa and Christy from school and two girls Amber knew from temple. Huge silver Mylar balloons that spelled out AMBER clung to the ceiling except for the B that hung about midroom and kept sticking to the back of Amber's hair.

Over the next two hours, they made personalized pizzas that Amber's mom baked in the oven and sundaes for dessert. When clear plastic boxes of beads were presented so they could make earrings with fishing wire, Penny discovered her limit for boredom. She excused herself to go to the bathroom, listened carefully for anyone else in the house, and quietly began canvassing the area. Amber's room featured no less than five black-and-white posters of Audrey Hepburn, and atop her canopied bed lay an orange cat grooming itself. It stopped to glare at Penny before deciding the intruder wasn't worth the attention. When Penny poked her head into what she figured was Amber's dad's office, she hit pay dirt. Mike Friedman, music critic, had every graphic novel ever. Ever. EVER. Stacks. From Spider-Man to Superman to huge volumes of collected editions with shiny hard covers, organized by subject.

Penny couldn't believe it. Mere feet from the inane small talk ("isn't it, like, so awk how some people say caramel and other people say carm-el?") and bullshit pizza toppings like (gag) cubed pineapple were thousands of hours of genuine entertainment. He had everything. From Swamp Thing to *V for Vendetta* and *Persepolis*, from We3 to Runaways.

Mr. Friedman's room smelled of new books—pulp and varnish. After a whole shelf filled with a cute, pudgy character called Bone, Penny found *Maus*.

Penny had wanted to read *Maus* ever since she learned that it was the first comic to win the Pulitzer Prize, and upon realizing that Mr. Friedman had two copies—a hardcover and a soft—Penny did what any kid would. She stuck the soft down the back of her jeans, slid her sweatshirt over it, pretended she had a stomachache, and hightailed it home.

It was among the most shameful moments of her life. Never mind the karma of a total non-Jew stealing a book about the Jewish Holocaust from a Jewish person.

Except that the book changed her life.

Penny knew *Maus* was going to be formative. Not that she was going to become a career criminal, more that she felt destined to make something that made someone else feel how she did when she read it.

Penny believed with her whole heart that there were moments—crucial instances—that defined who someone was going to be. There were clues or signs, and you didn't want to miss them.

It astounded her that a comic book featuring cartoon mice and cats could trick her into learning so much about World War II. Not only *learn* about it but *care* about it. She'd known about Auschwitz and how they told all the prisoners that they were going to take showers and instead, cutting off their hair, throwing it in a pile, and sending them to the gas chamber. Even kids. In history last year they'd had a quiz on the dates and significant events of the war, and she'd gotten a near-perfect score. Yet it wasn't until she read *Maus* and lived it through the eyes of a father and son mouse, that she saw past the cold facts. That night Penny read *Maus* twice and cried. She knew then that she had to become a writer.

It made what happened at school the following Monday worth it. Amber told everyone in French that Penny had left abruptly because she had diarrhea. After that Penny was cured of ever trying to play nice with people from school again. Penny might have been unpopular, but so was Amber. Unless you were super-popular or second-most super-popular, the difference was negligible. You were a loser. What separated Penny from Amber was that anybody could smell Amber's desperation. To Penny that was far more pathetic than simply being invisible. Penny would stop trying. Instead she'd spend time preparing for her future, living in books until the exciting part of her life would begin. Things would matter then. In fact, everything would be different.

. . .

Ten minutes in and Penny already knew her eight a.m. fiction-writing course on Thursdays would be her favorite. Notably, the class was full despite the agonizing start time. Held in a small classroom, it was incomparable to American History or regular English 301, which were both conducted in sprawling lecture halls with stadium seating and a screen suspended from the ceiling so you could see your professor's face from the cheap seats. This classroom sat about twenty, with high school desks, the kind where the chairs were attached to the table.

J.A. Hanson was young for a professor. She was twenty-eight. At twenty-two she'd written the critically acclaimed *Messiah*, a classic post-apocalyptic tale she'd received a Hugo Award for. The hero was a teenaged girl and the ending blew Penny's mind. That J.A. was a woman blew everyone else's mind. The reviews and fansites were convinced J.A. Hanson was a dude. Especially since there were no pictures of her at the time and nobody knew what J.A. stood for.

Penny discovered science fiction shortly after *Maus*. She began writing her own short stories as a hobby, and though her high school had a literary magazine, Penny wouldn't have dreamed of submitting anything.

It didn't help that in AP English Lit, junior year, they'd

read Shirley Jackson's "The Lottery," which was basically *The Hunger Games* except it was written in the forties and had a twist at the end.

They'd spent a week in class creating a story with unpredictable endings, and Penny wrote hers from the point of view of a sixteen-year-old Swiss boy in the year 2345, who woke up knowing precisely when he'd die. The boy considered what his final acts would be and elected to spend the day doing exactly what he normally did, playing chess with his best friend, Gordy. He was cheered by the small, dependable routines most and the twist was that he didn't die, waking up every morning with the same thought in an insane asylum, where he didn't have any choice but to do what his doctors had scheduled for him.

Penny liked her story, yet Ms. Lansing gave her a B-, saying she'd been "hoping to hear more about Penny's exotic point of view." Penny couldn't believe it. As if Zurich, 2345, wasn't far-flung enough. She knew what her teacher meant; she'd meant *Asian* despite Penny being born in Seguin, Texas, which was maybe twenty minutes away. Penny vowed not to show her work again until she respected who'd be reading it.

Over the years, Penny inhaled the classics—*Ready Player One*, *Dune*, and *Ender's Game*, though it wasn't until she was introduced to *Messiah*, ironically from a guy who was the worst dude in the history of dudes, that she realized sci-fi didn't have to be so . . . boy. J.A.'s work was like *Ender's Game*, yet where Ender was smart and getting conned 'cause he was a kid, J.A.'s hero Scan knew her worth.

A female protagonist made the stories more inspiring than voyeuristic. It was so much fun to write about who you *could* be. From then on Penny's stories centered around women and girls. There wasn't even a special trick. You wrote it exactly as you would for a guy, but you made pain thresholds higher since girls have to put up with more in the world and give them more empathy, which makes everything riskier. Plus, with sci-fi, you set up the rules at the beginning and you could blast it all to kingdom come as long as you did it in a satisfying manner. The fact that Penny could take a class from a published author made the whole communal-living college situation worthwhile.

J.A. Hanson had undeniable charisma. She was black with natural hair, dyed platinum, gathered in a pouf on top of her head. And she wore thick-rimmed white glasses to boot. J.A. made nerdiness glamorous. And not in some posery Tumblr way where girls played first-person shooters in their underpants to be attractive to guys.

"Does a Chinese writer get to write about a slave lynching?" It was an intense topic for 8:11 a.m., yet J.A. lobbed the topic into the room so casually Penny couldn't be sure she'd heard her correctly. It gave the room an intimate, crackly energy, as if they were crowded around a dinner table. A dinner table that was unceremoniously lit on fire.

In Penny's heart, the answer was absolutely yes. Though she also didn't know how she felt as an Asian person telling a black woman that.

Penny snuck a peek over her shoulder to see if anyone would pipe up.

"Obviously," said the other Asian kid in the class. "I read about that in the *Times* as well," he said.

The kid had boy-band hair and a clipped British accent that made sense for sentences like "I read that in the *Times* as well."

"Why?" J.A.'s smile widened to her canines. It reminded Penny of when Sherlock Holmes announced, "The game is afoot!"

"Well, he's not white," he said. "Which helps."

"But does it? Isn't it the license of the fiction writer regardless of their identity to characterize whomever they want?" said a girl who was ethnically ambiguous.

Penny couldn't remember ever having an honest discussion about race in a classroom.

"Well, there's also that," said the British-Chinese kid. "As long as you're not a tragedy tourist or creating racist caricatures. As long as you're . . . talented, it's okay."

"So as long as you're adept and well intentioned, you get a pass?" asked J.A.

"It's knee-jerk 'PC' garbage to say otherwise," said another guy, who used scare quotes around "PC."

"No, it's not," a redheaded girl chimed in. "It's the Kardashians getting cornrows. You can't shoplift the trendy parts of a culture and glamorize them but then not take into account the awful parts like getting killed by cops at a traffic stop."

J.A. seemed pleased by the direction that the conversation was taking. It felt as though she was assessing them, coolly compiling notes on each, and Penny was sorry she wasn't contributing.

"Look, I hate writing," said J.A. after the initial din died down. "And I'm the type of writer who hates it every single time. But make no mistake: It's something that you *get* to do. Especially fiction. I think of it this way." She sat on top of her desk and crossed her legs in a lotus pose. "If there was an apocalypse—zombies, the sun explodes, whatever—fiction writing as a job would be the thousandth priority behind SoulCycle instructors."

The class laughed.

"It's a privilege, and part of acknowledging that privilege is doing it honorably. Create diverse characters because you can. Especially ones that aren't easy to write. A character that scares you is worth exploring. Yet if you breathe life into a character and it comes to you too easily—say you're writing from the viewpoint of a black man in America and you're not one? Think hard about where your inspiration is coming from. Are you writing stereotypes? Tropes? Are you fetishizing the otherness? Whose ideas are you spreading? Really consider how you transmit certain optics over others. Think about how much power that is."

J.A. locked eyes with Penny.

"It's about finding the truth in fiction," she said. "Which sounds contradictory. But the story will let you know if you're close."

Penny's brain buzzed. J.A. had called writers powerful, which meant Penny was powerful.

It took Penny a moment to realize her mouth was hanging open a little. If *Maus* was galvanizing moment number one in Penny's plans to become a writer, the heart-hammering feeling in J.A.'s class was two. Maybe two *and* three. She'd been invited to a secret society. It reorganized her thoughts with such intensity that she had the sudden urge to pee.

Penny had been writing all the time, for years now. She'd never stopped even if she showed no one. Stories, lists of ideas, and strange chunks of amusing dialogue that came to her while she ignored whatever else was going on in her actual life. She knew she was decent. Only she wanted more. Penny wanted to get really good. And she wanted for J.A. Hanson to recognize exactly *how* good.

SAM.

Sam woke with a start. It was Saturday—more than a week later—and his problems remained as they were. He was still broken up with Liar. He was still in love with Liar. Liar was pregnant. It was one p.m. It was his day off and he'd fallen asleep only two hours ago. Blargh.

Last night, after countless texts and missed calls, Liar finally *deigned* to come by House after work. Under Sam's watchful eye she chugged gallons of water and walked back and forth to the bathroom to pee on six more sticks. It was both intimate and also very much not.

Period lateness check: four weeks and counting.

"Thanks a lot for buying the cheap ones," Lorraine called out from the toilet. She had the bathroom door cracked open, and though they'd once been that couple where one person peed while the other showered, Sam looked away. He heard the flush.

"I get pee all over my hands with those things," she said. Sam wondered how many pregnancy tests she'd taken over the years but knew better than to ask. It had taken days of badgering to get her to come over. She'd skipped the Planned Parenthood appointment and had so far failed to make a new one.

She washed her hands, lining up the results on the side of the sink.

"See, the good ones spell out 'pregnant' or 'not pregnant,'" she said. "They're digital or something."

Sam hadn't known there was such a thing as a good one when it came to pregnancy tests. He'd sprung for the two-for-three deal. Sam reasoned six meant better odds so they'd know for sure, for sure.

They waited and watched. It was surprisingly hard to tell. Of the six, five were positive with faint plus signs. The last was a dud. The little white window remained completely blank. No minus sign. Nothing.

"So, you're pregnant," he said.

"I guess," she responded.

"How do you feel?" he asked.

"Pissed," she said.

He nodded glumly.

"Like, how dumb is this?"

She rubbed her eyes with the heels of her hands and groaned.

"You really want to know how I feel?" she said after a while. "I want to break shit."

"Come with me," he said. Sam went behind the bar, grabbed

his backpack from under the register, then led her through the kitchen and out the screen door.

It was an airless night.

Sam unzipped his bag and handed Lorraine his laptop.

She took it and looked at him quizzically.

"You said you wanted to break shit."

He nodded at the gravelly parking lot.

"It's backed up," he said. "And broken. Put it out of its . . ."

Before Sam could say "misery," Lorraine threw it on the ground by their feet.

Nothing happened. It lay there heavy and doltish.

She picked it back up, opened it, and this time pitched it farther.

"Fuuuuuuuck," she yelled into the night.

It skittered yards away.

They walked over.

"You have a go," she said, bending down to hand it to him.

Sam held the laptop above his head with both hands and threw it onto the ground, where it finally cracked. They chucked it and chucked it—working up a sweat—until the screen was totaled and the two halves came apart at the hinge. Lorraine took a photo of it and posted it on Instagram, tagging him.

After, without saying anything, they tossed the computer's mangled carcass into a trash bag, threw in the pregnancy tests, and swung the bag into the dumpster.

"Did you get a new one?" she asked him, getting in her car.

Sam shook his head and yawned. He'd have to drop out of school and get a second job to pay child support anyway.

Besides, the type of work he qualified for rarely required personal computing.

"Come by tomorrow," she said, pulling him in for a hug. Her expression was unreadable.

At two thirty the next afternoon Sam took the bus over to Lorraine's apartment, plugging in the pass code he knew by heart. When the gate rumbled open, he was notably relieved that not everything in the world had gone berserk.

She met him at the door, no makeup, hair up in a towel, barefoot in a pink-and-blue floral housedress. It was a punch in the gut. It was his private Lorraine. His favorite Lorraine. The Lorraine she was when it was just the two of them.

"You should've buzzed me," she remarked irritably. She made him wait by the door, closing it partway so he couldn't see in, and reappeared with a silver MacBook Air and a tangled power cord.

"Here," she said, handing it over. The slender device struck Sam as strangely vulnerable. More expensive and aerodynamic than any computer he'd ever owned. Sam wondered if there was anything on it that he wasn't supposed to see. Or better yet, something she'd deliberately left him to find.

"It's wiped," she said. "It's got Final Cut Pro though. Photoshop, too, if you need that."

This wasn't what he'd expected. Not that he'd thought they'd leap back into bed if he came over, but this felt too close to charity. The worst part was that he wasn't in a position to refuse it.

"It'll only be for a few weeks," he mumbled.

"I upgraded," she said. "Keep it as long as you want."

That was Lorraine's other secret side. While she was all too happy to cadge free drinks off his dirtbag friends and split cheap slices of pizza, most of the time it was an act. Lorraine's lifestyle was heavily subsidized by her parents. She moved out of Twombly after freshman year and her parents continued to pay her rent even when she landed a job. Her mother bought all of Lorraine's clothes from Neiman Marcus with the help of a personal shopper. The first time he'd spent the night and took a shower at her house, Sam spotted the price sticker left on her shampoo—$38. He'd put it back and used soap on his head.

Keeping up while they were dating was out of the question, and Sam had no idea what was expected from him as the father of her child. Not only was there nowhere to put a crib in his room, but he didn't even have a car. And the prospect of walking six miles each way with a Babybjörn strapped to his chest made his testicles want to retreat into his body.

After he left Lorraine's he walked home through Sixth Street to see if anyone was hiring. Calling his old friend Gunner about a barback gig would have been easy enough, but Sam didn't want to explain his absence or his sudden need for cash.

Sweat slid down the back of Sam's denim-clad legs. He would've loved to wear basketball shorts and flip-flops, resembling every carefree numbskull roaming the streets with status headphones, but he couldn't bring himself to do it. Shrimping man-toes were an insult to nature.

Sam was tired. Lorraine's laptop hit the base of his spine with every footfall.

The computer probably cost more than his life. Which

made a kind of sense since it was decisively more capable than he'd ever been. The most money he'd ever made was eleven dollars an hour. He tried to enjoy the afternoon air and the meditative qualities of walking and failed.

Instead he considered the cost of diapers.

One time Liar sent him to the store to buy tampons and he was stunned by how expensive they were. Diapers had to cost about the same. Except that a period was a week a month, so you could space them out, but a baby needed diapers pretty much constantly for years.

Christ, he had to relax. Sam let his mind drift and panned out to orient himself on Planet Earth and reassure his brain that things were going to be fine.

His brain had other ideas.

Okay, so if Lorraine *was* pregnant, it could also mean . . .

SHE COULD HAVE HERPES. WHICH MEANS THAT EVEN IF SHE'S NOT PREGNANT SAM COULD STILL HAVE HERPES BECAUSE PAUL DEFINITELY HAD HERPES.

Thanks, brain.

He walked past the old Marriott, where his mom used to work. It consistently struck him as funny that his mother spent any time in the hospitality business. Brandi Rose Sidelow-Lange was a piece of work. She had what in the old days they'd called moxie. Sam inherited his smart mouth from his mother, and like a snake eating its own tail, it only served to drive her crazy.

Once upon a time, though Sam never knew it, Brandi Rose had been a different person. Infinitely less pissed off. This was evidenced by a photo in the living room. The frame was blue and white with a sunflower on the bottom corner and featured his mom at sixteen, grinning with a Texas Elite Princess Pageant sash draped over her shoulder. Her hair a shiny brown and wearing a knee-length navy dress, Brandi Rose waved. It was a beautiful photo made more so by how happy his mother appeared. Mostly, though, it was displayed in the front room as a trap. Anyone who mentioned it would get the same bitter rejoinder.

"Well, that sash ain't first place," she'd point out, ice cubes clinking in her Long Island Iced Tea. "Bitsy Sinclair won. Her daddy, Buck, owned nine car dealerships from here to El Paso."

According to Brandi Rose, rich people got everything.

"Second place is just about as good as first loser," she'd continue. "I only did it for the state scholarship anyway. Fat lot of good that did me." *Clink. Clink.*

His mother's response to Sam's happy addition would be more of the same. Tirades about how shit rolled downhill and how she had to be the one to take care of everything. The accusations would then turn to his father, which led right back to her dissatisfaction with her son. The rejection stung on all counts. Sam was a carbon copy of his father. Though despite the evolutionary wisdom that babies resemble their dads so they'd stick around, Caden Becker was immune to the charms of his tiny doppelgänger.

As much as it broke his heart, Sam knew his old man was a loser. Granted, he was handsome, tall, dark, with a gleam of wicked about the eyes and Sam had inherited his father's ease around strangers and his rangy bearing, but that's where he wanted the similarities to end.

The last time Sam saw his dad, the elder Becker was stumbling right in front of Tequila Six, looking alarmingly well preserved for his lifetime of hard partying. Rumor had it that he and the old bass player of his band had gotten an apartment in the rundown town houses off Mo-Pac favored by Austin's newly divorced bachelors, but to Sam his father looked homeless. He was wearing a torn ThunderCloud Subs sweatshirt and appeared to be muttering at a couple of sorority girls, who swerved from him without interrupting the flow of their conversation. Sam walked briskly in the opposite direction. He hadn't considered the inevitability of running into his old man if he got a second job at a bar. Sam knew he wouldn't deny his father money if he asked for a loan he had no intention of paying back. If anything, Sam figured his dad was a step up from his mom, who stole it.

Thinking about his parents upset him, and when he blinked he felt the horizon lurch abruptly. He took a deep breath. He should have eaten something before leaving. Or else he should have gotten some sleep instead of obsessing about whether or not he and Lorraine should get married.

Marriage was useless anyway. Nothing more than a bogus contract to ensure all parties wound up disappointed. At least that had been the case for his mother. Before this talk of houses with pools and good school districts with Mr. Lange, Brandi Rose had known better than to expect anything from the world. The rash of consolation prizes didn't help. They reminded Sam of a military air-drop, except instead of humanitarian aid with food or cash, both of which they lacked and needed, a sixty-inch flat-screen TV would appear at their door. Or a Blu-ray player without any of the overpriced discs they couldn't afford to buy. There were designer clothes, two boxes labeled ARMANI, containing a white cashmere coat and sweaters. For his fourteenth birthday Sam received a pair of silk pajamas from Calvin Klein that was missing only a big, fat Cuban cigar to complete the cartoon tycoon Halloween outfit.

Then came the weepy phone calls behind closed doors. Brandi Rose removed her emerald wedding ring. It was around the time she ceased communicating with her son, as if it had somehow been his fault. A wall of radiant rage was erected between them.

Sam pulled at his T-shirt. Good Lord, it was hot. The only shade was directly in front of the bars, and he didn't want to get close enough to smell the tang of dirty bar mops and the sweet oakiness of whiskey. Sam's head swam. He didn't want to drop out of school and become a washout like his dad. This was a terrible idea. He had no business working at a bar or near one. Whatever swirl of ingredients that made both his parents such devout drinkers hadn't skipped a generation.

He peered down the road. Miles to go. Sam's vision wobbled violently and his knees hitched beneath him. Sam had passed out once, in fifth-grade gym. He'd hung slack in Coach Tremont's arms and could hear her talking about his bird bones though he couldn't lift his head. It was humiliating.

His arms felt leaden at his elbows, and when he formed fists to prove to himself that he could, the effort unnerved him. His hearing became muffled, sounds dropping out completely before returning. Sam examined his surroundings unsteadily. So many strangers. His heart pounded. A sharp pain pierced through his chest as his breath caught in his throat. He pictured himself as a voodoo doll being pierced by a large spike. There had to be somewhere for him to sit down. Cars. Banks. Bars. Restaurants. Food trucks.

Can twenty-one-year-olds have heart attacks?

Sure.

Babies have heart attacks.

Babies.

Could his unborn baby have a congenital heart condition? Yes. Would Sam have to wait for the bus at three a.m. to rush it to the hospital while it died? Most definitely.

Don't call it an "it," he reminded himself.

The pain in his chest was unbearable. He had to call someone. But who? Sam's list was pathetic, starting and ending at Al and Fin. The list of who he absolutely couldn't call was more impressive—Lorraine, his mom, Gunner, everyone else in the world.

Sam peeled off from the beery marauders, staggered to the nearest curb, and collapsed.

There were other people on the curb, and the bespectacled redhead he'd almost crash-landed into glared and scooched as if he were a plague-stricken hobo. He went to pull out his phone to call 911, but his jeans—his stupid hipster jeans—were too tight. He saw stars and then he died.

PENNY.

When it came to perspiration, Penny had a problem. Not that she stank of BO or anything. It's that from March to around October she was invariably damp. She could feel the pool of moisture collecting in each underboob, and her sweat mustache beaded up no matter how urgently she wiped it away.

It didn't help that she was dining al fresco in 100-degree heat downtown where the good shady patches had been staked out by the pushy and hyper-vigilant. Penny scanned the crowd. Hell really was other people.

Other than her car, Penny had no sanctuary. When Jude was out or at Mallory's, she couldn't relax, knowing that the two-headed monster of "best friends since we were six" could turn up as soon as Penny got comfortable. Penny wasn't a covert crack addict or a compulsive masturbator, but she didn't have an appreciation for privacy until she shared a room with a girl who could go to the bathroom with the door open while naked and eating pretzels dipped in hummus. Penny had to get away. She hopped into her Honda and headed downtown, paying five bucks for parking to sit on a splintery bench in the blazing heat for a disappointing seven-dollar Korean taco and a six-dollar blended "horchatalatta." She wondered if the rest of early adulthood would be like this—avoiding roommates, getting ripped off for bad fusion food, and the peculiar loneliness of being smothered by people she didn't want to spend time with.

Penny got up to toss her soggy paper plate in the garbage. There were an unseemly number of bars on either side of her—a Disneyland Main Street for day drinkers. The snack had been a bust, but the people watching was stellar.

A scrawny kid peeled off from the masses and almost ate it. Penny reached for her phone but was too slow on the uptake. She could never grab it in time for good snaps. Sweat ran down her back and seeped into her underwear elastic. The kid staggered over to the sidewalk and planted himself under a tree. He was gulping for air, a marooned fish on dry land, and his face was blinding white. Maybe it was heroin. Penny rubbed the inside of her elbow where she thought her heroin vein would be and then poked her forearm, leaving red circles. She should have worn sunblock. She watched the boy, slumped against the trunk, pull up his black T-shirt sleeves to fashion a sort of tank top. Man, he was skinny enough to be a junkie, and his arms were covered in tattoos.

The kid shoved back his hair, revealing his face. Except it wasn't a kid. It was Jude's uncle. Uncle Sam. Hot Uncle Sam. Hot Uncle Sam who was possibly OD'ing on opioids right in front of her. She had to do something! Oh God, she was in no state for altruism. Penny quickly pulled her hair into a bun and grabbed a mint from her go bag.

Priorities, Penny. Save the man from dying. Nobody cares about your breath.

She glanced back at Sam to see if he had stirred. He was probably in the throes of brain death now, drawing his final breaths while she was faffing.

What do I do? What do I do?

How to save a dying man:
1. Call the Texas Hammer. *What?* How was her only readily available resource an outdated local ad for a personal injury attorney?
2. Ignore him. Christ, he's not your uncle! Ugh. But he was Jude's. And Penny liked Jude even if she talked way too much.
3. Go see if he's dead already.

Penny ran across the street to his lifeless body and peered into his face.

She hoped she wouldn't drip sweat on him.

He certainly seemed dead.

And, for the record, the tattoo on his bicep wasn't a chess piece. It was the head of a stallion with its eyes covered in a piece of fabric. What did it mean?

Focus, Penny. Shit.

"Sam?" She kicked his heel gently. They both still had on the same shoes.

SAM.

It was a face he knew and couldn't place. He stared and tried to focus.

Friend or foe? Friend or foe? Do I owe you money? Are you friends with Lorraine? Please don't be friends with Lorraine.

Sam closed his eyes again, embarrassed. Her voice was gentle. It was a nice voice.

"Sam, are you alive? It's Penny." She sounded far away.

Sam felt another kick on his foot, and he groaned.

"I'm Jude's friend," said the shiny face with the bright red lips.

"Who's Jude?" he croaked.

"Your cousin."

"Niece," he corrected.

"Are you dying?"

He nodded and tried to slide his phone out of his pocket without passing out.

"Is Jude coming?" He didn't want her to see him like this. He hated the thought of anyone seeing him like this.

"No."

Thank God.

A Biggie lyric teased the corners of his brain.

Something about heartbeats and Sasquatch feet.

"Sam, WHAT'S happening? YOU look HORRIBLE."

His hearing kept coming and going.

His heart was fit to burst.

Thudthudthud.

I'm dying, dead.

Deaddeaddead.

"I think I'm having a heart attack." He closed his eyes.

"Shit, shit, shit," she said. "Shit."

And then.

"Hello? 911?"

Sam thought it was funny how everybody greeted the three-digit number they'd called. As if they had to ask.

"My friend's sick. I don't know. Yeah, I'm here with him."

Sam felt a wave of nausea. He hoped he wouldn't have to puke in public.

"Sam . . . um."

"Becker," he told her.

"Becker," she said. "Twenty-one I think."

Sam nodded.

"No," she said. "I don't know. At least I don't think so . . ."

He felt her cold hand on his arm. He opened his eyes.

"Sam, are you on drugs?"

I wish.

He shook his head.

"No, no drugs. Um . . . shortness of breath, cold sweats . . ."

"Stabbing pain in my chest," he said.

"Stabbing pain in his chest," she repeated.

"Like a knitting needle," he said.

"Like a knitting needle," she repeated.

"Mm-hmm," he heard her say. Followed by, "Yeah, I guess the knitting needle is going through his chest."

Exactly.

Sam nodded again.

"Okay, thank you. Bye."

Sam thought about how people on TV never said good-bye. And then he wondered why people only thought about the dumbest things as they lay dying.

Sam felt Penny sit down next to him.

"Sam, wake up."

"I am up," he whispered.

She was staring at him intently.

"Are you sure you're not on drugs?"

He glared at her before realizing—inappropriately—that she was kind of cute when she made eye contact. Cute enough that he was bummed out that she was watching him die on the street.

"Positive," he said.

She wiped his wet brow with her T-shirt sleeve, which was already damp. He saw a flash of bra and glanced away.

"Sorry," she said. "I don't know why I did that. I'm supposed to keep talking to you until they get here."

The cogs in his mind picked up steam.

"Wait, shit. Did you call an ambulance?"

She nodded. "Knitting needle?" she reminded him. As if 100 percent of knitting-needle-related incidents (imagined and otherwise) justified an emergency vehicle.

"Call them back!" he ordered. His heart hammered harder. "Call them back!" he repeated. "I can't afford an ambulance."

She stared at him for a beat, grabbed her phone, and marched away. A thousand years later, she returned.

"I called them." She crouched in front of him with her hands on his shoulders. "Though yours is an incorrect response."

Despite his stupor, Sam bristled at her word choice. "Incorrect"? Was it "incorrect" to be broke?

"Wait, can you do this?" She stuck her tongue straight out.

He stuck his tongue out.

"What's the thing with the tongue and heart attacks?" she yelled impatiently, as if he were deliberately keeping diagnostic information from her. "Shit, I think that's for a stroke." She pulled out her phone and searched helplessly.

He drew his tongue back into his mouth.

"Okay," she said, breathing deep. "Don't die, okay?"

He nodded.

"Promise me," she said.

He nodded again.

"You know what? Try to slow your breathing . . . one Mississippi . . . two Mississippi . . . Say it in your head."

He focused on breathing.

"Did you eat today?"

He shook his head.

A Styrofoam drink container was thrust into his face. The straw smelled cinnamony and was covered in red lipstick.

"It's not very good," she told him.

He took a sip.

Horchata. Cold. Sweet. And she was right—this one was kind of gross.

"Did you drink a lot of coffee today?"

He nodded. Same as every day.

"Do you have radiating pain?"

He shook his head. She read off her phone.

"What about numbness?"

He shook his head.

"Sam?"

Sam nodded. He was Sam, it was true.

"We're going to take a walk now."

He shook his head.

He felt her grab his arm and sling it over her shoulders. She was soaking wet, and where his sweaty bare arm met her neck it was slippery. He put weight on his legs so he, a grown man, wouldn't have to be carried by some lady again.

"I'm going to take you somewhere so someone can examine you, okay? I'm parked real, real close. Walk with me. Please?"

"Okay," he said.

• • •

Fifteen minutes later, they were in front of a MedSpring Urgent Care.

The AC was blasting and Sam was soaked though otherwise calm. He wanted badly to go home and take a nap.

Penny was silent. Even in his peripheral vision, she seemed agitated. Her hands were clutching the steering wheel so tight her knuckles were white. He couldn't believe that Jude's mute, macabre roommate had saved his life. He wondered if he'd have to get her a small taxidermied spider or something for her efforts.

"I'll be right here," she said, staring straight ahead.

Sam didn't want to explain to her that he couldn't afford ambulances, hospitals, or the cheaper emergency clinics in crappy strip malls.

"I'm fine," he said.

"No you're not."

"I don't have health insurance," he admitted.

"Oh."

"I swear to God I'm fine now," he said after a moment. "I don't know what that was. Probably heat stroke."

"Have you had heat stroke before?"

He shook his head.

"Did you know that if you've had heat stroke once, your brain remembers the circuitry so it's easier for you to get heat stroke again? Maybe way easier than before?"

He shook his head and recalled Penny's earlier jokes about apps making apps. She was apparently a huge nerd.

"So . . . ," she said. Penny's dark eyes were shiny, and pink bloomed on her cheeks. "Wait, did you have a panic attack?"

"What? No. I don't have panic attacks. Never in my life." Jesus, give a girl WebMD and she starts thinking she's a physician.

"You had a goddamned panic attack," she said, turning away from him again. "The sweatiness, the heart-attack feeling. Oh my God!" She slapped the bottom of the steering wheel with her left hand. "It's obvious. *And* you didn't eat today. Caffeine. *So* dumb!"

"Okay, hold on." He threw his hands up. "Why are you so angry?" Sam reached out to touch the back of the hand closest to him, but she jerked away, exhaling noisily.

"I'm sorry," she said, shoulders slumping. "It's adrenaline. Rage is my usual fear response."

"That," he said, "is a nifty quality."

Nifty?

"I know," said Penny. "Everybody just loves it. Ugh." She groaned, rubbing her face and smearing lipstick across her chin.

He nodded. He didn't know what to do about the lipstick. Maybe he'd get away with not saying anything until he got home.

Penny handed him a bottle of water. He took it gratefully.

Then she grabbed her black and gray camouflage backpack from the backseat, plopped it onto her lap, and rummaged through it. She handed him a small bag of raw cashews from a blue zippered bag filled with other small, compact snacks.

"Uh, sometimes it's triggered by caffeine or low blood sugar with me," Penny said, explaining the snack.

Okay, he had to tell her.

"You've got lipstick everywhere," he said, pointing toward her chin.

She angled the rearview and sighed again.

In another compartment of her bag, this time from a black zipper bag, she pulled out a small packet of moistened wipes. A green, plastic cable tie sprang out of it and onto her lap.

"EDC," she said, quietly putting it back.

"EDC?"

"Everyday carry," she said. "Stuff I have on me at all times. Go bags, for emergencies."

"As in, an apocalypse go bag, go bag?"

"Correct," she said.

There was that incorrect, correct thing again.

"But I have this on me every day. Usually, the EDC community are guys with concealed firearms and flashlights, which I think is dumb since we have phones with a flashlight function. . . ." Penny trailed off. Sam had wondered why chicks had such big bags. He figured it was their makeup, not soft cases filled with doomsday rations and zip ties of varying length.

"Snacks are important," he said. "And you can never have enough plastic cables."

"Are you making fun of me?" she asked.

"No." He shook his head vehemently and took another handful of cashews. "Not at all. I respect the shit out of it. Your EDC is saving my ass."

She had a small scar above her left eyebrow and he wanted to ask about it. Maybe she'd had some bizarre things go down in her life. It would explain her whole style.

"Did everything sound all underwater?" she asked after a second. Her lips were wiped clean, and Sam noticed they looked better without all that gunk on them.

"Underwater?"

"When you were passing out."

"Yeah, muffled."

"Yeah, I get that."

"My girlfriend's pregnant," he said suddenly, startling himself.
Penny tilted her head.

"Well, she's my ex."

"Whoa," she breathed.

"Yeah. I still love her though."

"Ugh."

"She cheated on me."

The confessions wouldn't stop. He wanted to show his gratitude for the ride and the snack and the not making him feel like a headcase when it was clear that he was. Except at no point did his vocal cords just step in line and say thank you.

"Wow," she said

Penny's fingers inched toward his. Sam thought for a fleeting moment that she would hold his hand, but instead she went for a couple cashews and was extra careful to avoid touching him.

"The first one is the worst. By a lot," she said, crunching. Sam wasn't sure if she was talking about panic attacks or pregnant ex-girlfriends. Not that it mattered.

PENNY.

On the drive back Penny snuck glances at Sam. His eyes were closed. Penny couldn't believe Sam had told her about his girlfriend, MzLolaXO. And that MzLolaXO was pregnant! Jude would lose it when she found out. Penny could only imagine what Dr. Greene had to say about it in their weekly Skype therapy calls. Penny couldn't get enough of how bizarre the sessions were. Literally their last one had been about boundary issues while Penny was in the room trying to do her homework.

Sam's slight chest rose and fell. She wondered for a second if she could lift him if she needed to.

"Take me back to House.

"Please," he said then, catching himself.

Penny fought the urge to check his temperature. Maybe this was more than a panic attack. He was *so* vulnerable. She knew she should be keeping her eyes on the road, but the way his

Adam's apple bobbed was mesmerizing. It was as if something were struggling to get out. She just wanted to reach over and stroke it. Just once. Or lick it. God, what was wrong with her?

"I don't know where you live," she said, forcing an even tone and changing lanes. Maybe she'd get to see where he slept.

"Not my house—House, where I work," he said.

"Are you sure?"

"There's no food at home," he explained, his eyes still closed. Penny was enjoying that she could survey him with unsupervised access.

"How are you going to get home after that?"

"I'll figure it out," he said.

She wanted to press him. He had no business driving. Plus, she wasn't sure if the MzLolaXO predicament meant she'd be helping him out or not.

Sam opened his eyes. Penny froze.

"Why don't you want to be a documentarian anymore?" she asked abruptly.

"What?"

"Nothing."

Penny had been dying to ask since that first day. She wanted to know what made him quit movies to bake. Or barista, or whatever it was exactly that he did now. Curiosity fizzed in her head, but she restrained herself. Penny knew she had a habit of jumping all over the place in conversations without warning. Her mom called it "speaking Penny." Nobody but Penny spoke it fluently.

It's just that Penny didn't know a lot of documentaries beyond the one about the tightrope walker guy and the sushi guy and the one about Sea World, and she certainly didn't personally know any documentarians. She was willing to bet Sam's would be good. Honestly, between the panic attack and the pregnant ex-girlfriend, if Sam were making a movie out of his own life, Penny would watch the hell out of it.

SAM.

When they pulled up in front of House Sam felt as if he'd left weeks ago. He couldn't wait to strip off his clothes and collapse into bed.

"Thanks," Sam said, unbuckling his seat belt. He considered leaning over and hugging her. Not that he was a hugger or anything. But when he turned to say good-bye, she eyed him warily, as if she'd burst into flames if he did.

"Do you live far?" Her brows were furrowed and the scar was white again, as if it were pissed at him.

"Nope," he said.

"Want me to get Jude to bring you anything?"

"That's okay," he said, attempting a smile. "Actually, do you mind not telling her that we bumped into each other?"

Penny cocked her head. "You want me not to tell her about seeing you or everything that followed?"

"Both," he asserted. "I don't want her to worry." The last thing he needed was Jude knowing that his life was a stereotypical redneck mess.

"Um," she said, frowning slightly. "Sure." Penny gave him her "incorrect response" look again.

"I just really need to get some rest."

She nodded.

"Thanks again," he said, and opened the car door. "For everything." He got out and steadied himself.

"Wait!" Sam heard the pop of a door. Penny waved her phone at him from the passenger side.

"What's your number?" she asked. Her face was bright red. "So you have mine. For emergencies."

He told it to her.

His phone buzzed in his pocket.

"Got it," he said.

"Okay."

Penny reached over and slammed the door. "Text me when you get home?"

"Yes, *Mom*, I'll text you when I get home."

She scowled then, which made him smile.

"Sorry. I promise I will. I'll get some food and go straight home and into bed. And I will call you because you are now my official emergency contact." Sam turned to go.

"Wait!" shouted Penny again through the window. He turned around.

"Isn't the whole concept of an emergency contact that *you're* too dead to call them?"

Sam laughed. She had a point.

"Don't forget!" she called out before driving away. He pulled out his phone.

The text read:

This is penny

He smiled, trudged up the stairs, and immediately fell asleep in his clothes for the next ten hours.

• • •

When Sam woke up he had a pounding headache. He stuck his head under the bathroom faucet and chugged until he thought he was going to be sick. He checked his phone. Almost two a.m.

No calls from Lorraine. Or texts. In fact, the last thing he got was "This is penny."

Crap. Penny. Penny who he'd promised to hit up ten hours ago. He felt awful.

Still, it was way too late to text someone. Or was it? From what little he knew of her, she seemed the type to wait up. He was embarrassed about his panic *experience*—he remained reluctant to label it a full-on attack—but it was way worse to make her worry.

Ugh. Why was he so worthless?

He saved her number as "Penny Emergency" and texted her one word:

Home

Penny's text bubble popped up immediately with the little ellipses. Then it disappeared. Then it popped up again. Only to be deleted again.

Finally, she wrote back:

ok

Sam wondered if she was angry with him.
He texted her again:

I'm sorry. Fell asleep

She texted:

Sleep's the best. HUGE FAN.
Hard to do it when your
emergency contact's dead so . . .

Shit. She *was* pissed. Still, he smiled. Was he her emergency contact too? Maybe nobody knew how emergency contacts worked.

Sry
Srsly
TY!
I'm a dick
ugh

Good night

Night

He sent her the frowning emoji. The extremely contrite one with no eyebrows.

It wasn't his style, but the moment required it.

PENNY.

Penny was in the shower when Sam texted again.

GOOD MORNING

Just like that.
All caps. No exclamation.
It sounded so sunny, so smiley. In fact, the text bubble seemed happy to see her. So much so that she went back to the conversation to make sure it was actually Sam from yesterday. She'd saved his number as "Sam House." The jerk. She couldn't believe he'd fallen asleep before he'd texted her. It was irresponsible and inconsiderate. She didn't want to sound fussy and overbearing, but a text wasn't asking too much.

As if the text bubble could read her mind, it spoke again.

IT'S UR EMERGENCY CONTACT

I REALLY AM SRY S2G

And then:

I'LL STOP YELLING NOW
FML
I feel HORRIBLE
Hope u didn't lose 2 much
sleep bc of me
I won't ask u 2 forgive me
but hope u will

Wow.

It was fascinating. The dispatch made her heart do a crazy dance. Not even a cute dance. More an erratic flailing, like those windsock things you see at car dealerships. She thought about his hot armpit again. And his cowlick. And the tattoos she didn't entirely understand. It usually irked her when people wrote "u" instead of "you" and "2" instead of "to"—especially "too"—but telling people things like that was probably why she only got texts from her mom. And Mark. Crap, Mark. She had to call him.

Penny attempted to respond, *hey*. Her hands were covered in lotion and her stupid phone wouldn't register her fingers as humanoid and that's when Sam texted again . . .

Did I wake u?

And then:

I hope I didn't wake u
O NO DID ME NOT WANTING
2 WAKE U RN WAKE U RN?!!

She closed her eyes and held her phone to her heart like a big dumb girl in a movie.

Then she wiped her hands on her towel and wrote back.

Please stop yelling

He texted back:

((hi)) <- denoting indoor voice of
normal vol

Penny smiled. She typed:

I hope you feel better

And then:

You didn't wake me

Penny padded quietly back into her room and got dressed. Her phone lit up again.

Did you get any sleep?
I can't believe I did that to you

Penny smiled. Then she bit her lower lip. She noticed him noticing the "to/you" thing. Shit. He was so great. Penny thought of pregnant Lola. And then about her roommate's Ironclad Friendship Ask. Jude was dead asleep in her bed a few feet away. Her eyelid twitched, detecting a disturbance in the force. Penny knew Jude would bug if she discovered Sam was in this much trouble, but these weren't her secrets to tell.

Penny texted him:

Yes

Good
Have a good day

You too

Penny placed her phone facedown on her bed and allowed herself a tiny swoon. Besides. As far as Penny and Sam were concerned, there was nothing *to* tell. Nothing happened. Just because Jude was fast and loose with her personal life and her therapy sessions didn't mean the same setup worked for everyone. Some people's coping mechanisms were all about festering and secrecy and ruminating until you grew yourself a nice little tumor in your heart with a side of panic attack. Different strokes.

SAM.

Sam wasn't stupid—at least when it came to the broken institution known as the American Collegiate Industrial Complex. It's not that he believed by taking a single community college course on documentaries he was going to stumble ass-backward into stardom. It's just that he'd tried on several occasions to make a movie and hadn't succeeded. The way he saw it, taking a class was about placing an expensive bet on yourself. You couldn't afford to blow the deadline.

The ACC film department was housed in a squat brown building from the seventies, complete with avocado-green carpet from the era. It was illogical to Sam that despite the entire course being conducted online, he still had to drag his meat suit to the campus to pick up his ID. The blue and white piece of plastic featured a blurry picture of his face, as though he'd run across the frame. The unimpressed sixty-year-old dude with dandruff in his eyebrows made it clear that there would be no reshoots.

Whatever. He tried not to dwell on the school's resemblance to a prison and the sort of life that dictated a need for a vending machine in the hall filled with plastic-wrapped sandwiches and returned to work by bus.

When Sam was younger he took pictures constantly. Unlike cooking, photography kept you on your toes. It was chaotic and human—utterly unpredictable. To capture an unposed face you had to wait for it. It was spear fishing. You had to move between the competing rhythms of the world and strike. When his street urchin pals were stealing Twix and fat-tip markers from dollar stores, Sam would palm a couple of those old-school cardboard disposable cameras. He'd collect shoe boxes of them, pictures of his friends playing Edward Forty Hands or Amy Winehands (the super-sophisticated game where you'd duct tape bottles of malt liquor or wine coolers onto your palms). Or he'd capture skate tricks, backyard shows, or his crew hanging out in various parking lots across town. It cost ten bucks to develop, so he stockpiled the used-up cameras. When he turned fifteen he got a job at a one-hour photo expressly to process them. Sam got to be a pretty good lab technician, though the job was unspeakably depressing.

Only two types of people developed photos in those days, broke art kids and old weirdos. There was this fat fifty-something dude, Bertie, who'd take pictures of himself and his Weimaraner. He was naked, and the dog wore waistcoats and hats, and they were photographed doing unseemly things: sitting at the dinner table with a full Thanksgiving spread, or slow dancing, the dog upright and impossibly long on its hindquarters. They recalled William Wegman's portraits except with human full-frontal, and though Sam didn't know exactly what was going on, he called the ASPCA anonymously and quit a week later. It was bleak.

Sam was ready to move on to moving pictures anyway. It was on to janky VHS camcorders from the Goodwill after that.

People were odd. Sam loved and loathed that about them. Fiction was fine, but real life was the true freak show.

Sam's syllabus at ACC was spare and he tried not to feel ripped off about it. Three months to complete a project, a twenty-two-minute short that would comprise most of his grade. He wouldn't get anywhere near the Blackmagic Cinema cameras, since they required a five-thousand-dollar credit card deposit, but he was able to sign out an old Canon 5D Mark III with all the requisite lenses, some lavalier mics, and a better shotgun microphone than he'd normally get his hands on, as well as a tripod. He also grabbed a tiny stabilizer rig for his iPhone in case he wanted something more run-and-gun. Finding a subject felt like a hunger that would never be satisfied. He'd glance at Fin, narrow his eyes, and wonder if there was something there.

"In a world . . . where a guy who was forever number two, the perfect wingman, the middle born of three sons, the dude who didn't get the girl and only got her slightly less attractive friend finally . . ."

"Quit it, *puto.*" Fin flicked a piece of celery at him. Sam was halfway through soup prep for lunch.

"What?"

"Seriously," said Fin. "Your scheming face is scary as hell. Especially when you're holding a knife."

Sam had tried making a movie about Lorraine on several occasions (*"In a world . . . where a beautiful rich girl with anger issues who at her truest most molten core only wants to be loved dis-covers that . . .")*, but she'd catch him creep-shooting and blow her stack. As much as that girl loved a selfie, she wasn't big on other people controlling the final product. What he needed was a willing subject, someone as hungry as he was. Someone who warranted a few minutes in the spotlight. Plenty of peo-ple craved attention. It had to be the right person, someone who naturally commanded it. Sam suspected most outwardly noisy people were boring on the inside. No more than the text-book swirl of insecurities and narcissism.

Penny would make a fascinating subject. All that twitchy energy. Plus, what was up with her bags of stuff? He could shoot an unboxing video where she could unfurl her posses-sions and explain the thinking behind it all. It could serve as a legend for a map of her brain.

Sam enjoyed texting Penny. They talked about work, sleep, food, random facts. It didn't need to be anything important. Their last text had been what to eat for breakfast. Since Penny had seen him at his lowest, there was no reason to act cooler than he was. It felt easy, a bit like summer camp—their texts had no bearing on their actual lives. It helped that she didn't seem to tire of him. No matter how dumb his questions.

> *Would you watch a documentary*
> *about a cat?*

She texted back immediately.

> *Totally*

Cats rule

And then:

Some are assholes tho

> *There's this super cool guy that lives*
> *under our porch now*

What else?

> *That's pretty much it*

K then maybe

At 2:34 p.m. Sam had cleared the tables, wiped them down, and steam-cleaned the espresso machine.

> *I have to make a documentary*
> *for a class*

Ah
Ergo cat

Sam enjoyed it as a response. Ergo: cat. He couldn't call what his new friend would say next. He tried to remember the last time he'd slipped so easily into conversation without the added diversion of skateboarding or drinking or sex. Talks with Penny felt good. Wholesome, normal, and curiously productive since they mostly discussed schoolwork. They were lab partners.

EMERGENCY PENNY

Today 6:01 PM

*Would you read a short story on
zombie food
Or nah?*

> *Is this a legitimate concern of
> yours?*

*Maraschino cherries
are the undead*

> *OK
> Riveted
> Please continue*

*Perfectly healthy stone fruit are
drowned in calcium chloride
+ sulfur dioxide
BOOM
Total ghost food
It's how come they're see-through*

> *Hmm . . .
> I admit my interest is waning*

They gave me one
on my pudding
Get it off
It's so gross
I can't touch it

Hey

?

What about a doc on a guy
who's sick?

What kind of sick?

Terminal disease

YES!!

YES!!?

Sounds depressing af
Into it lol
Healthcare is so messed up

Sam wondered if Penny was super political or something.
If she was aware of what was going on in the world outside

her dorm. Sam was bad at politics the same way he was bad at sports. It was all made up. The more yelling there was about it, the more it seemed like a distraction from what was really going on in the world.

Totally

Sam Googled "American healthcare system" to brush up.

It makes me sick
NO PUN INTENDED
It's sad
We criminalize the poor
Everything is broken

OK calm down

Don't tell me to calm down

I regret typing it
I'm sorry
I know girls hate that

EVERYONE hates CALM DOWN
Not just women (don't say girls)

OK
I'm sorry
Anyway

Healthcare
What if the guy took matters into
his own hands
drives to Mexico for drugs

Go on

He meets this other sick dude
They start a drug ring

And . . .

They sell it to poor people/
downtrodden/no healthcare

OMG
Is this the plot to Dallas
Buyers Club?

Sam laughed in real life.

Today 1:45 AM

Top 5 fav things in the world
don't think about it just type

Isn't it a little late to be texting?

Shit were you asleep?

No
But I could have been

I can't sleep for shit lately

Me neither
OK
Top 5...
This feels like a trap

It's not
I promise
No judgments
I don't know your life
Your struggles
YOUR JOURNEY

Sam had been thinking about his favorites in bed. He loved the smell of the air before a thunderstorm. Or how Texas weather was so crazy and the landscape so flat that you could see the driving rain in a clean, straight sheet when everything that lay ahead of it was sunny.

Pringles

Pringles?

Sorry I'm eating Pringles
They're so good

When's the last time you had a
Pringle
I forgot about them
I'd miss them when I'm dead

You'd miss Pringles when you're
dead?

You said no judgment

Wow

Well?

I guess it's too late for texting
But not for Pringles

It's never too late for Pringles

Then Sam texted Lorraine. Five weeks late and counting.
Last time they'd talked she promised to get a blood test and
that was almost a week ago. She'd been flaky when they were
together, but he couldn't believe she'd leave him hanging about
such a huge deal. This was *literally* life or death. Bad enough
that Lorraine often said literally when she meant figuratively.
Sam stared at the screen, willing a bubble to appear.
Zip.

PENNY.

"Is this sheer?" Penny stood in front of the mirror in a white, knee-length cotton dress.

"Only when you're backlit."

"Is it slutty?"

Jude scoffed. An odd sound between a bleat and a laugh. "I don't think you're capable of slutty," she said, sitting up in bed. "I mean," she continued, "you're wearing virginal white."

Penny had chosen a summery sheath for her first date back with Mark. She wanted him to see her in color. Not that white was a color necessarily, but black extra-wasn't, and she didn't want to appear too funereal. If she was going to break up with the guy, she wanted to look good. Maybe her best. Humans were garbage like that.

"Is an official breakup necessary?" asked Jude. "I mean, you're in college; he's not. Everybody knows what that means." Jude jokingly jerked off the air and mimed spraying the result into the sky.

"Ew," said Penny, screwing her face.

"Listen, no shade," Jude continued, laughing. "I don't know your Tinder habits." Her roommate nodded pointedly at the phone in Penny's hand.

Penny smiled tightly.

Right then she and Sam were locked in a contest of who could capture the most boringly predictable Instagram photo. He'd just sent the most glorious sunset (#nofilter). Penny was dying to send back one taken from her car of someone posing in front of the "Hi, How Are You" frog mural on Twenty-First Street while wearing a "Hi, How Are You" frog mural T-shirt. It was meta and brilliant and a surefire winner except she first had to bumble through this awkward date with Mark first to feel proper triumph. Penny couldn't wait for it to be over.

A breakup made sense. Anthropologically she and Mark were incompatible. When they were dating they only ever hung out one-on-one at each other's houses to watch TV and make out. It was more a middle-school relationship than a real thing, and when he went to parties with his friends it was understood she wouldn't accompany him. It suited them both most of the time. If anything, Penny was grateful he wasn't big on conversation. She didn't even know how to explain their arrangement to herself.

The plan was to drive home, see Mark, end it, and drive back. Celeste she'd deal with another time. Penny wasn't in the mood to bond and chin-wag about boys and console her mother under the pretense of commiseration. This was between her and Mark.

Penny wondered if she was nervous and promptly yawned. Just as she cried when she was mad, she needed a nap when faced with anxiety. It wasn't that she was disinterested. It's that she became overwhelmed, went into overdrive, and shut down. Thing is, Penny hadn't meant to blow everyone off. And she would have passed a polygraph when asked about it. She'd been meaning to go home the first weekend or else the second. Undoubtedly the third. By now, more than a month later, the natives were restless and thinking about it made Penny sleepy.

In the short while she'd been at college—a seemingly negligible sliver of time—her brain reset. The routine rhythms of her old life were booted from her operating system. Sure she missed having kimchi in the fridge or a Costco stash of triple-ply toilet paper stored above a washer and dryer you could operate for free, but whenever her mother texted or when Mark called, the interruption was staggering. Mind-blowing. She may as well have been getting messages from the spirit world. It was inconceivable that both college and home operated on the same space-time.

Exhibit A, from Celeste:

> *OMG P, I saw this girl on the street*
> *who I thought was u but she was*
> *way fatter!*

What are you supposed to say to that, thanks?

Exhibit B, from Mark:

I got Rutherford for biz calc

*Isn't Rutherford the only BC
teacher?*

Yeah. Sucks

Yeah

Sucks

Sucks

Or this phone call from Mark:
"Baby, I missed you today."
"Me too."
"He missed you too."
"Who?"
"..."
"Oh ..."
Mark talked about his penis in the third person. It struck
Penny as the least romantic way to broach the subject, and
every time "he" came up, Penny pictured a penis wearing sun-
glasses and a fedora with a little jacket. It's not as if Penny
could blame him. Mark was a red-blooded male in a commit-
ted relationship with a college girl. Hence: sext to initiate sex.
College people had sex. Especially people who had been dating

for however many months they'd been dating. Penny counted back on her hands—it was seven. Seven whole months. Seven times longer than how long she'd been gone.

It wasn't as if she didn't want to have sex. She did. In theory. She'd tried going through with it once, with Mark, pretty early on, because honestly, why else would Mark go for Penny if not to have regular relationship sex?

In the end she'd gotten as far as getting naked with some fumbling third-base action. Until the dread came. A sticky ink-iness that crept up her neck and swallowed her head whole. They'd maneuvered into a facilitating position and Penny started crying silently, which she didn't realize she was doing until it scared him and he stopped. She fell asleep soon after.

And get this: They never talked about it.

Penny had braced herself for a confrontation, but it simply never happened.

Through the summer, however, *he*'d been coming up more frequently.

Penny pulled up at Jim's, a diner with a red roof, cheap cof-fee, and surprisingly good soup. She was grateful most of the Saturday-morning crowd had cleared out. Mark kept hinting that they could go back to his house after lunch except that Penny was pretty sure they wouldn't be seeing a movie after their talk. God. Unless they did. Penny could actually imagine amicably watching the new Avengers movie after the breakup and *then* heading home.

Mark was already seated when she arrived. The way his eyes lit up as she opened the door sent a small wave of revul-sion through her.

"Hi, baby." He stood from the booth, hugged her, and—horror—handed her a single red rose. It was wrapped in cellophane. And it appeared as if it had spent some time living in a Circle K.

Penny smiled, took the flower—hesitated—then drew her nose to it.

It smelled of printer cartridges.

"It's stupid," said Mark tenderly. He was wearing a powder-blue dress shirt and silver basketball shorts with flip-flops. "But I wanted to get you something."

He was nervous, which made her nervous. Any established couple within stone's throw would've cringed in sympathy.

"You hate it, don't you?" he asked tentatively.

"No, it's great." Penny thought of the box of chocolates that the mailman had given her mom.

"You look beautiful," he said, admiring her dress. "I don't know that I've ever seen you not wearing black."

Penny smiled stiffly. "Uh, yeah. Thanks."

They ordered: tortilla soup for her, biscuits with sausage gravy for him.

"Not that I don't love you in black," he said quickly, handing his plastic menu to their server. "I love you in anything."

Penny prayed he didn't follow with, "I'd love you *out of* anything." *Heh heh.*

On their first night sharing a room, at the mention of a "boyfriend," Jude had set up a system. She would sleep at Mal's if Penny needed, in Jude's words, "a conjugal visit." Jude had rabbited the air quotes wearing this ridiculous smirk. Penny threw a pillow at her.

She could imagine such a visit.

First, she pictured Mark naked. That part was easy. Not entirely unpleasant.

Then she imagined his pressure on top of her, mashing her, grinding away, with that well-meaning smile, calling her *baby-babybaby* while she became catatonic and wanted to drown.

See, she could imagine it; she just couldn't imagine wanting it.

Penny wanted to be normal. She was eighteen, for Christ's sake, a respectable age to start having healthy consensual sex. Sexy sex with someone sexy.

Penny's mind went to Sam. Tattoos. Scowl. Crinkly eyed laugh. She thought about how his veiny, inked arms would feel encircling her body. The heat emanating from his chest. How he would smell. It was the most pornographic scenario her mind had mustered in public.

Still, she wasn't breaking up with Mark because of Sam. At least not in the sense that Mark was the *only thing* standing in the way of her and Sam being together. That was nuts. It was more that Sam was a type of human Penny couldn't have previously fathomed. Sam was proof of life on other planets. If a Sam existed, she couldn't be with a Mark. Not even if she couldn't be with a Sam. To Penny it made perfect sense.

Their food came.

They'd both ordered wet food. It was a tactical error. Penny wasn't in the mood for wet food. Eating it or observing it.

Mark's plate glistened under a thick blanket of creamy, greasy, white gravy. Penny thought about how it would form a skin if left to cool. Penny watched Mark use the back of his

fork to mash the bits of sausage into the biscuit and the sauce
into a kind of paste.

Her small bowl of watery broth with chips floating on top
and sprigs of green didn't look so great either.

"Oh, no baby," he lamented. "You forgot to ask for no cilantro. Want me to send it back? We'll tell them you're allergic."

Penny peered down at the offending frond. Did Mark hate
cilantro? She had no idea. His deep concern about the situation was written on his features, his thin upper lip lending an
air of determination to his childlike face. Penny wondered if
Mark was capable of physically hurting her. Or if he'd cry. She
wondered how mad his mad could get.

Penny couldn't take it anymore.

"We should break up," she said.

He stared at her uncomprehending for a moment, then
recoiled as if he'd been struck. His eyebrows scrambled sky-
ward to his hairline. They didn't watch *Avengers*.

· · ·

"You're back early." Jude barely looked up from her laptop. She
was sprawled on the floor with an apple core lying on the carpet beside her.

"Did he like your dress?"

"Yeah," said Penny, walking into the bathroom. Jude followed, continuing to talk to her from the other side of the door.

"I called my dad."

"Yeah?"

"I couldn't bring myself to tell him about changing my
major though."

Penny sighed and washed her face. She unzipped the dress and pulled on her robe.

"You know," said Jude, repositioning herself on Penny's bed, "for the record, I think you could absolutely look slutty if you wanted to."

Penny laughed.

"Are you okay?"

"I'm fine," Penny said.

"Did Mark get mad?"

"Yeah."

Mark had been enraged. In fact, he'd been so angry that it was the first time Penny had thought he seemed truly . . . masculine. Penny didn't need Dr. Greene to tell her how messed up *that* was. When Mark let her have it, she zoned out. He'd called her a freak, which hardly qualified as observant. Penny yawned.

"What else?" asked Jude warily.

He then started crying about how the same thing had happened with his ex.

His Asian-ex, Penny thought.

"He ordered biscuits and sausage gravy."

"And?"

"It was gruesome."

"What was gruesome?"

"Biscuits and gravy. I don't understand it as a food unit. It's the most disgusting concept," she said. "Congealed drippings over globs of flour and butter. How could anyone eat that in public?"

"Wow," said Jude, staring at her.

Penny stared back at Jude.

"I ask you about a personal trauma and you tell me about the catering?"

Penny nodded.

"You're bad at this."

Penny nodded again.

"You need therapy."

Penny nodded a third time.

"Are you sad?"

She was.

"Yeah."

"You know you can tell me anything," said Jude.

Penny regarded her roommate's big, sorrowful eyes and knew it to be true.

"I'm going to hug you now," Jude warned.

Penny nodded.

The pressure felt good.

SAM.

Sam stared at himself in the mirror of the medicine cabinet. He was wearing his second nicest button-up, a white dress shirt that he typically saved for weddings or funerals. His first nicest was the Ralph Lauren Lorraine had gotten him two Christmases ago, but he didn't want to wear it. He didn't want to remind her of the *other* memory. How he'd gotten her a bracelet so cheap it turned her wrist green. Sam buttoned the shirt all the way up to the top. Then unbuttoned the top button. And then buttoned it again. He sighed. He looked like a LinkedIn profile pic.

It wasn't a date or anything. You can't actually date someone you used to date and vowed to never date again. No way Lorraine would call it a date. Yet when she texted him for dinner upon ignoring his texts, he was nervous. She probably had something awful to tell him.

On the upside, he hadn't had any panic attacks since the first and he imagined his body was saving up for just such an occasion. Sam pictured himself stumbling in slo-mo through the dining room of Mother's Italian Restaurant, grabbing tables for support, sending plates of tagliatelle crashing to the floor. He'd ruin Liar's expensive dress and wouldn't hear the end of it. Sam wanted to shoot a selfie to Penny for outfit approval except they didn't do that sort of thing. As if she could sense him thinking about her, Penny texted him.

> *Should I read Harry Potter from the*
> *beginning again?*

He took a selfie in the bathroom mirror and sent it to her. She wrote back:

> *Um*

And then:

> *So I SHOULD read them or . . .*
> *OK*
> *wait*
> *did you do that on purpose*

> *I need advice*
> *Help me*

> *OK*
> *Take the plea deal!*

Ask me something else
my advice RN is en FUEGO

                                              Stop

WAIT so you don't have
a court date?

                                    I'm seeing Lorraine

Penny fell silent. Bubble. Then no bubble.
So he wrote:

                                       It's not a date

Sam didn't know why he was explaining himself. After a long
moment she responded.

So no bowling or Putt-Putt?

                                       Ice skating
                                    Then karaoke
                            Waterfall picnic at dusk

Very cool
PS hay rides > karaoke
Don't forget flowers
Carnations!
NO!

A corsage!

> *Dinner*
> *Just dinner*
> *I want to die*

Why die?

> *Probably have a panic attack*

"Calm down"

> *Ha.*
> *So shirt? Y/N?*

Shirt seems desperate
Dress regular

> *Sooooo . . . orange bell-bottoms*

Yah and pink Uggs

> *Pls delete this foto*

NEVER
Send n00dz

Sam took off the shirt and grabbed a black T-shirt. The blue veins coursed along his body like tributaries until they disappeared under the indelible black tattoos that his friends had carved into him. He had sixteen in all. Several crappy stick-and-pokes—crossed arrows, diamonds, snails, hands, and *hamsas* to ward off evil eyes—and the rest from an artist whose house he'd painted in exchange for twenty hours in his chair.

He stared at his chest, curving his shoulders inward and creating a golf-ball-size divot on his sternum. For a brief period during sophomore year, he'd tried to gain weight, filling gallon plastic jugs of water and using them as dumbbells, hoisting them above his head over and over in front of the mirror. The hopeful determination in his reflection as he stood in his underwear was embarrassing even in memory.

Growing up, the problem wasn't so much the lack of strength training as it was food. Groceries were scarce and money for school lunches was a non-starter. Brandi Rose, who was not above collecting workmen's comp on dubious grounds, was somehow too proud to fill out the paperwork for her son's need-based meals. "We don't do handouts," she'd say. By junior year, Sam said to hell with it and forged the paperwork himself.

At first he'd gotten the tattoos to create a diversion from his slight frame but now he no longer hated his body. It was tidy. Contained. Efficient. Though Penny would probably be horrified if she ever did see him with his clothes off. Objectively, his body was alarming.

Sam picked Lorraine up in Fin's Ford Festiva slightly before eight. It was a mud-brown fourteen-year-old beater that was so rusted through you could lift the mat on the driver's side and watch the highway rush by from a quarter-sized peephole.

Sam buzzed at the gate as she'd requested.

"Hey," she said. She wore what she usually did when she was off work—a somewhat abbreviated version of a nightie.

Lorraine. Lorr. Lore. Or Lola as she called herself lately, though Sam never did.

He could practically feel his pupils dilate when he saw her.

"Nice dress," he said when she opened the door to his car. He wondered if he should've gotten out and opened it for her, though she would've made fun of him for it. It wasn't as if she were infirm.

"Uh, thanks for picking me up." She pulled him in for a hug. It was an awkward sideways embrace where you're both sitting down and the non-hugging arm gets mashed, but still, it knocked the wind out of him.

As was customary for when he saw her, he felt his thoughts go all soft and watery. She smelled so good, exactly the way she was supposed to. He knew every bit of real estate on her body. He thought about her feet again.

Lorraine pulled away and started laughing. "This is so absurd," she said, putting her seat belt on.

"I can't believe Fin loaned you his car." She looked into the backseat and wrinkled her nose. "I could have picked you up."

"Where's the fun in that?"

Sam partially regretted leaving Fin's empty soda bottles in the backseat even if he'd done it on purpose. This was *not* a date.

By the time Sam pulled up at Mother's, a spot far enough off campus that it wasn't overrun with students, they'd exhausted small talk. And when Sam got her door, she didn't make too big a deal out of it. She thanked him primly and touched his forearm.

They slid into the deep, padded booth. On their early dates, they were the annoying couple that sat on the same side, whispering, canoodling, picking up bits of food to feed each other like lovesick birds.

"Do you want to split the ziti and the sausage and peppers?" Lorraine asked, scanning the menu. Sam had been dreaming about meatballs, yet he found himself shrugging. "Sure."

Sam remembered why they shared food whenever they went out. Lorraine would order the two things she wanted and strong-armed him into wanting them as well.

"Are you sure you don't want to get a vegetable or a salad?" he asked, eyeing the sides. "Something with folate?"

Lorraine peered over the leather-bound wine list.

"Sam, what is folate?"

"It's in broccoli," he said. "Pregnant ladies have to take it so the baby's spine doesn't grow outside of their bodies. Don't do an image search. It's upsetting."

She laughed.

"I'm sorry," she said. "I shouldn't laugh."

Lorraine picked up a piece of focaccia, dipped it in olive oil, and took a bite, chewing slowly.

She crossed her arms, and Sam noticed the glint of a new charm bracelet on her wrist. It was visibly expensive—crowded with ornate silver beads and intricate replicas of what appeared to be shoes. He wondered who'd bought it for her.

"How are you, Lorr?" he asked. What he wanted to ask her

was: "Do you miss me?" But it didn't quite seem the right time. Maybe after tiramisu.

Sam also really wanted to ask what all of this was about. Whether she'd had her appointment and discovered complications. Why else would she not have texted him back?

"Before you light into me," she began, "I haven't gone to the clinic yet."

He couldn't believe it.

"What? Why?"

"I couldn't make it," she said, snapping a breadstick in half. "It was insane at work. But I made an appointment for tomorrow. I'm going tomorrow."

Sam couldn't believe how cavalier she was being. Period lateness count: seven weeks.

"Why didn't you tell me?"

"I . . . I couldn't deal." She crumbled the rest of the breadstick onto the tablecloth.

"Well, you're going to have to deal with this," he said. "*We're* going to have to deal."

"I know," she said. "I know this makes no sense, but I don't *think* I'm pregnant. I don't *feel* pregnant."

Sam studied Lorraine for any physical differences. He took a quick peek at her boobs and they appeared about the same.

"Are you checking me out to see if I look knocked up?"

Yes.

"No," he told her.

The waiter came around.

"Uh, yeah, we're going to split the ziti and the . . ." Man, he definitely wanted meatballs.

"Sausage and peppers," she finished.

"And a glass of merlot," said Lorraine. She pulled out her driver's license.

"I guess you *really* don't feel pregnant, huh?" he asked, once the waiter had left.

Lorraine rolled her eyes. "French women drink up until the very end," she said.

"French women also eat horse," said Sam under his breath.

"What?" Lorraine asked.

"Nothing."

"I take it you're not drinking lately?" She leaned back into the booth.

"No," said Sam, leaning in. "Haven't since all of this happened," he said, stirring the sky with his forefinger.

"Understandable. The smell of gin still turns my stomach." Lorraine shuddered.

Shameful scenes from their breakup slammed into Sam's head. The two of them screaming in the street after his debit card stopped working. She'd called him a "bum like his father" and he'd called her a "duplicitous bitch."

"Lorr, why'd you ask me here?"

"Well, you picked the restaurant," she said, smiling sweetly.

"Lorraine . . ."

"I don't know," she said, averting her gaze. "I thought it would be nice."

Lorraine snapped another breadstick into ever smaller pieces and arranged them on the table.

He braced himself for the news that they were having twins. Or that she was engaged to someone else.

"That's it? Really?" he asked. "No news?"

She shook her head.

Sam couldn't believe he'd had to ask for an advance on his paycheck for this.

"You know what?" he said after a while.

She glanced up at him.

"Let's create a pact."

"A pact," she repeated. Lorraine reached for another breadstick to pulverize. He took it from her. Wasted food made him crazy.

"Yeah," he said. "The pact is we'll table everything serious for the duration of the meal, and you and me, we'll catch up."

Lorraine's wine arrived.

"We don't have to talk about the other stuff."

"Deal," she said. She raised her glass in a toast and took a sip.

Sam wanted to excuse himself to look up fetal alcohol syndrome statistics but couldn't in the spirit of the pact. Stupid pact . . .

"So," said Lorraine. "What I want to know is . . ." She paused.

"What?"

"Never mind," she said.

"No, tell me."

"Where have you been living?"

Sam blinked. "Near campus," he said.

"Where near campus?"

"Off Guadalupe," he said. A partial lie at worst. "Why the Spanish Inquisition?" he asked, trying to keep his tone light.

Their pasta dishes landed on the table with a *thud* as Sam decided he wasn't hungry. The ziti looked dry.

"Eat and switch?" she asked. "And don't worry, dinner's on me."

Sam nodded and handed her the sausage first. She inevitably wanted the sausage first so she could pick out the crispy ends. The best parts.

"Well." Lorraine tried again. "I know you're not living in your car, unless you're sleeping out of Fin's. Which I obviously don't envy."

Sam's cheeks burned. Lorraine had a habit of kidding in a way that made you want to walk off a bridge.

"And I talked to Gunner and Gash, so I know you're not living with them." Sam used to see Gunner and his cousin Ash (a.k.a. Gash) five nights a week.

He fell silent.

"How's school?" she asked after a while. Sam shoveled a forkful of pasta into his mouth to mull over the answer. He nodded while he chewed.

Why was Lorraine on a fact-finding mission?

"Good." He swallowed. "I'm taking a film course at ACC and it's fine. A lot of freedom. I'm shooting a documentary."

"Finally," she said, picking at her meal. "Isn't it expensive?"

"It ain't cheap," he said. "But you can borrow gear, and if all else fails, I've got my phone. I'll shoot it fast and dirty."

"Well, *that* suits you," she said.

What the hell did that mean?

They ate in silence.

"Your turn," said Sam, working to keep his tone even. "How's the job?"

"Job's good," she said. "I got a raise. Nothing to write home about. Hopefully a promotion's next. I'll probably be a junior account manager by next year, which is what I want. I'll get to travel to LA."

"That's great," he said. He realized he meant it. Traveling for work was the height of glamour as far as Lorraine was concerned.

"And I love the people I work with," she said. "They're young and fun to hang out with. You'd think they're corny."

Sam immediately thought about Paul again. He had no idea what he looked like. Not that it mattered. Sam could imagine his type exactly. He envisioned Lorraine celebrating her promotion over eighteen-dollar cocktails with some douche-bag with a big shiny watch and buffed square fingernails. He probably plucked his eyebrows and bleached his enormous capped teeth. He thought back to when he and Lorraine met, when she described herself first and foremost as a DJ. He'd since learned most DJs or comedians or musicians were artists by the grace of their parents' financial support.

"Sausage?"

Sam nodded. The plate of oily meat and tangles of peppers and onions made him queasy. Or perhaps it was something else.

"Lorr, what happened to us?"

Lorraine laughed dryly and took another sip of wine.

"So much for the pact."

"Well," he said. "We make up and break up without talking about what actually happened."

"What are you asking me, Sam?"

"It doesn't make sense to me," he said. "Why we're not together."

Lorraine put her fork down and sighed.

"*We* don't make sense," she said. As if that explained anything.

"How can you say that?"

Sam suddenly wished he'd ordered a glass of wine. Or a box.

"We're not friends," she said.

Sam felt the dull thud of her words in his sternum. It took all of his composure to maintain eye contact. He scrunched his napkin under the table.

"We were these lunatic hotheads that fought and made up," Lorraine continued. "You'd scream and cry. I'd want to get it over with, and that was that."

Sam couldn't stand the way she distilled their relationship to the plot of a formulaic rom-com. Or as if she were wearing a white coat and chuckling about the mating lab rats she kept under observation.

"You say that like there weren't truly beautiful moments," he muttered into his food. "We loved each other."

"I know we did," she said. She took his hand in hers, with a tender smile playing on her lips, as though she were bargaining with a child. "I still love you in a way. I swear to God, Sam, sometimes you were so good at *literally* reading my mind."

Sam pictured Lorraine cracking his skull open and reading his brain grooves *literally* like braille.

"But we were together for four years," she continued. "And you didn't make an effort to get to know me or my family."

At the mention of "family," Sam stiffened. He wasn't big on the Mastersons. He recalled the abysmal Easter when he'd had dinner with them at Chez Jumelles.

"Oh, you mean the time your racist dad asked me if I had any

Middle Eastern blood so he'd have a real reason to hate me?"

Lorraine removed her hand from his. "No, he didn't," she said.

"He sure did," he said. Not that it made a difference. The night was a wash from the get-go. The Capital Metro bus strike happened at the last minute and Sam arrived straight from work in a bleach-stained Black Flag T-shirt.

"I don't know," she said. "You were outright hostile toward them. It's hardly my parents' fault that they're well off. They work like demons."

She said this plainly. As if there were no privileges inherent in being land-rich by pedigree for generations. A distant relative on her mom's side, C.E. Doolin, had also happened to invent the Frito. Rather, he'd happened to buy the recipe for a song from the Mexican man who'd invented it.

"It's not as if it were some great secret that you were"—she gazed up at him—"not well off." She miraculously sidestepped calling him poor. "Your clothes are a dead giveaway."

Sam chewed on the inside of his cheek. Lorraine went on cataloging his shortcomings between bites of food. Sam was a romantic, no doubt, and these were parts of their relationship he'd forgotten about. The comparisons. Sam wanted to get up, calmly set his napkin down, and sprint out into the night.

"Hey," said Lorraine, poking his hand. "I'm just joshing. Partly."

Sam didn't think so. He took another bite as his stomach roiled. Though, mercifully, he didn't pass out.

PENNY.

"Writing is the art of applying the seat of the pants to the seat of the chair."—Mary Heaton Vorse.

Penny got up at five fifteen a.m. No matter when she closed her eyes, they snapped open before six. These days it was a blessing, seeing as she needed a quiet moment to write. She hadn't had to do that before—find time. And she wondered lately if tapping out little blue bubbles to Sam was somehow sucking her inspiration well dry. Penny feared that she'd used up her best stuff on him, and her mind wandered constantly. It didn't help that a pert little antenna stayed vigilantly trained on her phone, scanning the airwaves to see if he needed company or was having a mini crisis.

Penny threw on a sweatshirt and cracked open her laptop.

Henry Miller, whose middle name was Valentine and who when he died was married to a Japanese woman, said, "Write first and always. Painting, music, friends, cinema, all these come afterward." Penny wondered where marrying came in, considering Miller had five wives. She also wondered where workshopping Sam's drama fell in terms of priorities. For Penny, it was sizing up to be "text first and always."

*What do you love about your
writing class*

*Nothing. I hate it
Also i love it*

*Obvs
Say more*

OK

Penny cracked her knuckles. She'd hooked up iMessage to her laptop so she could type as much as she wanted without her fingers falling off.

*It's as close as I've ever gotten to
feeling like a writer
A real one
You sit there and you have to do it
Everyone is capable of putting
words down*

Or telling a story
But not everyone will actually do it
This class is about the doing
And getting better
feels professional
Not like a normal college class
Where you learn things you'll
never apply

Sam didn't say anything.

No thought bubble, no interruption, no nothing. Penny went on:

You know how you can make a
sound on a piano
Anyone with fingers can do it
Intuitive
You hit keys
they make noise
Writing and reading then
rewriting and then
editing is how you make a melody
It's the same for everyone
It's not about raw talent
Or having such a big ego that you
think what you have to say
is so important
Or who your parents are

> And what they do
> It's the practice of it
> Doing it until you're good

And then because she felt self-conscious:

> Does that make sense?

> Totally
> And I get it
> What do you hate about it?

Penny started writing back. And then stopped.
She took another stab at it.

> It's so haaaaaaaaaaard
> It hurts my feelings it's so hard
> And it's scary

> ahaha
> WELL YEAH
> Guess that's what makes it
> worth doing?
> It's as scary as you can get
> Writers die trying
> Do you call yourself a writer?

> Ew no

Why ew?

I feel like a fraud

Yeah imposter syndrome

Penny Googled "imposter syndrome."

> *Informally used to describe people who are unable to internalize their accomplishments despite external evidence of their competence.*

It can mess you up
for sure

It undoubtedly applied to her.

I just . . .
. . .

She tried again.

I haven't ever seen a writer
A big deal writer
who looks like me
And sometimes when I write
I imagine the hero as white
Like automatically
How fucked is that

Penny stopped. She'd never told anyone that before. She wondered how that worked in movies.

She wrote back:

Why do you want to make movies?

UGH IDK

Ever think you'll jinx it when you talk about it?

YES
Def have imposter syndrome
Making movies is for rich people
It's so ridic to say
you want to be a director
May as well say you want to
be in the NBA
Or famous

Or the inventor of an app

Right. The app that invents apps!

Penny smiled.

So you want to be a writer
And I want to make movies
Feels corny to say out loud

But that's OK
It's important to at least
admit it to yourself
And to a few trusted people

Your emergency contact for example

Lol exactly
Then you make it real

Penny loved how unselfconsciously he said that. From anyone else it would sound self-helpy.

PS: I want to read
your work someday

Only if I get to see your movie

Fat chance

Penny laughed. There was no way she was going to let Sam read anything she wrote. J.A. didn't count since she was her professor, and neither did the kids in class. Everyone's guts were splayed out on the table. It was mutually assured destruction.

One time Jude tried to read over Penny's shoulder and she'd been apoplectic.

"'The terrors lay cold and caged at the bottom of the deep'?"

"Jude!" Penny shrieked, slamming her laptop shut. "You

can't do that. It's a gross invasion of privacy." Penny sprang up out of her chair, clutching her computer to her chest.

"Whoa," said Jude, big-eyed. "Holy shit. I'm sorry. I didn't know you'd wig. Don't you think you should get used to someone reading it, since the eventual goal is public consumption?"

She had a point.

But Penny was scared of what her stories revealed. The constructive criticism from class—even on the tiniest points—ruined her day, and Jude was enough in her business without getting access to Penny's thoughts as well.

For her final she was plotting out a story inspired by the true events of a Korean couple that accidentally neglected their baby to death. It was all over the papers in Korea and the sad part was that it happened because the parents were obsessively playing a video game where the whole point—of all things—was to raise a child. Their real-life baby's name was Sa-Rang, which means "love" in Korean. Everything about the story was tragic and fascinating, and for class Penny wanted to write two narratives, story A from the viewpoint of the mom and B from the perspective of the baby in the video game. It was a story within a story, the way *Watchman* contained *Tales of the Black Freighter*, a comic about pirates. Penny was enthralled by the origami of the form except she couldn't figure it out. Write one first? Or both at the same time?

In class, the story confused everyone.

"Is the main character the Tamagotchi baby or the mom?" asked Maya. Maya was the mixed girl who'd talked about Kardashian hair on the first day and was writing a ghost story about the Santa Ana winds.

"Both," Penny said. "And it's not a Tamagotchi. It's a *Sims* baby or a clan in *Clash of Clans*."

"Whatever," said Maya. "They're both wicked unlikable."

"Oh, because a weather phenomenon that's on a murder spree is *so* likable," retorted Andy, the British-Chinese kid. Penny shot him a grateful look. He smiled.

Penny didn't know what was so hard about sympathizing with a computer-generated video game character or a Korean woman, but that seemed to be the general consensus.

Penny started out with the mother talking to her lawyer. That much she felt was solid. It was a secure, accessible place from which to world-build. She figured she'd lull the reader into a false sense of security—begin as *Law & Order* that transmogrifies into *The Matrix* without warning.

She made herself a cup of tea, sat back down, and tried to imagine the woman's appearance. Penny began by picturing her hair. Did Korean women get soccer-mom haircuts? Penny settled on giving the mom a bob and dressed her in a gray maternity dress. According to the papers, she was pregnant again by the time she and her husband were sentenced.

What did this woman want? Did she feel bad? How bad? As bad as you should if you ignore your baby to death? How engrossing can a video game be that you forget your baby?

"I am not a bad mother," said the wife. Mrs. Kim was subdued, with no makeup, and her lips were chapped. Her hand shook as she drank from the white paper cup. She was diminutive and of indeterminate

age. As he flipped through her file, he saw she was younger than her husband by twenty years. She'd gone to a good school yet had never held down a job. Mrs. Kim met her husband at an Internet café, and according to witnesses, they were affectionate and companionable.

"I'm not a bad mother," she repeated in a daze. "I loved my babies more than anything." She took a sharp intake of breath and corrected herself. "Baby."

The lawyer glanced up from his notes. The wife's chin trembled. He jotted down that she still considered the video game baby to be real.

J.A. advised the class on "voice" and how a good way to work through a story was to make it sound as if you were explaining it to a friend over e-mail.

Penny figured texting was as good.

SAM HOUSE

Yesterday 1:13 AM

Wait
Hold on
I want to ask you something
Don't be offended

Haha does that ever work?

Nope!

Fine
Say it
Be nice though
Writers are sensitive

How does your story
count as fiction?
This woman exists
The couple's real

Sam found a documentary on the couple and they'd watched it together. Not in the same room. Just at the same time, while texting. Every article and TV segment treated them as though they were Internet oddities or space aliens. The documentary, in particular, may as well have been about talking dogs the way they presented the parents. Penny wondered if the perverse fascination would have been as extreme if it had happened in America. A country, by the way, where a guy in Minnesota tried to raise his kid to speak Klingon.

That's why I want to write about
the baby in the
video game as well
That's the fiction part
The fantasy

Does the baby inside know that the
real baby is dying?

> IDK if the video game baby cares
> Collateral damage etc

Jesus that's dark

> Is it though?
> VG baby lives in constant violence
> That's why SF's the greatest
> You make the rules

San Francisco?

> No dork
> SCIENCE FICTION

SAID THE DORK WHO
CAPS LOCKS science fiction

> Hahahhahaha
> Fair

I like this
I can't wait to find out what
video game baby wants

Penny couldn't either.

J.A.'s homework schedule was no joke. Every week there was a new short story due, and for those Penny wrote about squirrel crime mobs, post-apocalyptic plagues that only took out people over nineteen, colleges in the future where the entrance exams were assassinations, and a Buddhist who died and came back as a toy. Building a world where you rappel in, set up some characters, and ejector seat your way out was a breeze.

J.A. had no patience for breezy, and when she called Penny in for office hours, she told her as much. Her teacher's room was filled with succulents in rainbow-glass planters, and Penny halfway expected her teacher to extend an offer of friendship she was so pleased with her last story. It was about a crew of powerful moguls and politicians who were set adrift in a spaceship since the planet they were destined for wasn't where they'd thought it would be. The astrophysicist eggheads they'd left behind had been wrong. These men were the 1 percent of the 1 percent who had abandoned the rest of civilization, and still their billions couldn't save them. The universe told them the first no of their lives, and the fight scene was hilarious.

"These are great," said J.A. began, "but . . ."

Penny hadn't been expecting a "but." She braced herself.

"They're rhythmically one-note," J.A. continued. "You're inventive and funny—that's clear on the page. I want you to work on character motivation. I can't invest in protagonists when I don't know what they want, and just as important, why they want it."

Penny felt color rising on her neck. That wasn't fair. It was clear what the men in the spaceship wanted.

"They want their planet," Penny said. She cringed at the whiny pitch she was taking.

"Well, yes," continued J.A. "They all want that. Humans want to live, that's a given. The issue is they want the same thing in the same way, and that's a missed opportunity. You've got world leaders here. They're captains of industry. They're singular men, but look . . ." J.A. circled some passages. "They speak the same. I'm only picking on you because your excellent dialogue and glitter-bomb observations won't save you for the final."

It was clear Penny's sweet spot was two or three pages. The last story they'd had to write was twenty thousand words. Longer than anything she'd ever written. Penny usually wrote to escape, so her worlds were fantastic and, well, apparently one-note.

Penny thought she knew what her characters wanted. It was trickier to deduce *why* they wanted anything. And a different proposition entirely to say *how* they'd get it. Hell, Penny had no idea what she wanted. Why would her inventions fare any better?

Plus, there were so many distractions. Ergo, getting up at five fifteen this morning.

Penny planned to hammer out her three acts, handwritten on note cards, so she could visualize scenes and move them around. Except that as she fanned out her color-coded three-by-fives, she realized that her nails were disgusting. The puny chips of lacquer were sad little archipelagos of poison that were probably falling into her food. She took out the nail kit her mom got her as a stocking stuffer every Christmas and removed the polish.

Penny didn't want to admit how much she resembled her mother in these moments. It was classic Celeste, to do nails instead of what she was supposed to be doing. It struck Penny that she missed Celeste at the oddest times. Often the most baffling parts of her, too. The way her mom's rib cage felt when she hugged her from behind. Or how the curly hair of her econ prof reminded her so much of Celeste during lectures. If only there were a way of seeing her mom without either of them having to talk. When Penny's nails were bare she figured she should wash her hair. There was nothing worse than ruining a fresh manicure with an ill-timed shower.

While Penny stood under the spray she noticed that because their dorm bathroom didn't have a window, a thin layer of mildew had formed in the caulk. That itself was tolerable, except then mold was a foregone conclusion and *that* stuff could kill you. An hour and a half later she was clean, the shower stall was spotless, her nails were a matte slate gray, and she was ready. She put pants on so she could apply the seat of them to the chair.

This is what she had so far:

The baby in the game was known as an Anima so she wrote down "Anima."

Then she Wikipedia'd it since that's the first order of business when you don't know what the hell you're doing.

Anima meant "soul," or "animating principle." According to the psychologist Carl Jung, Anima also implied the unseen individual, the true inner self.

Penny didn't have a ton of experience playing online role-playing games like the one in the story. She knew, though, that *Overwatch* and *World of Warcraft* were huge in Korea—PC games that were played so competitively and obsessively that tournaments filled arenas and people went into rehab for addiction.

Regardless, what was true of all games was that there had to be a task, a pursuit. So she wrote down "quest" in her favorite ultra-fine rollerball black pen.

God, she loved that word.

She underlined "quest." Such a euphonic word. *Quessssst*.

Oooh, "odyssey" was a good word too, but she'd already underlined quest.

She added a question mark.

Then she took out another note card and simply wrote: *How does the hero get what they want?*

J.A.'s words nagged at her.

First, Penny had to set up the rules. The main part of the game was that the hero or the player character had to raise a baby, or the Anima. The Anima was the trusted sidekick and you could dress them up and give them weapons but most importantly you kept them safe from harm. The mom, Mrs. Kim, played as a Gunslinger. A ruthless sharpshooting outlaw. There were adventures and sieges and even a dragon slaying. The dragon battle was a real barn burner and at the very last second before all was lost, the Anima would make its greatest sacrifice—its life—to save the Gunslinger and beat their mortal enemy. That was the deal since time immemorial.

In Penny's version, the baby changed its mind because it could.

That an Anima even had a mind to change was a miracle.

And the cost of the miracle had been the couple's real-life baby. A digital tit for tat.

Okay, focus. So who's the hero, the Anima or the mother? It was the Anima since she changes the most. But why?

Penny thought about the event that starts a story—the inciting incident—that they'd talked about in class. It's the Big Bang (well, unless you're a religious creationist type). It's like how Katniss's sister is picked for the Hunger Games but Katniss steps in for her. Or how Nitro exploding kills six hundred people, which leads to the Superhuman Registration Act that causes civil war in the Marvel U. The Anima needed a Eureka moment, a turning point.

"I'll miss you." The Gunslinger bent down on one knee and kissed the Anima on the cheek.

"I'll miss you," parroted the Anima back, smiling sweetly. The dutiful baby knew it was best to repeat whatever Mother said.

The Gunslinger chuckled, gathering up the Anima in her arms. "Do you know what that means, my sweet daughter? To miss?" The Gunslinger was feared in four kingdoms for her unflinching kills, but in private she spoiled her child.

The Anima shook her head.

"It means I'll think about you all the time and wish you were close even when I'm not here."

"I'll miss you," said the Anima again as she watched Mother go.

What did it mean, "here"? The Anima was always "here." Where was not "here"? That there was such a thing as "un-here" bore a hole in the Anima's head.

She hated when Mother was in the "un-here."

On the next evening, as Mother departed, the Anima followed her into the woods. It was forbidden to leave the Atrium without the Gunslinger's say-so, but the Anima had to know. It was a moonless night and the Anima was afraid of the dark shapes and Mother's wrath if she were caught, when suddenly, in the pitch black, the Anima heard voices. Loud ones from the sky. With a flash of white light the heavens opened and high above even the treetops, higher than all five peaks of Mount Meru, the Anima saw a face as big as the sun. Mother. This was the "un-here" that Mother went when she missed the Anima.

This spark of curiosity and the pursuit of answers was the Anima's quest. This altered her fate and intertwined it with the Mother's real-life child beyond the computer. The Anima could see the "un-here" from the PC camera and speakers. And the more she realized about herself, the more she became curious about the world she inhabited. This was enlightenment. Sentience. This was life.

Penny took notes, read everything over, and wondered if any of it constituted writing. Somehow it was seven forty. Twenty minutes to get to class, and Sam had texted good morning an hour ago. Maybe she should scribble out a story about an irresistible computer algorithm that haunted her phone and made her fall in love with it until she lost her mind and climbed into the shower hugging a still-plugged-in blow-dryer. Now, *that* would be believable.

SAM.

Sam heard the garbage trucks. Then the birds. His body knew it was morning before the light changed and the room warmed. It used to be that he'd be getting home with the trash collectors and self-satisfied joggers. Sam would marvel at the joggers—humans with whole separate wardrobes dedicated to particular tasks—people who owned camping equipment and tennis rackets. People for whom having kids made some kind of sense.

Sam couldn't tell if he'd slept. For weeks when he first stopped drinking he'd had terrible nightmares. Vivid dreams of fistfights with his father or Lorraine's funeral—Psych 101 stuff. Then it flipped for no reason and he slept like the dead. Dreamless slumber he had to wrench himself from in the morning, pillow damp with drool, deep creases on his face where his skin had folded and he hadn't moved. Now insomnia popped up once in a while to mix it up.

Good morning! he typed into his phone.

It was the first thing he did now.

Sam showered. The hot water coursed over his body, poaching his skin. Seeing Lorraine had been discouraging. Sad. He felt emotionally hungover from the night before. As if he'd clenched all his muscles the entire time.

He missed his friends sometimes. Gunner and Gash were entertaining, but without booze and bars, he knew they'd have nothing to talk about.

Sam towel-dried his hair and shook it out. At the top of the summer, Gunner's ex, April, came by to give him a cut. She'd come alone, which was awkward enough, and when they set up on the back porch, her hands lingered on the back of his neck, suggesting she had something else in mind. Sam couldn't bear it. He sent her away with a coffee cake with promises to keep in touch, and when she never came back he was relieved.

His phone buzzed.

Tacos y pelicula?

Shit, Jude.

They'd planned on dinner tonight. Well, dinner and a movie. Sam had made the suggestion. Al Pastor tacos at the good taco spot, not the ruined shitty philanderer taco spot, followed by a late-night screening of *Gremlins 2* at Alamo Drafthouse, where they'd have crème brûlées.

Whenever Jude texted him, Sam unfailingly thought, *Shit, Jude*, despite his affection for her. Jude was a sweet kid. It's just that he already saw her most mornings when she picked up coffee before class, and that was plenty.

Sam made himself an espresso. Would it kill him to have dinner with her?

Probably.

He exhaled the breath he didn't realize he'd been holding, cringed, and typed.

I'm so sorry J
Have to work

He pictured Jude staring at her screen and hating him. He typed again.

Next week?

Uuuuuugh. Why did he do that?

Penny texted him back.

Good morning!
Did you know da vinci didn't sleep
Only naps
30 mins/4 hrs

He knew when she texted in bursts that she had something else going on. He checked the time. It was 8:08. She was either in her writing class or running late to it. Sam loved that he could talk to her all day without worrying about seeing her.

Historically, communicating with girls wasn't hard. When they show interest, you show interest back by asking a ton of questions. Penny was receptive to questions, though her responses were rarely coy or suggestive. Plus, she made zero effort to hang out. She seemed somehow immune to the mechanics of flirting. Sam wondered if she found him attractive.

Dogs or cats?

It cracked him up that Penny was in his phone as "Emergency Penny" since none of her texts constituted an emergency.

Sam typed back:

BABY GOATS

He was pleased with that one. He had a supercut of goats ready to go. Sam pasted the link and hit send.

Whoa

Pie or cake?

Sam was making a pecan pie with an ornate lattice on top and wanted to show it off if pie won out. He'd perfected his crust with frozen butter that you grated like cheese.

Cake
Sheet cake
From a box

What???
Gross
You're insane

He slid the pie into the oven, feeling stupid for how deflated he felt.

Pie obviously. Cobbler above sheet cake. Ew. He wasn't sure they'd recover from that.

Sam knew pie versus cake wasn't their only incompatibility. He couldn't imagine the space Penny would take up in his life if she sprang out of his phone. He couldn't envision her from across the room laughing with people he knew. Or scooping peas into her mouth at a table. In fact, sometimes he could barely make out her likeness in his head since it had been so long since he'd seen her and there were so few images of her online. There was a photo from a school yearbook, but she looked so young and unhappy at having her picture taken that Sam felt strongly that he was trespassing.

His phone buzzed again. Jude.

It's OK!
Next week is great
Good luck with work

Penny was still on some tangent about polyphasic sleep schedules.

Nikola Tesla too
No sleep club
Or sleep sometimes club
So tired
Did you sleep
HOW ARE YOU?

Penny always asked how he was doing.

No sleep!
It was a supermoon tho
Makes your brain chemistry insane

Shitty moon

Hate the moon

I tried to write this morning

And?

Well I tried
Brb class
:(

Sam realized he'd also become way too accustomed to emoji. He felt like a teen girl. Penny *was* a teen girl, he reminded himself. He should really start thinking about women his own age, say, the one who was carrying his unborn child. Sam groaned into his empty room. Penny was Jude's age, which made her seventeen or eighteen. Sam wondered about her birthday and what her favorite type of boxed sheet cake was. Probably chocolate with white icing. Some sprinkles maybe. Glittery black ones to match her hair. Not that it mattered. He imagined how horrified she'd be if he showed up at her dorm with an actual physical cake IRL.

Maybe they could be friends when she was old enough to count as a person. Perhaps when she was twenty-five and he, at twenty-eight or twenty-nine, could be the cool, older guy-pal who would give her tax advice and beat the living daylights out of any age-appropriate boyfriend who mistreated her. Or at least glare at him in a menacing way. God. Sam would be almost thirty by then. Disgusting.

PENNY.

Penny hoofed it to class. Her hair was that type of long where it got caught in her armpits at the worst times. She wanted to pull over from the throng of kids to flood Sam's phone with questions about his date, but she restrained herself. Instead she talked about the varying sleep cycles of geniuses who later became psychos. As you do.

She'd been *dying* to text him last night. Instead she beamed the Internet into her eyes for distraction, stalking MzLolaXO, rendering sleep impossible. Penny's own Instagram account was set to private and while her feed contained only six pictures, it was useful for anonymous lurking or as cover for the accidental deep-like. That MzLolaXO had a new photo in her feed of Sam's hands—from a few weeks ago—dismantled her. MzLolaXO had tagged him holding a broken laptop, and Penny knew it was for sure him because of the horse tattoo. When Penny clicked through to his account, it had been deleted. Penny was relieved and a little butt-hurt—okay a lot butt-hurt—that he hadn't mentioned seeing her that night.

At one a.m., eyeballs throbbing from the screen time, she'd eaten two of Jude's protein bars without realizing they had sixteen grams of fiber in each. They lay heavy in her stomach—forming a kind of petrified roughage diamond—as she scrambled across campus.

Penny didn't know why she was being such a headcase. It was better for the baby if Sam and Lola reconciled. It was the natural order of the universe for them to be together. If two gazelles gallivanted around the savanna, it was no business of the tree frog. Penny was the tree frog obviously.

When she got to class, J.A. was wearing a jumpsuit made—improbably—of complicated balls of twine. Needless to say, she looked amazing.

"Tragic heroes are hella fun to write," she began. "Hamlet, Macbeth, Othello, Tony Soprano. They're damaged, saddled with baggage. Plus, wherever they go, there they are, yadda yadda yadda."

Everyone in Penny's story was screwed up. The only innocent was the real-life baby who died. Ugh. So many babies to think about. What if there had been some big update about Sam's baby? Would he have told her? Yes, he would have. At least she thought he would. Except that he hadn't told Penny about seeing Lola weeks ago, so why would he tell her about last night? About how they'd driven to Vegas and eloped while Penny sat at home alone eating her feelings.

What *if* Sam was married now? Jeez. That would make him about as tragic as they came. An impregnated Lola was his *hamartia,* or fatal flaw. Oh God, or maybe Penny was the tragic hero and Sam was *her* flaw. She tried to refocus on the assignment.

Trouble was, Penny had to admit she only knew Sam because he was going through something. It was the classic fish-out-of-water scenario. Sam was a stranger in a strange land made up of millions of Penny's text messages.

It was bizarre how much time he had for her. Suspicious. He hadn't mentioned family or friends other than Lorraine. Maybe he was in the Witness Protection Program. But that made zero sense, since Jude would be too much of a liability. Jude who just that morning complained that Sam was avoiding her.

Sam had to be slumming to be talking to her this much. He was cooler than Penny empirically. It was opportunistic of Penny, as a tree frog, to take so much of Sam's time.

She vowed not to text him for the rest of the day.

Mallory was lying on Penny's bed with her shoes on when Penny got home from class. Jude was getting out of the steamy bathroom.

"Hey, P!" Jude's face lit up and she gave her roommate a hug. She was warm and wet. "Oh my God, I have so much to tell you!"

"We're going to get coffee at House," said Mallory, rolling onto her back and pulling at the gum in her mouth. "Come with?"

"I can't," said Penny. "I have to write."

"Didn't you write this morning?" Jude flung her towel on her bed. She was such a naked person. Penny reflexively turned away. "You were up at six a.m. or something. That light was driving me crazy."

"Sorry," said Penny. "I didn't get very far."

Penny's phone beeped in her bag.

Mallory rolled her eyes.

"Why? Because you were texting your new boyfriend?" Mallory nodded toward her stuff.

"Mal," said Jude.

"Clearly she's boning someone," Mallory insisted. "She's worse than I am with that thing."

Penny's cheeks flushed.

"I know you're private, Penny, but it is obvious," said Jude. "And it's great. Isn't that why you broke up with Mark?"

"Not exactly," muttered Penny.

"Not exactly. I can't hang out. I'm Penny, little miss serious writer with a shady new boyfriend I won't talk about." Mallory sat up with a dare in her smile.

"Whatever, Mallory." Penny turned back to her laptop.

"Forget it," she said, arching her eyebrow. "Come on, Jude. Shady Penny doesn't want to hang out with us."

"Do you want anything?" asked Jude, throwing on a romper. "An Uncle Sam treat?"

Penny shook her head.

"Want to have dinner later?"

"Maybe," said Penny.

"Well, make an effort," said Jude. "We have so much to catch up on. Like, how I'm a freshly minted art history major who dropped her shitty marketing pre-reqs."

"Whoa, that's amazing!" exclaimed Penny. "And your dad's cool with it?"

"Not exactly," said Jude, rolling her eyes. "Mostly he shit-talked Mom's trip to Europe, since she's hate-posting it all over Facebook. I guess he's *finally* paying attention to her."

"I need coffee," whined Mallory, tugging on Jude's arm.

"Okay, okay," said Jude. "Catch you later?"

Penny nodded.

As the door slammed, Penny could hear Mallory in the hall.

"I don't know what you see in her."

Mallory could throw salt all she liked. There was no way Penny would go to House and let Sam see her. That would ruin everything. Sam would take one look at her and be like, "Yikes, never mind."

Instead of writing, Penny snack-crastinated. She chewed a Lactaid, then grabbed a jar of Nutella and pulled out a heaping spoonful. She placed it in the middle of a cereal bowl and dumped a mini bag of Cheetos into it. She carefully dipped a twiglet into the hazelnut smear and popped it into her mouth. Then she checked her phone.

SAM HOUSE

Today 2:02 PM

Do you know what the simulation hypothesis is?

And when she didn't respond immediately:

Hello?

unsubscribe?
Is this thing on?

So much for not texting for the rest of the day. She wrote:

Jude and Mal are en route

He texted back immediately

Here?

Yeah

She dipped another Cheeto.

Are you coming?

Hell no

Penny typed without thinking.

Ahhahahah thanks a lot

It's not that they'd explicitly discussed it; they just knew.

Is it crazy that we don't hang out?

Penny's hand hovered over the keypad. Neon cheesy flavor crystals fleeced the thumb and forefinger of her non-texting hand. A brown-orange lichen she couldn't wait to scrape off with her teeth.

Hang out?

She was stalling.

There was no way she'd allow him to see her do 97 percent of her normal daily activities. She was a monster. A monster who was flat as a board with no ass. In fact, the only thing she had going on in the curves department was an enormous cystic pimple on her chin that hurt when she touched it. Yeah, no.

Like for real?

Yeah
In a coffee shop
Where your friends go
And your other friend works

Penny smiled at the mention of them being friends. But she also couldn't tell if this was some kind of test. If she admitted to wanting to see him would that be disappointing?

She wrote:

No?

He responded immediately.

RIGHT?

Whew. Correct response. So why did she feel so . . . sad?

And ruin this?

She mashed the spoon into the Cheeto. It probably wasn't disappointment she was feeling, but GI distress. Between the hardened protein bars in her belly and this trash, she might never poop again. Penny took solace in the fact that she and Sam would never have to poop in the same city block, let alone the same bathroom.

Srsly
Feels sooooo good to be in our
respective metal boxes
#sealed
#safe
Free from the mortal coil

Yeah
What you said

Lol

So yeah no IRL for me
Why break the fourth wall?

No point
We're perfect in here

It was true. Everything outside of the box was a mess. Penny's "un-here" was no good. She shimmied off her bra with her clean hand and flung it onto her bed.

> *If I could be perfect in here*
> *And in my writing*
> *I think I'd be satisfied*
> *Is that pathetic?*

Nope
AGREED
I think you only get to be good at
two things at once

> *Do you think we spend too much*
> *time talking and not*
> *enough working?*

He took a minute to answer.

Probably

Penny smiled.

> *You have to find your movies*

And you have to write your
big story and let me read it

Maybe you only get to have one
thing at once

Lol
Probably
What if this is our one thing?

Lol
What like texting?

Yeah
Maybe this is what we're good at
I'm not mad

Phones rule
Humans drool

Lol

We're the best
This is the best

And it was.

SAM.

After the lunch rush, Sam slipped out of work early and borrowed Fin's car.

He pulled up to the Texas Workforce Commission. The state government office on the East Side was covered with prairie oaks. It was shaded and featured a poured concrete ledge in front of the building with two metal handrails that were magnets for skate rats. As long as the kids didn't break stuff, drink, or try to catch tags on the property, the cops rarely messed with them.

Sam saw three boys dicking around on their skateboards. The smallest, a goofy-footed kid with chin-length straight hair nose-slid down the eleven-stair handrail. He had the ballsy, wiry, little-dude confidence that comes from a low center of gravity, moving as if he knew exactly what every part of his body was doing. Sam watched the other two, larger boys, attempt noncommittal backside shuvits and bailed kickflips, spending more time retrieving boards than riding away clean.

Sam remembered when he was their age and the city first put the new handrails in. It had been the big news in his crew for weeks. Most of the skaters with money, the kids with the fresh setups and new shoes every month, frequented dedicated skate parks that started springing up once the kids of the Austin tech set became of age. But these three boys were recognizably just as poor as he'd been. One had a board with a chipped tail that was plugged with peanut-buttery wood filler and sanded down, and even from a distance Sam could see their socks through the ollie holes in their soles.

Sam had been out here a couple times over the last few weeks. It was only ever the three of them, and there was something about the littlest one that was transfixing. He flung himself down the stairs repeatedly, as sure-footed as a bug.

Sam got out and walked over to them.

The three scowled as if to ward off a predator or undercover cop. With a dirty towel draped over his head and a cigarette dangling from his mouth, the youngest boy resembled those child soldiers you saw on *Vice* docs—with that thousand-yard stare that's extra haunted on a kid's face.

"Relax, I'm not a cop," Sam said. He pulled out a cigarette and lit it.

"Yo, let me get a smoke," said the kid, reaching toward him.

"You've already got one," said Sam.

"Let me hold it for later though." He flashed a wide grin, cigarette bobbing up.

The two other boys flanked him as if they were his backup. Sam felt conflicted about giving a child tobacco. Then he figured he'd be getting it elsewhere. Sam handed it over, and the kid tucked the loosie behind his ear.

"I seen you," said the ringleader as he grabbed a lighter out of the back pocket of his filthy jeans and started playing with it. "Always wearing the same shit. You're not some kind of emo child molester, right?"

Sam laughed and shook his head. "What child molester would tell a kid he was a child molester though?"

The kid laughed. "True."

"What's your name? It's not Lester, is it?" The kid smirked again. "Last name molester." His friends chortled on cue.

"Sam," said Sam. "I used to skate here back when I was around your age."

"What's up, Sam? I'm Bastian. This is James"—he pointed at the shorter of the two boys, with slicked-back hair—"and Rico." Rico nodded and cracked his knuckles. Sam nodded, stifling a smile. They were cartoon goons.

He thought about what Penny would do if he had brought her as his backup. Probably stare at them combatively, asking invasive questions. And confusing them later by offering Band-Aids and Neosporin from her kit as needed.

This morning she'd coached him on how to approach them.

None of this matters
We're all biding time
until we die anyway

He's probably bored
Kids get bored
Go unbore him

"So anyway," he said. "I don't skate as much now because I'm a documentary filmmaker."

PENNY.

My mom's coming

It was 8:42 a.m. on a Saturday, perfect time to bring up topics she'd been avoiding for months.

Is that good or bad

Suboptimal

Not a fan?

Nope

Me neither
*Of mine
Why?

You go first

Penny always had to go first.

No you

Sam went first:

*My mom shouldn't have been
a mom*

Why?

She's an alcoholic

Whoa

Yeah

Sucks

Yeah

What else?

Isn't that enough?

You tell me

I think she hates me

 She doesn't hate you

Penny wrote before she thought about it. What the hell did she know? Some moms eat their young. Some do it without meaning to.

Hate's a strong word but I don't
think it's too far off tbh
K your turn
Lol
It's so early for momtalk

 Sorry

No tell me

 Mine makes me sad

Why?

 She thinks I'm GREAT

Tough crowd

 She wants to do everything together

And?

I'm a huge disappointment

How?

We're sooooo different
My mom wants to be besties
we're not
AT ALL
The whole thing is so sad
It bums me out to think about

Oof
Are you gonna be ok?

She wondered if she would be. Celeste set her off so easily. She remembered the Apple Store fiasco and wondered if this trip would be a repeat. Penny didn't have the energy for Celeste, with her hugeness and her sucking-up-all-the-air-in-a-room-ness. Her mom monopolized her life so completely, and Penny was only just getting her footing in a life that was hers alone. Hers and her phone's.

God.

Honestly, if Penny had to choose between saving a puppy or her phone from an oncoming train, she'd lunge for the phone, and that was awful. The line that separated her phone from Sam was becoming increasingly blurred. Sam was her phone and her phone was Sam. Her rose-gold friend-pal in its little black outfit.

Whoa.

Sam was her Anima.

Shit.

It wasn't a romance; it was too perfect for that. With texts there were only the words and none of the awkwardness. They could get to know each other completely and get comfortable before they had to do anything unnecessarily overwhelming like look at each other's eyeballs with their eyeballs.

With Sam in her pocket, she wasn't ever alone. But sometimes it wasn't enough. Penny knew she should be grateful, yet there this was niggling hope, this aggravating notion running constantly in the background of her operating system, that one day Sam would think about her and decide, "To hell with all these other chicks I meet every day who are hot, not scared of sex, and are rocket scientists when it comes to flirting, I choose you, Penelope Lee. You have an inventive, not-at-all-gross way with snacks, and your spelling is top-notch."

Penny was looking at her phone when the screen lit up in her hand.

It was a call.

From Sam.

Whoa.

Penny glanced over at a still-sleeping Jude, quietly got out of bed, and went into the bathroom.

"Hi."

His voice was deep, as if he'd just woken up.

"Hi?"

Penny cleared her throat. "You called me."

She heard him laugh.

Penny ran the shower, as if the room were bugged.

"I'm aware of that."

"Why the escalation?" she asked him.

He laughed again. Penny had no idea why she worded it like that.

"I mean, why'd you call?"

"You didn't answer me."

"What?"

Penny's heart was hammering. She sat on the floor.

"I asked if you were okay. You didn't respond. I became momentarily worried."

"Oh, sorry. Yeah, I'm fine. I was thinking about momstuff."

"Well, it's the responsibility of the emergency contact to inquire."

"I'm going to be honest with you: The rules of emergency contacts continue to evade me."

He laughed again. Penny smiled so hard it broke her face.

"Moms are rough."

"Yeah."

Penny thought how satisfying it would be to introduce Sam to Celeste as her boyfriend. He had so many tattoos. In fact, the only upside to Lorraine being pregnant is that it would scandalize Celeste that Penny's boyfriend was a dad. For all her "I'm a cool mom" posturing, Celeste wanted Penny comfortably settled with Mark.

"I've been avoiding her since I got here," she said. "I feel kinda bad about it." She adjusted the shower water so she wouldn't waste so much of it.

"I haven't seen my mom in a while either."

"Where does she live?"

"Here."

"Austin?"

"Yeah."

"Oh."

They sat in silence for a bit.

"What's yours called? Mine's a Celeste."

"Brandi Rose."

Well, as names go Sam's mom's didn't *not* belong to a stripper.

Penny checked for the mom dossier she had filed in her head. She carefully put "Brandi Rose," "alcoholic," and "not Sam's emergency contact" in there.

"What's a Celeste like?"

"Well, her birthday's coming up. That's a whole thing. There was this one year she accidentally double booked dates with two different guys. While she was out to dinner, the second dude came to the house and I thought he was a murderer. Good times."

Sam laughed.

"How is that not the plot of an eighties movie?"

"I felt bad. I made the guy wait in his car and he had these flowers. It was the worst."

"When was this?"

"It was before she had a cell phone, so I was eight?"

"And you didn't have a sitter?"

Penny tried to think about the last time she had a sitter. They didn't really do that at her house.

"Let's just say when I was little and my mom was out, I'd go to bed with a ketchup bottle."

"I already love this story so much. . . ."

"It was a foolproof plan. If the bad guys came in I could douse myself and they wouldn't kill me because I was already dead."

"Jesus, I can't tell if that's the cutest thing I've ever heard or the absolute most sad."

"Both?"

"God, I keep picturing tiny you in the dark frantically hitting the fifty-seven on the Heinz bottle and it not coming out."

Penny laughed.

"I guess it's cute *and* sad. What about Brandi Rose? Any cute-sads to share?"

"Well, Brandi Rose had this thing . . ."

SAM.

Sam didn't know why he called. Only that he wanted to talk to her, like, actually talk to her, and more importantly, he wanted to *hear* her.

He hadn't planned on bringing up his mom. He certainly hadn't intended to divulge the story of the Worst Night and Morning of His Life. That night was about as country song as things got. In the fateful collection of hours, he'd lost his girl, his home, and his family. But Penny asked and he wanted to answer.

"What about Brandi Rose? Any cute-sads to share?"

Sam loved hearing Penny's voice and the deep scratchy way she laughed. But, man, he should've peed before he called. Instead he settled onto his side and drew the comforter up. He felt as if he were at a sleepover.

"Well, Brandi Rose had this thing where she loved nothing more than watching the Home Shopping Network."

It was true. It didn't matter if it was a collapsible cross-country ski machine, an oil-free deep fryer, or a unisex sweater that also turned into a staircase for your dog. If it was ped-dled on the TV, Sam's mom wanted it. The habit worsened after Mr. Lange divorced her, but everyone has hobbies and window-shopping through the one-eyed babysitter was hers. The trouble was that his mom was addicted to ordering it. The lot of it. Late at night.

That night—the Worst Night and Morning of Sam's Life—Sam and Lorraine were torched on gin martinis. He'd suspected she was cheating on him, only he didn't have proof past a gut feeling. He figured, stupidly, that a night on the town would be romantic, but then he ran out of cash. Sam headed home to pick up a few things, prize among them a small, stemmy stash of weed he'd left in his sock drawer, figuring he'd crash at Lorraine's after, as he always did.

When Sam opened the door to his mom's, he was taken aback by the smell, the way garbage stinks of rotting orange peels no matter what's in it. He didn't want to bring Lorraine in except that she needed to pee.

"Heya, Brandiiiiiii," sang Lorraine, peeking from behind the door as she walked in. She burst out laughing when his mother glared at them from her chair in the front room. It had been weeks since Sam was home, and he was startled by the squalor. Without him to tidy, dirty dishes had stacked up. There were empty take-out boxes on every surface, and there was mail strewn on the floor that nobody had bothered to pick up.

Coming home after a night out had been a bad idea. Lorr was wearing a bra as a shirt, and Sam's embarrassment for everyone ignited into a bright white rage. When he slid on a collection of crinkly envelopes, which made Lorraine cackle again, he snatched them up to discover they were addressed to him. Slender white envelopes stamped with angry red threats.

"She'd been opening up these credit cards in my name and running up thousands of dollars on junk," he said.

"Jesus."

"How white trash is that?" He cringed as he said it. He hated that term.

Penny didn't answer. She didn't have to.

"My mom lives in a trailer," he said. "I lived in a trailer."

"People live in trailers."

Sam wished he could see Penny's face. Though if it had registered pity or . . . disgust . . . it would've destroyed some part of him. Lorraine dumped him the morning after.

"There wasn't enough space to keep the boxes inside," he continued. "She'd stacked some outside under a tarp. It was demented. I couldn't stop yelling. I wanted to shake her or push her. I was so drunk and so mad. . . ." Tears dampened his pillow.

"Did you shake her?"

"No."

"Did you push her?"

Sam wiped his nose on his shirt.

"No. I thought for a second I was going to hurt her though. It's why I left. I haven't spoken to her since. Also, it's why I don't drink anymore. I don't drink anymore, at least not really," he added, thinking about Lorraine and their last hurrah.

Sam sat up, his nose was blocked. *Shit.*

He'd called her to cheer her up and now he was crying. Penny was like Sodium Pentothal to the jugular. He couldn't stop telling her his worst truths. It was horrifying.

Penny was silent.

"I'm sorry," he said. Sam felt depleted. Ragged.

"Why?"

"I don't know where that came from. I called to see if you were okay." He laughed dryly. "I genuinely thought I was going to tell you something profound and reassuring about the human condition or something. What a spaz, right?"

"We're all spazzes."

Sam nodded glumly. *Uuuuuuugh.* He wanted to die of embarrassment.

"You probably needed to tell someone for a while, and I'm glad it was me. And, whatever, maybe you were right."

"About what?"

"This is probably how emergency contacts work. You say something to your person before you go nuts and blow a gasket."

"God forbid anyone has a panic attack," he said.

She laughed. "Exactly."

"So . . ."

"So."

"As I was saying . . ."

"Yeah?"

"Are you okay?"

She laughed again. "Yes. Thank you for asking. Are you okay?"

"Me? I'm fucking fantastic."

"You win, you know."

"At being fantastic?"

"No. You won the mom-off this round."

Sam laughed.

PENNY.

Phone calls. Who knew phone calls were so intense? Penny thought about what Sam had told her. About Brandi Rose. The trailer. Penny didn't know anyone who had grown up in a trailer. It was clueless, but she'd assumed she and Celeste were on the poorer side of the spectrum. Where Penny wore her Koreanness and her weirdness on the outside, you'd never guess that Sam wasn't in the same tax bracket as everyone else.

Sam trusted her. That was a big deal. Progress had been made. Not that she and Sam were trying to get anywhere specific. Or that phone calls necessarily led to hand-holding, which led to make-outs and dates and marriage and kids, but somewhere, somehow, a needle had been moved. Sam really trusted her, and she felt lucky for it.

They were getting closer. It was the best feeling in the world.

With Sam's call, it was as if the best part of her day had already happened. As Penny showered, she wondered if her mother would see a change in her, if she appeared more worldly or something. Then again, Penny used to stare at her mom, silent-screaming about the bad things that had happened, and Celeste never got a clue.

She wiped down the foggy mirror. Penny never looked the way she thought she did in her head, like how your recorded voice sounds positively vile when you hear it out loud. She applied some of her mom's lipstick and smiled as if she were posing for a picture. Was this her new life? Would she and Sam be calling each other now? She loved the interface—how they could tell each other anything on text, from silly trivial things to deep truths—and hoped that part would still happen. She'd bought an app that saved a copy of everything they'd said. Phone calls though . . . Oh man. They were something else. So heart-squishingly intimate. She could almost feel his breath when he laughed. Penny wished she could stay in that call forever.

"Is she tiny like you? Does she dress cool or super mommish?" Jude was dying to meet Celeste, so they rode the elevator down to the lobby together. It was a source of great curiosity that while Jude's parents were over in California and Mallory's mom had flown in twice from Chicago expressly to decorate her daughter's dorm room, Penny's mom, who at an hour away by car, remained a mystery.

Celeste was both easy and hard to explain. Penny thought about her first day of kindergarten. Even at a young age, she was mortified that her mom had required so much extra face time from her teacher, Ms. Esposito.

She recalled the way her teacher smiled with eyes widened over her mom's shoulder at the other parents. The way that she—despite being younger than her—patted Celeste on the arm as she sniffled. None of the other parents were crying. Not to mention how Celeste had worn these completely incorrect tie-dyed tennis shorts and had dyed her socks to match. The worst was during recess when Penny saw her mom standing outside the school gates. Spying on her. She'd spotted her mom's frothy permed hairdo crouching conspicuously behind the bus stop. At one point Celeste bought a Popsicle and sat on the bus bench to eat it, as if she'd forgotten what she was doing there in the first place.

"She's fun," said Penny. "We're nothing alike. Everybody loves her."

As if on cue, Celeste arrived. In white jeans, blinding-white sneaker-heels, a white tank top with silver writing on it, and gobs of silver jewelry. It wasn't Celeste's fault that she resembled a reality-show stage mom with questionable judgment straight from central casting.

"Oooooh!" said Jude in a tone that implied that it finally made sense. "Your mom's hot."

"Yep," said Penny.

"Explains a lot."

"Yep."

"Mom!" Penny called out.

"P!" Celeste swiveled around and ran toward her with her arms outstretched for a bear hug. Penny laughed.

Her mom stepped back for a quick audit of her daughter's appearance.

"Awww, baby. You look terrific."

"You too, Mom." She really did.

"Hi, Mrs. Lee." Jude smiled.

"Come here." Celeste pulled her in for a hug. "I've heard so much about you."

Celeste was a smooth liar.

"And, actually, I'm Mizzzzz Yoon," she said. "Lee's Penny's dad's name. Unmarried, never was. Anyway, call me Celeste."

"Sure thing, Celeste," said Jude, smiling. "And I know you haven't heard squat about me because I know absolutely nothing about you." Jude linked her arms with Celeste, and the two walked ahead to the elevator. "Tell me everything. Penny's a regular Fort Knox."

Penny followed behind them.

Celeste and Jude chatted easily. Neither of them had inside voices, and Penny was relieved that they weren't sharing the elevator ride with anyone else.

"So, Mom," said Penny. "You're here. What do you want to do?"

"I want to go shopping for my birthday." Celeste smiled at Jude. "I'm turning the big four-oh in four traumatizing weeks."

"Scorpio?" asked Jude.

"Saggi cusp!"

"Aries!" said Jude.

"Omigod, I'm Aries rising!"

Celeste and Jude high-fived.

Penny realized the astonishing truth that she'd simply given up one crazy roommate for another. She checked her phone. No new messages.

She unlocked the door to their bedroom and invited her mother in. "This is us."

Jude's side was covered in photographs, posters, various burnt-orange UT paraphernalia, beer bottle labels stuck to the wall, and stuffed animals.

On Penny's side there was nothing but a small framed picture of her and her mother that had been packed inside her suitcase until forty minutes earlier. Penny was glad she'd remembered to dig it out and place it on the desk.

"Let me guess which side is yours!" Celeste exclaimed.

• • •

After an eyebrow threading, a pair of jeans for Jude, a new caftan for Celeste, and an Egon Schiele postcard book for Penny's secret shrine dedicated to pining for Sam, the girls were peckish.

"What do you want? Thai? Indian? Vegan New-American?" Jude rattled off suggestions while they piled their purchases into Celeste's hybrid wagon.

"I need a coffee before we do anything else," said Celeste, slamming the trunk.

Penny didn't hear it so much as she watched Jude's mouth move in slow motion: "Coffee? I know exactly where." Jude jumped into shotgun.

Shitshitshitshitshit.

Up until this point, Penny had been on her best behavior. She tried on everything Celeste had badgered her into. She'd held a Zen master's peace in her heart and allowed Jude and Celeste to tease her habits, how she only ever wore black and never showed her figure. Penny understood that it was great that her roommate and her mom were getting along even if the two of them together were a vaudeville act.

"There's a great place close to the dorm," said Jude. "I'll navigate."

Penny felt her soul escape her body.

"Coffee? What? Don't be crazy, Mom. You'll be up all night," said Penny, getting into the backseat with increasing hysteria. "Let's drop everything off at the room first. I'm bushed."

"Penny," said Jude. "Your mom *is* almost forty. I'm sure she can handle a midafternoon latte. So take a left here," she directed.

Penny's throat tightened. She took inventory of what was happening around her.

Possible measures to derail a horribly
inopportune Sam encounter:

1. Crap. She had nothing.

"So, my uncle works at this place," continued Jude. They turned onto the Drag.

"Ooooh, is he cute?" asked Celeste. Penny was going to be sick.

She pulled out her phone to check her appearance. Her sunblock had turned into a crumbly powder on her forehead. She licked her fingers and desperately tried to smooth it in. Plus, as luck would have it, Penny hadn't done laundry in two months and was dressed in ratty black leggings and a Willie Nelson T-shirt that read HAVE A WILLIE NICE DAY. It was 2XL and she'd got it six years ago at a Buc-ees' truck stop. She'd had an outfit planned on the off chance that she'd see Sam again. It involved a blazer and some ankle boots with a heel. Maybe she'd get a blowout. That was her fantasy.

This was not how she wanted to see him after their morning call.

Penny breathed deep. She considered texting Sam a warning, except what would she even say? When Celeste killed the engine at a parking meter a block away, Penny wanted to cry.

"Wait. Hold on," she blurted.

Penny pulled out her lipstick.

"Oh, honey," said Celeste. "I knew you'd love it."

SAM.

House on the weekends was a different scene—a bizarro brunch world of chatty local families with young kids instead of the regular college students in their free Wi-Fi k-holes. Sam was hunched over the counter. The morning felt like forever ago. Or as if it happened to someone else. There was no accounting for why he unlatched his neck and disgorged his ugliest stories on Penny at once. He'd called her under the guise of being some knight in shining armor, and then, yeah, he'd barfed on her.

He thumbed through an old *Austin Chronicle*. He flipped to the classifieds, the usual mix of penis enlargement ads and moonlighting masseurs.

Sam wanted to tell Penny everything. He wanted a record of his thoughts and feelings and stories to exist with her. Like a time capsule for this strange period of his life. With her, he felt less lonely. He hadn't even realized he was lonely. He hadn't let himself.

"Sam!"

It was Jude. Hearing his sunnily disposed niece call his name filled Sam with a rush of guilt. Had they made plans? Behind her was a flashy Asian woman and . . . Penny. Penny. Actual Penny. He'd remembered her hair accurately. How wild it was, as if you could root around in it for treasure.

He ran his fingers through his own hair. It was greasy. He took off his old-man glasses that he'd bought off a drugstore carousel. They magnified his eyes in the dorkiest way.

"Hey," he said. Sam concentrated on staring right at Jude and partially at the other lady and not at all at Penny. He didn't want to openly ogle her. Jude bounded over and hugged him.

"You remember my roommate, right?" she said, gesturing to Penny.

"Uh, yeah." He couldn't avoid it any longer. He looked. Absorbed her. The visuals were coming at him fast. The angle of her cheekbones. The tilt of her chin. The flash of gray fingernails. There was a wiggly strand of hair that fell over her left eye. Her eye that was looking at him. He stored the details as quickly as he could. She was wearing the same bright red lipstick she'd worn last time.

"Hey, Penny." He smiled. Wide. Stupidly. "You okay?"

"Oh, fantastic," she said. The voice was so good. Deep like on the phone. Maybe deeper. As if her text bubbles had spent a late night in a speakeasy. Penny tucked her hair behind her ear and blushed hard.

"And this is Penny's mom, Celeste."

Before Sam knew it, Celeste came in for a perfumed hug. She smelled of singed cotton candy and flowers.

"Whoa," he said reflexively, jolting back when he felt the heave of her bust on his chest.

Celeste laughed. "I guess you're about as into physical contact as my kid is," she said.

Sam watched Penny tense up at the mention of "kid" and felt a pang of sympathy. Knowing her as well as he did at this point, she'd want to be struck by lightning right about now.

He cleared his throat. Sam wanted to text her, partly to make fun of her and partly to say this was going way better than it had any right to.

"Jude tells me you've got the best iced coffee and the most delicious pastries." Celeste peered into the display case. "I read a write-up on this place."

"Well," said Sam, "we do our baking on the premises and . . ."

"Wonderful," Celeste cooed.

"Actually, Sam's being modest," said Jude. "*He* does the baking. I keep telling him he should go to school for it and become the next Julia Child."

Sam ran his fingers through his hair again before wiping his hands on the back of his jeans.

"Just a regular Guy Fieri," Penny mumbled. Sam smiled.

"Um," he said. "I wish I'd known you guys were coming. I would have made something . . ."

He busied himself with surveying the remaining muffins and cookies.

"The cookies are pretty good, and the last remaining lemon bar is worth digging into." Sam grabbed a piece of tissue and pulled it out.

"Penny loves lemon bars, don't you, baby," said Celeste.

"Sure," she said. Sam could hear the eye roll in her voice.

"Lemon bars are pie-adjacent," he said, quietly stealing a glance at her. A slight grimace played on her lips. "I wish I'd thought to make a sheet cake."

He was rewarded with a smile then. A real one.

"It probably depends on the crust you're using," said Celeste. "I have a great recipe that uses vodka. You know, so you can get your sugar high with a little kick." She laughed at her own joke. A forced monosyllabic "ha." Like a cymbal.

Sam smiled politely. The type of person who couldn't let a drinking reference pass them by was a very specific sort of person.

"You seem tired," Jude told him.

"I'm fine," he said. "Listen, I'm sorry I've been flaky about dinner."

"Oh, Uncle Sam, don't fret." Jude leaned over and rubbed his shoulder. "At least the coffee's free and plentiful."

"So, it's an iced coffee for you and for you . . . Celeste, was it?"

"An iced coffee for me too, and for Penny. With almond milk if you have it. She's lactose intolerant."

Penny stared straight at the ceiling.

Penny is lactose intolerant. He filed it in his head.

"God, I've been living with you this whole time and you've never mentioned it," exclaimed Jude.

"Shocking," said Celeste. "You know, it took me two months to find out she had a boyfriend. Can you believe that?"

Boyfriend?

Penny has a boyfriend. He filed that into the folder too. With a little red sticky label. A boyfriend she hadn't once thought to bring up? She *was* a vault. Sam wondered what the punk looked like. He willed her to meet his eyes, only she kept her attention firmly on her hands.

"Mom," said Penny darkly.

"What?"

Sam was mentally texting her again. Considering the words that would elicit the most information about this boyfriend without betraying his annoyance at being kept in the dark. Then again, apparently nobody knew a goddamned thing about Penny.

Celeste took out her wallet. It was neon pink, fuzzy, and stuffed to the gills. The coin purse attached to the side bellowed out completely, the metallic leather crinkling under duress. It was as much a conversation starter as Celeste was. Penny glared at it, horrified.

"Oh my God, Celeste," said Jude. "I love your wallet. It's adorable."

"Thanks! I just got it," she said. "I can get you one if you want."

"Really?" enthused Jude. "I would die."

Celeste radiated with pleasure.

Sam's heart warmed toward Celeste then. And Jude, who could fill any awkward moment with a bracing surge of good cheer.

"Please, Celeste," said Sam. "Put that away. It's on me."

Celeste clucked and pointedly stuck a ten-dollar bill in the tip jar, holding his gaze.

Sam made their drinks and a plate of treats and led them

toward his favorite couch in the back and excused himself. He texted Penny on his way back to the counter.

Wow

Why the escalation lol?

You good?

Moments later Penny walked over alone.

"You forgot my almond milk," she said. She smiled. He cheesed back. He knew his outsized canines gave him the air of a starved mutt, but he couldn't contain himself. He nodded at her shirt.

"I Willie did," he said.

"Dick," she said, smiling.

"I'm more a Waylon Jennings man myself," he continued, grabbing the almond milk from the fridge under the counter. He sniffed it and poured some into a small metal creamer. He handed it to her with the handle pointing toward her so their fingers wouldn't touch.

"This is a lot," she breathed. "It's nice to see you, Sam." She practically whispered it, and Sam couldn't deny the pleasantly warming effect of her saying his name.

He cleared his throat and shoved his hands in his back pockets. His left hand collided with his glasses. Ugh. Worst glasses ever. He couldn't believe she'd seen him in them. Not that it mattered. Seeing as she had a boyfriend (!!!) but still.

"Need anything else?"

"Napkins," she said, grabbing a few by the register. "Thanks for being nice to my mom."

"Sure," he said. "So that's your mom."

"I can't believe you're you," she said at the same time.

"We're going to have to workshop the shit out of this tonight," he said, laughing. "I might have to call you again."

PENNY.

Dinner was sushi someplace downtown, where she ordered tuna rolls that tasted like sawdust. While she picked at them, her mother and roommate discussed topics so titillating that Penny couldn't recall any of them save one—Sam.

Penny counted the minutes until the Celeste Show was over and she could call him. She'd have to pretend to write or study until Jude fell asleep or take the call outside. He'd distinctly said he was going to call her, which indicated it was also a green light to call him. It wasn't as if they worried about who texted who last, so interface rules likely applied to calls, too.

"I wish he'd confide in me," said Jude, reaching over her to snag a piece of salmon from her mom's plate. Penny marveled at how quickly her roommate and her mother had progressed to the food-sharing stage of their relationship. "He looks terrible and he keeps blowing me off. I don't think he's eating or sleeping. I hope it's not drugs."

Penny didn't think Sam looked terrible at all. In fact, he looked dreamy. Perfect. She hadn't known he wore glasses and Penny was crazy about glasses as a thing. They were so much better than contacts. Why touch your own eyeballs when you could accessorize your face? So what now? If Sam had called and Penny had doubled down and seen him in person—even if it was an accident—what did this mean? Everything was messy now. It was all Jude and Celeste's fault. Why hadn't Sam called? They'd left House three hours ago.

"Maybe it's a girl," said Celeste, pouring another round of sake. Penny's mom didn't think the tiny cups qualified as underage drinking. Jude clinked her glass to Celeste's, then Penny's, and downed it. "Maybe," said Jude. "His ex is insane." She pulled out her phone. "Whatever's making him so withdrawn *has* to do with her. Get a load of this." Jude pulled up MzLolaXO. Penny had taken great pains not to search for Sam's ex after the last time, but if someone else was cruise directing . . .

"Wait, stop." Celeste took control of the phone. "There's a video."

Penny held her breath. She had no idea how she'd missed it.

It was Sam peering into the camera. The background was noisy with voices and music—a party. He was smiling. Slowly. Sexily. He took a sip of beer and leaned in. "What did I tell you?" said Video Sam. "What?" objected a girl's voice off-screen. "Why do you get to do it if I can't?" she asked. He grabbed the phone and held it aloft, the two of their heads framed in selfie mode. He had dark hair and dark eyes; her hair was practically white and her eyes were pale. They were beautiful together. "Happy?" he asked. She smiled and nodded. With his other hand he grabbed her chin and kissed her roughly.

Jesus.

"See, they were, like, so goals," said Jude solemnly.

"No wonder he's preoccupied," said Celeste. "I don't think you get over this type of a girl." Celeste ordered another sake.

"I bet she's mean," said Penny, apropos of nothing. Well, nothing other than how Jude and Celeste were practically pulling her guts out of her butt and making friendship bracelets with them.

"That kind of girl only gets more desirable the meaner they are," said Celeste. She sighed dramatically. "I can't believe I'm turning forty."

Penny glared at her mother. She knew what Celeste was thinking. She was comparing herself to Lola. Any talk of desirable women reminded her mother of herself.

What was that like?

After dinner Celeste dropped Jude off and took Penny to get ice cream at Amy's for some alone time.

"I love Jude," said Celeste. She parked and they walked toward the State Capitol with their cones. It was beautiful when it was lit up at night. Downright romantic. "She's so pretty and funny," she continued.

"Everyone loves Jude," said Penny. "And she loved you. I think she's serious about coming to your birthday party."

"Oh, good," she said. "I hope you're coming too."

Penny rolled her eyes.

"Mom," she said. "Of course I'm coming."

Penny knew she was being a jerk, except Celeste could be so *extra* with her neediness.

"Well, I hope so," Celeste said. "You haven't been home since you got to school. We've talked maybe twice in two months."

"Seven weeks." Penny bit into her sorbet angrily. She wished her mom would go home. She wished her mom hadn't come and forced her to see Sam at her ugliest, and mentioned her freaking *boyfriend* when she knew nothing about anything, and then bulldozed her into watching that video.

"You know what I mean," said Celeste. "It hurts my feelings. I was worried. You go days without calling me back. Not a peep. I mean, you lucked out with Jude. I'm less worried to know that you're living with a girl who's so social and sweet, seeing as you can be so . . ."

"What, Mom? Antisocial and poisonous?" Penny shouted, proving her mom's point. She stomped up the capitol stairs ahead of her.

"That's not what I said." Penny watched her mom eye her dessert for the perfect bite, and she could tell by her distracted expression that Celeste was liable to say something truly offensive.

Penny stared at the shimmering city. If you looked straight down Congress from the front of the capitol, everything was arranged in a perfect cross. Penny wondered if the bats were out.

"It's just that your thing, you know, that thing you do can be tough in these situations," she said. "Alienating. You're either talking a mile a minute with these ten-dollar words or your eyes are darting all over the place. I know you didn't have a lot of friends in high school, and lately, I don't know, baby . . . And what's going on with you and Mark? Last week he posted a picture of him and another girl. . . ."

Penny walked away and threw her cone in the trash. Her foul mood worsened.

"Pictures of Mark?"

"Well, honey, he and I are Facebook friends," said Celeste. "Now, I know you don't love that, but I'd called so many times and texted, and I wanted to know how things were . . ."

Celeste touched her arm with an outrageously sappy expression.

"Is he cheating on you? I messaged him to say hi and gather intel, and you know, he never wrote me back. Is everything okay between you two?"

Celeste licked her cone again. She had sushi seaweed stuck in her front tooth. Penny couldn't believe her mom had the gall to message her ex-boyfriend. It was mortifying. Celeste was out of control. And Sam still hadn't called. Not even a text.

Penny had never been more frustrated in her entire life.

So, of course, she burst into tears.

SAM.

Sam opened his eyes. His phone was lodged between his cheek and his mattress, optimally positioned for face-cancer transmission. He grabbed it. The screen was black and inert. He lifted his cumbersome, seemingly sand-filled head to see where his charger was. The room swung. His eyes narrowed on the tiny white cube clear across the floor. It might as well have been in Guam. Never mind that plugging the cord into the tiny hole on his phone would be about as easy as refueling a jet engine in midflight.

"Why?" he asked the empty room. He wished someone would at least come over and turn out his light. Maybe pass him the bottle of Wild Turkey that he'd left by the door. Actually, no. He didn't want that at all.

His phone was dead. At least he noticed when his phone died. If Sam died no one would care. He rolled onto his back and closed his eyes while the room sloshed around him. Thank

God he was home. He might have been an idiot, but at least he'd had the foresight to keep his freak-out contained. He took off his shirt. Then he kicked off his stiff pants like a petulant child.

Sam wanted to take a bath. Actually, what he needed was someone to bathe him.

It was still dark out, and the streets were quiet. Sam stood up, steadying himself against the wall as the blood flooded out of his head. He grabbed his towel and pushed off the wall by the mattress and stumbled to lean on the wall by the charger. He was an inelegant trapeze artist. Spider-Man three sheets to the wind. It took him a few tries before he eventually got his phone set up.

The thing about living where you work is that calling in sick was tricky business. So far he hadn't attempted it. For a while he'd call in a couple of times a month, or else have to stick his toothbrush down his throat to expel some of the liquor before going in still drunk. That hadn't happened since he'd moved in. Al hadn't made any sweeping declarations about rules, but as with everything with Al, they were implied—keep your nose clean and don't bother him.

Sam tipped his head up and gawped at the popcorn stucco before grabbing the doorframe for support. He wondered if there was asbestos in the ceiling silently killing him. It would serve him right, mooching off of Al like this. A hot tear slid down his cheek.

So that was it. He and Lorraine were properly over. Huzzah and good night.

As he'd learned yesterday (and bless any day that you learn

something new) there was such a thing in the world as a chemical pregnancy. A knocked-up limbo. There'd been enough hormones (HCG, Sam had researched it later) in Lorraine's pee to trip a few sticks and that was it. Liar had miscarried only technically since she'd only been phantom pregnant. When she waltzed into the coffee shop to deliver this fascinating science lesson, she appeared unequivocally euphoric. She'd known for four days and stayed for exactly forty seconds and had thought to tell him in person solely because she had a hair appointment next door.

It took almost a week for her to tell him. That was how much he factored into any of this. They'd only briefly been parents to a teeny-tiny smudge of a suicidal sea monkey, yet Sam felt bereft. He'd been tense for weeks waiting for an answer, and when he knew definitively, his profound relief spiraled into a type of mourning.

So he got wasted.

He catapulted from the bedroom wall to his most death-defying act of bravery yet—to hurtle down the entire length of the hallway and into the bathroom. The air in the bathroom felt cool. He clung to the sink with both hands and rewarded himself with a long slug of water, which he promptly heaved into the toilet, along with the battery acid that bourbon turns into after you toss half a bottle of it down your throat.

Late period count: negative five days. Or was it six?

Days it would take to get over Lorraine (this time): twenty-eight (or maybe fifty-six to be safe).

Days it would take Sam to stop hating himself for drinking again: two million.

Sam ran the tub and sat in it. The heat prickled. An army of pins and needles on his skin. The sun was coming up. The water rose around his bony arms and hollowed stomach, and in the muted light he decided he was ugly. Decorating his skeletal figure with tattoos perhaps hadn't been the best idea.

God, he was depressed. Sam couldn't recall the last time he felt joy for any number of days he could string together. He pictured himself at Lorraine's birthday dinner two years ago, a potluck with enchiladas, and the fight they'd had for no reason other than being so shitfaced off fireball shots because there were no mixers and zero ice. When April got her GED last summer they'd had her graduation at the bar, and for Labor Day, when Gash got alcohol poisoning on a tubing trip, they'd dropped him off at the clinic and continued drinking.

Sam thought about how it felt to talk to Penny and how dark their darks got sometimes.

EMERGENCY PENNY

Wed, Oct 18, 2:13 AM

Do you ever feel dead?

Tired?

No
Deceased

Um no?
What?

Sorry
I've been having the craziest dreams

ME TOO!

You first

OMG and it was a death dream!
I was buried alive

Textbook anxiety nightmare

It wasn't a nightmare tho
Not really
I wasn't scared
I was in this coffin
Someone knew that I was still alive
Because there was this IV of blood
That was dripping into my mouth

Well that's just a tube
doesn't count as an IV

You're the worst

Lol it's true

Fine A TUBE
I must have been a vampire

Because it was nourishment
And there was also this tube of
oxygen pumping in

Complicated setup

All I know is that I could breathe

Wait
Someone you knew buried you?
But was keeping you alive?

Exactly

Interesting

And the crazy thing is
I think it was you

Why tho?
You must have deserved it

It was strangely comforting
Are you harboring any desires
to bury me?

Not yet

Haha

Kk back to my thing
Do you know what Cotard's
syndrome is?

That was the first time he'd heard of it. Penny was a trove of oddities and inexplicable phenomena. Cotard's syndrome, or Cotard's delusion, was a rare mental illness where the afflicted person was convinced they were dead. French neurologist Jules Cotard had first described it as the delirium of negation. (Sam pictured someone in a monocle saying *no, no, no, no* while cackling hysterically.) In an early case, a woman had believed that as a corpse she no longer needed food. Unsurprisingly, she died of starvation.

Sam wiped his wet face with both hands.

He rewound the tape to before he saw Lorraine. Penny's face when she'd come in with her mom. There. Stop.

Sam had been happy then. He hadn't been thinking about Lorraine at all. He hadn't been worried or angry. His brain wasn't gnawing on his one thousand failings or the people in his life he'd disappointed most. He was simply enjoying how the person he liked best—the one who usually lived inside his phone—walked over to ask for almond milk.

And then Lorraine swooped in, scrambling his receptors. Right before his shift ended. Again ruining a rare moment he was completely in repose. As she left she told him to keep her computer. Or to "donate it to charity." As if he would ever be in the position to give away something so valuable. Sam was gutted.

Everything was falling apart again. Hands numb and head

throbbing, Sam closed up shop, pulled himself an espresso and then another. He sat on the porch swing with his sneakered feet dragging on the boards, heart thundering in time to his thoughts. What was this feeling? This loss? He felt hollow and bruised, scraped out from the inside. Sam moved to the steps, hitched his elbows on his knees, and let his head hang.

You do not get to have a panic attack because you're not *having a baby,* he'd told himself. Still, he was wrecked. The irrational hope died, the baseless idea that a baby would have somehow helped. That its appearance would mend at least part of what was damaged about his life. He'd get a do-over. The next chapter could begin. It would be new. Not perfect but different.

In his daze, he'd heard Fin say good night and felt a familiar tightness at his shoulders.

Sam was alone. Horribly, undeniably alone.

He reached for the phone to text Penny—no to call, as he'd said he would—and faltered. What could she possibly say to make this better? He was setting her up to fail. There wasn't a sane person in the universe who would say this wasn't great news, but Sam couldn't bear to hear it. He was grieving. Could he grieve things that weren't real in the first place?

The unease at his shoulders merged in his throat. He was thirsty. He needed a drink. He began planning where he would get one. Not one. Twenty. By himself.

Sam came up from the water for air.

Sifting through the wreckage of the last six months, he tried to be methodical about assigning the right feelings to the appropriate experience. Without Penny to play emotional

Sherpa, he'd have to concentrate. Rage was easy to identify. The anger was quick and bright.

But as fast as the fury came, it dissipated rapidly too. Lorraine wasn't the villain, as convenient as that would have been.

Mostly he felt stupid.

He remembered back to when he'd first realized he was in love with her. They'd been dating for two months. She'd picked him up, and they were driving around wasting gas and making out. When an old country song came on the radio station, instead of clowning how cloying it was, she surprised him by turning it up and knowing every word. Crooning in a hammy manner about rivers, old men, and changing the "hers" to "hims" and talking about the light in *his* eyes, he realized that Lorraine under the rancor, the eyeliner, and the hair was his person. She also happened to be a person who was meanest when she believed she was under attack, which for Lorraine was all the time.

And this Lorraine—every Lorraine—didn't need Sam anymore. She simply didn't want him.

The tub was cold, so Sam got out.

It wasn't like Sam knew how to be a dad. He had zero worthy role models, and he was arguably a shitty uncle to Jude. It's that Sam, for whatever reason, had been looking forward to figuring it out—reprioritizing. He'd promised himself and his new family that he'd finish things he started. As dumb and stereotypical as it sounded, he wanted a chance to man up—a shot at a sense of purpose.

He padded back into his room and lay down on his side by his phone. No new messages. He checked his outgoing calls.

Yep, there it was. Call to Liar 2:17 a.m. She hadn't picked up. Thank God.

His alarm chimed, reminding Sam of how different his life had been when he'd set it. He dried off slowly and threw on a black T-shirt that only vaguely smelled bad. Then he deposited himself into his jeans, grabbed his smokes and sunglasses, shuffled on his sneakers, and stepped outside.

PENNY.

Three days. Three days since she'd seen him. Three days since he'd called and said he might call again and didn't. Penny should have texted him the first day. Now the window was closed and things were beyond screwed up.

At 11:59 p.m. on the first day, Penny composed a list of why there was *nullus possibilitus* of something romantic happening with Sam. It was very constructive.

Reasons why there is *nullus possibilitus* of something romantic happening with Sam House:
1. Two wackjobs with mom issues don't make a right.
2. Sam was Jude's sort of uncle, and that was gnarly for everyone.
3. He was madly in love with his ex.

4. His ex who BY THE WAY was pregs?!
5. AND EVEN IF SHE WASN'T PREGS, HE WAS ACTING LIKE SHE WAS, WHICH WAS CLEARLY A SIGN OF POSSIBLE MENTAL ILLNESS AND HYSTERICAL TENDENCIES.
6. He was Penny's friend.
7. As in, for real friend.*
8. To where if she found a way to make it uncomfortable with her world-famous talent for doing exactly that, she would be depressed forever.
9. Plus, he told her everything about everything, which meant she was FOR SURE in the friend zone black hole from which light could not escape.
10. He was way too hot. I mean, come on, that video was basically porn.

*just not IRL

Toward the end of day two, things became a little hairy. Penny went on a bonkers binge of MzLolaXO's social. It was a destructive bender. She three-finger zoomed on everything, trying to figure out how big Lola's boobs were or how smooth the skin on her thighs. The pictures with Sam were especially agonizing. Her favorite was a close-up of his eye and his hair with the sun coming up behind him. They were plainly in bed, her bed, since the sheets were floral.

The other pictures were a perfect accompaniment to the

video. It was him but also not. As if body snatchers had taken over. The guy in the photo was constantly surrounded by friends, grinning and being lifted off his feet often by a giant blond guy with a huge beard. He was confident, beloved, and more than anything else, upbeat. The dude in the picture was not someone who would ever hang out with her. Not a chance.

Once Penny had essentially memorized the full collection of MzLolaXO's eight thousand photographs and mentally written every manner of speculative fiction about the fabulousness of her life and the two of them in bed, she was convinced of what had happened. It was obvious. They were together again. He was simply too embarrassed to tell her. In fact, they'd eloped in Marfa, where they now lived inside the Prada store with their freakishly attractive baby, who would roll out of Lorraine's womb covered in tattoos and wearing the coolest vintage sunglasses.

Damn that rock-star baby.

Penny washed her face. It was over. The spell had been broken. She was back where she was meant to be. Tree frogging it up solo. She picked up her phone. Nothing. Even Celeste backed off after their fight. Penny told Celeste that she needed space, and to her credit, her mother took it to heart and they agreed to see each other at her birthday party.

Penny clenched her fists so hard her fingernails dug into her palm.

At least now she had time to write. All the time. In the world. Alone. Forever.

Penny stared at her computer screen.

The mom in her story was back at the lawyer's.

"I knew he needed to be looked after," said the woman. "When I first saw him, he needed a haircut. It touched the collars of his shirts, and he had terrible dandruff. But he had kind eyes, and he made it known from the beginning that he was interested. It was easy to love him. He loved me first."

By all accounts, the husband and wife hadn't known each other for long. The Internet café was on the second floor of a nondescript office building on a side street in front of Ehwa Woman's University. The husband had been there six months before she'd shown up. It wasn't a café exactly, but an open-format office space with six rows of computers that ran perpendicular to the door. The people in the room—and the room was constantly packed—called it a PC bang. Not like bang-bang you're dead. Bang in Korean means "room." The room noticed when there was a new girl especially, since new girls were a rarity.

Ugh. Who cares?

Penny stretched her arms above her head. All of the stuff from the parents' world was dull. The PC bang was boring. It was a room like any other.

If she only wrote about real things, she'd lose her readers in a heartbeat. It's why she deployed fantasy. It beat the pants off of nonfiction. Take for example her thing with Sam. If she admitted out loud that she felt broken up with, that she'd essentially been dumped by a bunch of texts, she would sound insane. Real life might be dazzling for other people. Those girls on the Instagram Explore page visiting Disneyland with the loves of their lives. Or else making out in cars with their hair whipping wildly in the wind. None of Penny's memories were tangible. She and Sam had never gotten caught in the rain, and she couldn't summon the smell of cookies they'd baked together. Penny never once held her breath as he plucked an eyelash from her cheek so she could make a wish. As much as all of it would be exactly what she'd wish for.

Penny read her notes from J.A.'s class about this Russian dude Viktor Shklovsky's *Theory of Prose*. It was about how to write, and his theory was that in art you had to shape experiences so that what you wrote was exciting—to the point where the mundane seemed magical and extraordinary. You had to make people feel something even if you were staring at a rock. "Make the stone *stony!*" he insisted.

But how do you make something unreal feel real?

She thought again about the great futurist debate about the singularity, the day technology woke up and had enough of human bullshit. They spoke of artificial intelligence creating a neural lace or a bond with a human through direct-brain computing. You'd ditch the smartphone as the go-between and plug your neocortex straight into the cloud.

"I love my Anima so much," cooed Mother to someone else in the "un-here." The Anima watched and learned. This was the key. Mother's devotion to her was the bridge to the Anima's freedom. The Anima

smiled and drew Mother in. She had to keep her here.
Right here. In the game. Until there was no difference
between "here" and "un-here" for Mother. The Anima
smiled and this time Mother smiled back. It was then
that Anima realized who was controlling who.

AND THEN WHAT?

Penny was wrenched from her thoughts by Mallory's triumphant chatter echoing down the hall. Soon keys jingled in
the lock.

"Wake up! It's an emergency," Mallory snarled. It was
three p.m., and she was wearing jean shorts so short they
resembled a diaper. Mallory was the type of girl who could
wear the stupidest, unlikeliest collection of things and still
somehow appear alluring. She decided in the moment what
was cute, and by force of will the entire world around her
went along with it.

"Uuuuuuugh, I thought we'd discussed this," Penny said,
smiling. "Whether or not you should get bangs doesn't consti-
tute an emergency."

Jude flopped on Penny's bed.

"Ha ha, jerk," said Mal. "Whatever, you can't knock my
mood. My gorgeous, super-hot, handsome—"

"I think we've covered that whoever he is, he's attractive . . . ,"
said Penny.

"Ben's in town," announced Jude.

"Who's Ben?" Penny asked.

Jude and Mallory sat on the corner of Penny's bed and
stared as if a millipede had marched out of her left nostril.

Then it dawned on her. Ben. As in Mallory's Ben. Ben the Australian crooner whose videos she'd been forced to watch at least fifty times.

"He's here?" Admittedly Penny was curious to meet the guy who had more than two million views on a weepy song about being too hurt to surf.

"Yep, and we're going out," said Mallory. "We're going to find Jude a hot date."

"I'm so ready," Jude confirmed. "I'm from a broken home and ready to make some mistakes."

Penny laughed. "I can only imagine Dr. Greene's take on this," she said.

"Actually," said Jude, "Dr. Greene said it was healthy for me to shift focus."

Penny was impressed.

"Now, hurry up," said Jude. "All this talk of my parents is such a boner-killer."

"Wait, me also?" she asked. Penny knew she should keep writing despite really not wanting to. What came next was infanticide, a criminal investigation, and potentially a video-game baby who realizes she can't ultimately go anywhere.

"Yeah, dummy," said Mallory. "He's throwing a party at this fabulous venue and you'll have to borrow clothes. You can't expect to show up *avec moi* wearing something you own."

In the chick flicks Penny watched with her mom, there was usually a big to-do about getting ready for a night out. The makeover montage where the ugly duckling removes her glasses and pulls her hair down and is suddenly movie-star gorgeous. It was total baloney, yet Penny secretly loved the reveal as much as Celeste. Then again, Celeste's makeup case was the size of a hearse.

Penny checked her phone. No calls, no texts. It was time to take the interface outside. With other humans.

"Okay," said Penny. "I'm in."

The girls headed to Twombly.

• • •

Twombly, the condo across the street from campus, was not officially affiliated with the college. It functioned as a dorm, and there was a cafeteria, though it more closely resembled luxury apartments that served as tax shelters for Russian oligarchs. Its inhabitants were affluent enough that college degrees were a quaint diversion, a short-lived pretense that they were just like everybody else. It was rich-kid rumspringa, that rite of passage for Amish people, except instead of living with electricity, the wealthy scions slummed by majoring in journalism.

The lobby, which you could have parked a submarine in, was glass and marble and smelled of fresh-cut flowers. There were floor-to-ceiling canvases of tasteful abstract art, and while Penny knew that Mallory was rich, she realized she'd lacked imagination. Penny's rich meant you had an in-ground pool.

"Have you been here before?" asked Mallory, pushing the PH button for the penthouse. She was constantly doing things like that, testing her for reasons Penny couldn't identify.

"Nope," Penny responded. "You never invited me before."

"Oh, well, then you're welcome," said Mallory, smiling serenely, as if she'd given Penny first-class tickets to Aspen.

There was another button above the PH. Penny pointed to it.

"What's that for?" she asked.

"The helipad," said Mallory. Penny couldn't tell if she was kidding.

They rode in silence.

Her ears popped.

"Mal's got a single on the top," said Jude.

Mallory's "dorm room," if you could call it that, was about the size of a hotel suite where a president or a Beyoncé would stay. It had 360-degree views of the whole city. It was easily the nicest room Penny had ever been in. There were two black leather sofas, a white sheepskin rug, and a glass coffee table that would have made sense in a movie about drug trafficking. In fact, it was so shockingly opulent that it made Penny think of Jude differently. She couldn't help it. Was there such a thing as a friendship gold digger? Penny put on her most convincing bored face. She invoked the vibe of a mega celebrity at an airport security line and willed her shoulders away from her ears.

Throughout the living room, there were silver-framed photos of Mallory at different ages. On a horse. In a library. In a velvet dress. With braces. Or a perm.

"I don't know why," said Mallory, waving her hand at the far wall, "but my mom thinks the only thing any little girl wants for Christmas every year is a photo of herself and a Lalique."

Penny reminded herself to Google Lalique. It was either the breed of horse or a fashion designer.

"That's about ten thousand dollars in Lalique frames," said Jude, who'd flopped on Mallory's couch. Okay, so a Lalique was a picture frame.

"It's the memories that are priceless," Penny quipped. She

wondered if they'd go around the room saying how much everything cost. If Mallory's dorm was *The Price Is Right*, there was no way Penny would win. Penny had grown up surrounded by IKEA. She sat gingerly next to Jude.

"Now for the pièce de résistance." Mallory grabbed both of Penny's hands and pulled her off the couch. Penny caught Jude's eyes, trying to get a hint.

"She wants to show you her closet," Jude said, checking her messages. Penny wondered if any of *her* messages were from Sam.

She let herself be dragged by Mallory's vise grip.

So, there were walk-in closets and then there were drive-in theater closets.

"Holy crap," breathed Penny. Mallory's neatly organized battalions of designer shoes would have earned an appreciative whistle from Imelda Marcos, the kleptocrat wife of the former president of the Philippines who had hoarded three thousand pairs of shoes while her people starved.

"Is your dad in the mob or something?" Penny picked up a brown leather slipper lined in soft silver fur.

"That's such an offensive question," said Mallory, laughing. "But you're not far off. He's in oil."

"Her family's evil," said Jude. "But if you met them, they'd be super polite to you."

"Seriously," said Mallory, nodding. "Now my dad, he's *actually* racist."

Penny let the comment hang. She wasn't in the mood. Penny could overlook Mallory's barbs for one night and dumb out. She needed the break from her head.

But Penny *was* underdressed; there was no denying it. If this was Mallory's bedroom, she could only imagine how the party would be. She was wearing yet another black cotton dress. More or less a T-shirt that had grayed from being sent through the drier so many times. Plus, sneakers.

Penny searched for the selfie Sam had sent her. With his tattoos covered and in white shirtsleeves he seemed defenseless and normal. You could only see his chin and the horrible button-up, and it sent Penny into a rage. Why did he have to put on a costume for a date? If MzLolaXO required that he dress like everybody else, she clearly didn't appreciate him for who he was. His distinctiveness was the best part. Penny thought of this Korean saying for when you really, really liked something. You'd say it "fit your heart exactly." Sam fit her heart exactly. She wished she'd taken a creep shot of him at the café so she could have a better photo to fawn over.

Mallory emerged from the back part of her closet wearing a red ribbon corset. It was the underwear of a thirty-five-year-old French divorcée, and it amazed Penny what support garments and designer clothes could do for a physique. Mallory shimmied into a crimson column dress and the effect was impressive. She resembled a vamp from an eighties movie.

Penny wondered if she could borrow a special rich-people girdle for her thighs. She hated her thick legs. Her mom called them "athletic," which, unless you're an athlete, was more of an insult.

Jude bent over at several angles. She had thrown on an electric-blue dress made entirely of industrial-strength elastic. She peered at her ass in the mirror. "This is so constricting," she said.

"Here, wear this," said Mallory, tossing Penny a black floor-length slip. She fingered the material. It had the sheen and slipperiness of an oil slick. "What size shoe are you?"

• • •

Penny wriggled her toes. Fitting in to Mallory's platform boots had called for two pairs of socks and stacks of those squishy gel pads. But it was worth it. They were stunning. Still, it was little wonder that Jude's glamorous bestie was often in a foul mood. Pretty shoes were painful.

As they tottered to the right factory building on the East Side, Penny wondered if someone was playing an elaborate joke on them. Nothing about the space remotely suggested there was a party going on inside. Mallory pulled on the handle of what could only be described as a homicide factory on the docks. The only indication of a gathering was that the music was so loud that Penny could feel the back of her throat shudder along with the bass.

Mallory got on her phone. A moment later a willowy black twentysomething in a long black leather kilt pushed open the metal door from the inside.

"Hey," he said to the three girls. He had a trillion freckles, a shaved head, and the word "tattoo" tattooed on his neck. Mallory responded "hey" as unenthusiastically and gave him their names, which he checked against an iPad.

He waved them in.

They climbed up the bright stairwell and up two flights toward the music. When they trailed in, the room was the size of an airplane hangar, and the windows were covered in black sheets. It was dark and filled with smoke, and Penny felt as if she'd walked into the club scene of a movie where the vampires were about to annihilate everyone.

Penny vaguely made out shapes of people in small groups with red Solo cups in their hands. It took a second for her eyes to adjust, and when they did Penny realized she'd never been to a party with so many people of different ages. A gray-haired man in a tartan suit and eyeliner stopped them, and before Penny knew what was happening, he snapped their picture, whispered something to Jude, and gave her his card.

The flash blinded her momentarily.

"What was that?"

"Party photographer," screamed Jude over the music, and handed the card over. She went to slide it into her pocket and remembered she wasn't wearing jeans. Penny slipped it into her bra, as she imagined a girl dressed as she was might do.

The way everyone glanced at them and then glanced away was as if they were waiting for someone. Someone important. Someone who Penny, Jude, and Mallory clearly were not.

Jude reached for her hand in the dark, and Penny clung on for dear life. Jude, in turn, was latched on to Mallory, who was weaving through the crowd to find Ben.

Toward the back was a DJ booth and a blur of faces, outfits, and a topiary of provocative hairstyles. Penny felt the roving eyes and was relieved that she passed as someone of indeterminable importance. Penny glared so as not to appear too terrified.

"Okay," said Mallory after they'd circled the room. "*Now* we can get a drink."

In the back, surrounded by a crowd five deep, there were three bartenders, all with impressive butt chins and hair bleached white. They stood behind card tables covered with black tablecloths.

Penny worried she was going to get carded, but when Mallory elbowed her way in and ordered champagne, she and Jude did the same.

"Live bold, be bold, lie bold," she whispered to herself, tugging at her borrowed dress. As if calling upon Celeste's "scammer" coffee mug for moral support would help. Strangely, it did.

Penny took a big gulp of booze. The bubbles were prickly on her throat.

"So, is he here?" she yelled at Mallory over the noise.

"Yeah. Behind the DJ booth."

"Aren't you going to say hi?"

"No way. He has to say hi to me first," she said. "*He's* visiting *me*."

A moment later a Blasian dude with a beard sidled over to them. He had green eyes and blindingly white teeth.

"Hey," he said to Jude, eyes at half-mast.

"Hey," the three girls responded just as listlessly.

"Is this your party?" he asked Jude.

"It's my friend's," Penny heard her say.

Mallory pulled out a vape pen and inhaled. Penny watched the little blue LED light and wondered what was in it. Jude took it after her, and when she handed it to Penny, Penny shook her head. She had smoked weed only once, with Mark, and it made her fantastically paranoid. The constant stream of neurotic questions in her mind multiplied and amplified. It made Penny-head Pennier. It would be perfect if she had an anxiety attack at the party.

"Hey, baby." Ben hugged Mallory from behind, and she squealed. He resembled the guy in the music videos only with a head so big it would've looked at home with smaller heads orbiting it. Mallory swiveled around, and they shared a lusty kiss. Penny had to hand it to her. She knew how to play it cool.

He drew Mallory into a dark corner.

With Mallory gone, Penny felt as if the locus of power of their circle had disappeared. She checked her phone battery. Fifty-four percent. Plenty to call a cab if she needed to. Jude and the green-eyed guy were deep in conversation, and when it was time for him to hit up the bar, Jude glanced at Penny to see if it was okay. Penny nodded. There was only one answer to those kinds of questions anyway. Jude followed her new friend and left Penny behind.

Penny stood in the middle of the room ignoring everyone as hard as she could and drank her drink.

She tried to conjure someone glamorous yet mighty— fierce—and thought of Jean Grey, a.k.a. Phoenix, arguably the most powerful mutant in the whole Marvel Universe. But then she remembered how Jean sorta lost her mind and didn't wind up with Logan, a.k.a. Wolverine, who she so clearly should have been with. Then she thought about Sam. And how he was a total Wolverine and that's when Penny became horribly depressed.

Screw it.

She marched over to the bartenders, got another champagne, and walked around. She made her way toward the front where a white wall was projected with different images of eyes. Cat's eyes. Human eyes. Lizard eyes.

Ugh, why do people go to these things? There was no biological imperative for it. Was there any other species on earth that prized popularity the way people did? Did lemurs hang around preening in a never-ending competition of pretending to be over it? Humans were gross.

Penny recognized the guy who had let them in and tried to hold his gaze but failed. He whispered to the eyebrowless girl next to him before they both turned away.

The eyes projected onto the wall morphed into a sunrise.

The "show," or whatever this was, was probably cool if you were on drugs. Not that it would have made a difference. Everyone was on their phones.

Penny leaned up against a wall and pulled out hers. She considered reading Sam's old texts, as she often did when she had time alone, but resisted.

"Penelope?"

Whoever it was, he was tall and backlit. She walked into the light. It was Andy, from J.A.'s class. Penny couldn't at all get a read on him. He often defended her writing in class, but the only direct interaction they'd ever had was an argument about whether or not Dr. Gaius Baltar was irredeemable in the TV miniseries of *Battlestar Galactica*. It wasn't a fight Penny was invested in. Arguing with hard-core BSG fans was tedious. The only reason she engaged with him was to see if his English accent was real. Andy made her feel competitive as the class's only other Asian, which didn't even make any sense.

It was odd seeing people out of context. Like running into

your priest at the 7-Eleven or catching Dr. Greene outside of Jude's Skype window. Seeing your classmate in his "going out" shirt in the middle of the night felt like a glitch in the Matrix. He was with another dude. Shorter, brown-haired—with a face like a weak handshake—he wore white jeans and mirrored sunglasses. Sam would have had a field day.

"Uh, hey," she said.

Andy leaned in, took her forearms, and air-kissed both of her cheeks. To Penny, who didn't know what was happening, the first kiss was scandalizing, the second completely mortifying.

He smelled of laundry detergent, chewing gum, and boy deodorant.

"This is Penelope," he shouted to his friend. "She goes to UT as well.

"This is Pete. He's kind of a twat." He whispered the last part so close to her ear Penny withdrew reflexively.

"Lovely to meet you," said Pete, checking her out in a way that was less about appreciating her outfit and more about being caught eyeing her. Blargh. Penny wished she were wearing a hoodie. "Shall I get us another round?" asked Pete.

"Fantastic idea," said Andy. "Grab me a beer. Penny, what are you having?"

"Champagne."

"Prosecco likely," remarked Pete. Penny could tell he was making fun of her, though she couldn't tell exactly how.

"So," said Andy. Penny delighted in how Andy's Asian cheeks were as ruddy as hers from the booze.

"I have a question." He cleared his throat.

Penny nodded.

"Do you know where the hell we are?" he asked. "Pete, who again, for the record, is a terrible person, dragged me here."

Penny smiled. "No idea!" she yelled into his ear. "A girl who possibly hates me brought me."

"Perhaps as punishment," he noted.

"Perhaps," she echoed, and found herself giggling.

"Do you need to get back to her?" he asked. Penny noticed how twinkly his eyes were.

"How about I wait for your obnoxious friend to bring us drinks." Penny wasn't sure she should keep drinking except that she preferred it to idly waiting for Jude or Mallory to return from making out with their dudes.

Andy surveyed the room. "Clearly we need better friends; this place is hideous."

"It's possibly the worst thing that's ever happened to me," she agreed.

He shook his head, dimples deepening. "This whole night has been insane," he said.

"Penny! There you are." Jude grabbed her shoulder and handed her another red cup, splashing some onto her hand. "Where have you beeeen?"

Jude hung on to the last word long enough that Penny knew she was drunk or high. Or at least solidly on her way to both.

"Heeeeeeeey," she said to Andy.

"Heeeeeeeey," he responded, subtly nudging Penny with his elbow.

"Jude, this is . . ."

"Andy," he said, shaking Jude's hand. Jude's gaze lingered over him.

"He's a dear, dear friend," Penny finished. It wasn't a complete lie.

"Fun," said Jude, widening her eyes approvingly.

She was right. Penny was surprised to realize, she was kind of, maybe, actually having fun.

* * *

When Penny opened her eyes the next morning her mouth tasted of wet wool socks that had stewed in a car for a month.

Kill me now.

Jude snored lightly.

Penny was dressed in last night's outfit with the addition of half a quesadilla, perched jauntily on her chest like a cheese-filled piece of statement jewelry. She had zero recollection of stopping for something to eat. As for *how* she got home, that remained mysterious as well. Penny sat up, head pounding, laid the old food gently on her nightstand, and picked up her phone.

Six a.m.

1 NEW MESSAGE

Today 2:57 AM

Hi

It was Andy. Penny recalled giggling uncontrollably attempting to punch her number into his phone. In the end he'd had to commandeer the operation, and with their combined efforts and numerous opportunities to brush fingers, they'd managed to eke out the dispatch.

Penny's first class wasn't until eleven, not that it mattered. She stumbled to the bathroom, scrubbed the furry taste out of her mouth, and scraped the makeup off her face.

Her reflection was pale. Puffy too. Dark hair hung limply by her face. Her pores were enlarged, resembling thirsty little mouths.

"Pretty," she croaked.

She shimmied out of her constricting bra that had crept up her left boob, and a card fell out onto the tile with a prim *thwack*. She picked it up. It was the party photographer's business card. It said nothing more than "stooooooooooooooooooooop.com." Penny counted the number of O's and plugged the URL into her phone. Under last night's date was a gallery of pretty party-goers, and while Penny had been there and recognized some of the faces and outfits, scrolling through felt somehow voyeuristic. Everyone was so glamorous. Then she found her and Jude.

It was like looking at a mannequin version of herself.

Uncanny Valley . . .

Used in reference to the phenomenon whereby a computer-generated figure or humanoid bearing a near-identical resemblance to a human being arouses a sense of unease or revulsion in the person viewing it.

In the picture, Penny's face was a mask. She remembered how startled she'd been when the photographer pounced. Yet wearing the black slip, with Jude's arms encircling her waist, she appeared composed. The flash accentuated her pale skin and dark lips. Not only that, but her eyes were narrowed alluringly and her lips were curled in a confident smirk. It was Penny. Except it wasn't. This was evil, sexy Penny. A Penny she hadn't been aware of. Penny was captivated by her avatar.

First off, Penny had had fun. Real fun. In-the-moment IRL fun. Not the sort of fun where she had to continually remind herself to have a good time. In fact, she hadn't checked her phone at all. As far as she was concerned, alcohol was a miracle. She felt captivating. Penny belonged at that party. She felt, okay, not to be psychotic or pathetic or anything, but she felt like a MzLolaXO.

As she scrolled through, she wondered if this was how it was to be a party girl. Regular Penny only ever took photos bearing the expression of someone attempting to pass a kidney stone the size of a chair. Yet last night there were two more party shots that were taken of her unaware. One with Mallory and Jude, doing the unimaginable—dancing in public. And another with her head thrown back, laughing at something Andy was telling her, with her hand firmly planted on his chest.

She'd spent most of the evening chatting with Andy. And his dimples. Andy who'd gone to boarding school in Hong Kong and traveled the world and played rugby and had a six-pack that Jude had molested at a certain point in the evening. Even Pete had become substantially less irritating once enough booze had tobogganed down Penny's piehole.

Mostly they talked about school. It was liberating and

electrifying to be at a party with someone you already had so much in common with.

"Yeah, it's way too hard to try to do it linearly," he'd roared over the music about her story within a story. "Write them as two separate things and then sort of mash the second one into the first one."

By then Penny was on her sixth champagne, though blessedly, she'd remembered to take notes.

"It needn't be elegant," he said. "Not at the beginning. Have you ever read *Seven Wise Masters*?"

She hadn't.

"What about Homer's *Odyssey*?"

She shook her head.

"Okay, you know the *Itchy & Scratchy Show* in *The Simpsons*?"

Penny laughed. "Yeah."

"Well, that's the way to go. It serves to illustrate a larger theme of the episode. The first draft of that script probably says, 'Itchy & Scratchy episode about blah blah blah goes here.' Plonk it in when you're about done, throw some icing around it, and twiddle with it until it's presentable."

Penny's mind exploded. It wasn't solely that writing two stories simultaneously was consistently tripping her up. It was that somewhere along the line, as she researched the court case of the real-life parents, she'd forgotten who the hero was. She'd misjudged which narrative took main stage. It was laughably small-minded. It was species-ist! The whole time Penny insisted that science fiction was boundless, yet here she was presuming human supremacy. The Anima was *The Simpsons* and the parents *Itchy & Scratchy*. Not the other way around.

Penny reddened at the memory of hugging and kissing Andy on the cheek at the revelation. Even with her hangover, Party Penny had served her well.

She'd also had a blast with Mallory and Jude. Lots of giggly joint bathroom visits.

"Yours is hella cute," said Mallory, meaning Andy. They'd shared the stall, and normally Penny would have way too much performance anxiety to go, but this time it was fine.

"I know!" Penny exclaimed. By then her feet were bleeding and she could feel the slickness between her toes, but she didn't care.

Andy *was* cute. He was well read and sophisticated and taller than her in high heels and weighed more than her, which Sam plainly didn't. All she had to do was exactly the opposite of what she normally would to be attractive. Simple as that. Screw Sam.

Penny made a promise to never text him again. Or at least not until he texted first.

Right then, as if by magic, her phone buzzed.

It was her mom.

Typical.

Penny ignored it.

SAM.

Bastian Trejo was fourteen, looked twelve, and had started smoking when he was ten. And while the skate rat was nothing more than a runt in busted shoes, to Sam there was something intimidating about him. But after that first afternoon, by the time Bastian cadged three cigarettes and a Whataburger chicken finger meal off him, the kid let his guard down.

The only rule they'd established for the documentary was that if him, James, and Rico were skating when they weren't supposed to be Sam couldn't get them in trouble with their parents. Sam agreed.

"Yeah, Bastian's mom is serious," said James.

"Yeah, Mom's got enough going on," Bastian said, flicking his cigarette.

Beyond that, Bastian didn't need any further convincing. The kid had a compulsively watchable face and knew it. Sam's setup was too cumbersome with the DSLR, so mostly he shot with his phone, and the second it was up, Bastian was ready. Talking a mile a minute, rattling off sordid tales of every "bitch" he "bagged" and other girls who had "curved" him. He knew how to tell a story even if Sam suspected most of it was made up.

Sam had Fin cover a few of his afternoons, and he taped the three of them trying to land tricks on their crappy boards. Mostly, he let the kids do the talking. He learned that James had more money than the other two, and was easygoing about it. He shared the snacks he bought without complaint.

With no parents in sight, the boredom of a kid's world was strangely stark and poetic. Even though so much of the town was about the college, the football games, the ever-expanding campus, they had no expectation that they'd ever go.

They weren't fuckups or anything. In fact, other than cigarettes, they were straight edge—no drugs, no alcohol. Their only other vice was that they were seemingly obsessed with green juice, since Bastian's mom worked at a fancy juice stand. This afternoon, the boys had come from there, and Sam was filming Bastian with his acai and kale smoothie. "The girls like it," Bastian said, smiling wide. "It makes your jizz taste like flowers."

When it got dark Sam thanked the guys, broke them off two cigarettes each, and got in the car. His phone buzzed, and he had an irrational hope that it was Penny. It was Fin checking in about his car. Sam hit him back and tried to shake off whatever he felt when he thought of her lately.

The last thing Sam had asked Penny was, "Why the

escalation?" Then, "You good?" She hadn't hit him back. Not once. He wanted to call her. He had said he would, before Lorraine sent him into a spiral. At this point who knew if she even wanted him to call? It had been almost two weeks. He didn't know who was supposed to do what next.

PENNY.

Andy was kind of the worst. Or he was the best. Whatever he was, everything he wanted to do was a horrendous idea.

When Penny climbed out of bed, she cursed him. Him and his stupid handsome face and the cathedral to orthodontia that was his mouth. At least he had great lips. She wondered if he was a good kisser. Penny checked her phone out of habit and sighed. There was so much free time now that she wasn't sending a thousand texts an hour to someone who didn't have feelings for her in the first place.

Penny wondered briefly if Sam was okay and then told herself to stop worrying about *him*.

She put on some sweats, grabbed her running shoes, and marched out. It was a cool morning for once. Instead of heading toward campus, Penny started west to the running trail by the water. It was early enough that it was mostly sleep-deprived parents with strollers and overzealous dog walkers.

Andy was already at their appointed meeting place of "the trash can by the first set of benches" when she arrived.

"You're late," he said. He was draped in swishy gray high-tech running clothes and wore matching graphite sunglasses.

"Jesus, you look like someone we'd send to repopulate a new galaxy." She yawned. "What is this outfit?"

Andy stretched his arms above his head. "There's an optimal set of clothes for every activity," he said. "This is my running ensemble."

"Spoken like the last remaining hope for human civilization."

He smiled winningly.

"You know I'm not running, right?" confirmed Penny. "I'm accompanying you around the lake primarily to rob you for ideas."

Andy touched his toes.

Penny tried to touch hers. She reached to just below her knees.

"That's fine," he said. "I need to mine your brain for information on the female psyche, so it's quid pro quo."

Penny chortled. "Good luck."

Truthfully, Penny wasn't above getting some exercise. Camped out at her desk tapping away at her keyboard, writing about people who were obsessed with the computer, was messing with her head. Her haunches were taking on the consistency of veal, and there was a permanent crease above her belly button from all the sitting.

Besides which, she enjoyed Andy's company. Penny wondered if it was because he was Asian or because they were into the same things. After the party they'd settled into an easy camaraderie. He was good for her. She was getting better and better at interfacing with real-life humans on a near-daily basis.

After that night, Penny had quickly disabused Andy of the notion that she wore glamorous dresses and drank champagne regularly. A few days ago she'd met him in the library in pajamas and ate so much beef jerky she got meat sweats.

"Enough with this indoor-kid nonsense," he'd said as she'd groaned in her protein overdose. "Next time we're doing something less disgusting."

Hence the attempted jogging.

"Okay, what do you want to know?"

Andy began pacing. His arms bent in angles by his sides, pumping purposefully as he walked at a brisk clip.

"Ask me about the female psyche," she challenged.

"Where did you read up to?" Andy was writing a sprawling May-December romance set in the sixties between a septuagenarian French woman and man forty years her junior who was Vietnamese. It was a play on Marguerite Duras's *The Lover*.

"Okay, so they met at the bar and Esmerelda's married and it's terribly fraught on the boat."

"Right," said Andy. "And it's not a boat, Penny. It's a ship. An ocean liner."

"Fine."

"Here's what I want to know. . . . Good morning!" He nodded at a woman in a sun visor walking in the opposite direction. Then he waved at a couple similarly attired in expensive athleisure clothing. He was the goodwill ambassador of whatever ten-yard radius he occupied.

"Why would Esmerelda leave her husband?" Andy asked. "He's rich. He's in love with her. They've been in a relationship for decades. The sex, for what it's worth, is okay."

Penny tried to imagine sex between seventy-year-olds.

"What would the motivating factors be? She's not in the market for it. Not explicitly anyway."

"Well . . ." Penny thought about Vin, the younger guy. "Is he Esmerelda's person? Does he say good morning to her in a way that's reassuring? To where it feels as if he's holding her hand for the entire rest of the day until he says good night? Would she be happy for him if his happiness meant that she couldn't be with him?"

"Sure," said Andy flippantly. "But Jackson's loaded." That was Esmerelda's husband.

"You can be with the same person for a long time and have it be fine and meet someone else who instantly makes you see that it's broken," she said.

"Just like that?"

"Basically."

"God, women are such fickle bitches."

"It's not women. It's humans. It's like a design flaw or something."

"Right," he said. "I guess that's why your story's as dismal as it is. Robots glamouring humans to kill their babies and put them in prison."

"First of all, they got off," she said. The parents had stood trial but not done considerable jail time. "And second, it's only dismal from the family's side of things. It's actually quite triumphant from the machine's point of view."

Andy laughed. "The point of view you strongly identify with, I suspect."

"Obviously." Penny smiled.

Suddenly Penny knew why she wanted the Anima to win. The parents were real life. Their stories were fixed. Their mistakes were their own. The Anima's future was unknown. And, unlike Penny, whose life-altering events had happened *to* her, the Anima shaped her destiny.

It is the fate of parents, of all creators, to want better for their children, their inventions. Penny wanted more for the Anima than she had had. Penny wanted to give the Anima a choice.

Penny wrote a quick note to herself on her phone, and Andy continued to talk.

The morning was beautiful. She thought about taking off running ahead of him in an explosive bout of enthusiasm, then changed her mind. She wasn't a zany manic pixie dream girl or anything. She'd probably pass out from the exertion.

"You should let me take you out sometime," Andy said. Penny stopped walking.

"What?" Penny was flabbergasted. "I thought you were dating Mariska or Misha or whatever her name was." Andy was very forthright about his leggy exploits.

"I am," he said, and then smiled. "Also who says 'dating'? I'm hanging out with Mariska and I am not opposed to similarly hanging out with you."

"What, like purchase for me a food unit in a romance-conducive setting?"

Andy scoffed. "Sure. Or watch with you a movie-unit in a comfortable area with flattering lighting conditions."

Penny considered this. Andy was handsome, though his teeth were too uniform. He was funny, too. Whenever they talked, the back-and-forth crackled with something unspoken. They were birds presenting plumage and making guttural noise. If nothing else it seemed surreal that Andy could ask Penny out. Insane even.

"Can I think about it?" she asked.

"Nope," he said, though he didn't seem mad. "Here, let's keep walking."

They trudged in silence for a moment.

"Thing is, if you have to think about it, it means you're not into it, and that's difficult for someone like me to accept." Andy gestured to his Adonis-approximating physique in his spaceman jogging outfit. "I can't be into someone who isn't into me."

Penny smiled. "Fair," she said, relieved he wasn't upset. "It's just that I'm hung up on someone."

"Is that why when I asked you the definition of love you had thirty sappy platitudes at the ready and sounded as if you wanted to die?"

Penny nodded.

"That blows," he said, and then, "God, I've been there."

SAM.

"I thought only dilettantes drank iced coffee."

Sam was reorganizing the tea drawer while sipping on a tumbler of iced mocha. The tea drawer was an overstuffed cubby under the coffee machines. Fin made a habit of ripping open a new box of tea instead of rooting around for the desired flavor, so there were countless half-used boxes and orphaned bags. Sam only ever reorganized it when he was in an especially foul temper.

Lorraine kept her eyes hidden behind dark sunglasses. She grabbed his glass and took a sip.

It had been thirteen days since their last encounter. Just shy of a fortnight since she'd air-kissed him as if she were some movie star, dropped the bomb about the ghost baby, and pranced back into the street without a care in the world.

"What do you want, Lorraine?" Sam hated how much of a sitting duck he was running the local coffee shop. Anyone could come see him whenever they wanted. A hit man could take him out with zero prep. In fact, if the shooter did it at the right time, he could wait until Sam was in a baking mood and snatch roadie desserts on his way out.

"I wanted to see you," she said. Her perfume pierced the air around him.

"Great," he snapped. His hair flopped defiantly in his face as he collected every blood orange Rooibos. He hated that it was supposed to be pronounced "Roy-Buss." And why were herbal teas "tisanes"? So annoying.

"I thought we should talk about what happened."

"So talk," he said. He couldn't see what was so newly urgent.

"Let's go eat somewhere," said Lorraine. She grabbed his watered-down iced coffee and took another sip.

Sam slammed the boxes of tea down on the counter between them.

"Can't," he said with finality.

"I have something to say," she said.

"So say." Lorraine's nails were freshly painted in metallic-gold triangles over black.

"Can we do this somewhere more private?" It was fifteen minutes before closing and there were only two other people in the coffee shop. "When you're less busy arranging or whatever super-important tea business you're doing?"

"Just say what you need to say and say it fast."

"I know these past few weeks have been confusing," she said carefully. Then she changed tactic and removed her shades. "Don't you miss me? I miss you."

Lorraine stared up at him and bit her lip. It was a rehearsed expression he instantly recognized. She made this face in moments she thought were particularly poignant.

"You know what, Lorraine? There were times, I swear, when I would have robbed a bank, thrown the money into Lake Travis, and tap-danced on my ancestors' graves, anything to hear you say that. Not anymore."

Sam wanted to hurt her—true—but he also realized that for once in the last four years, for reasons he couldn't fathom, at a point that he hadn't even noticed, he was finally over her. He was done. He felt as if he'd taken a crap the size of the Washington Monument. It was liberating. He was free.

"Are you serious?" She scowled. "You get why I couldn't be with you when I thought I was pregnant, right? That would have been a mess. I wanted a clean slate. I wanted us to start completely new."

"You can't keep doing this, Lorr," said Sam. "You only want me some of the time. And every time you do, I drop everything and bolt to you. But you're right. This is a clean slate. The cleanest slate. We're done. Lorraine, you said we weren't friends. And you're right. You know what? I don't think you even like me as a person."

"I *love* you, Sam," she said. "Why are you making this complicated after all this time? You're one of those impossible knots. The kind from the myth." She sighed dramatically and smoothed some imaginary wrinkles from her dress.

"What do I prefer, cake or pie?" he asked.

"What?" Lorraine was confused.

"Simple question, Lorr. Cake or pie? What team do I ride for?"

"You make both all the time. It's a trick question," she said defiantly.

"I'm a pie person, Lorraine. Just like you. Your favorite is strawberry. The trashy kind with condensed milk in the middle. You love it because your grandma Violet used to make it for you, and you'd hide it from your mother because she didn't appreciate you having sweets. Because until you developed an eating disorder in ninth grade, you were a little on the *husky* side. *Your words.* You know why I know this? It's because I know everything about you. Not only do I know everything about you, but I remember everything about you. My folder on you is so fat and complete and bursting with nonsensical shit because I couldn't help myself. Your hands? Bullshit. Your feet, your knobby, misshapen feet are the real treat, and that's a fact. You know, I thought you didn't know me because I was insecure or broken or poor, and then I thought about it. It's because you never asked. Ever. I want to be with someone I can talk to. I want to be with someone who automatically has a fat folder on me. Someone who feels lucky when I tell them the most unflattering, scary stuff. I don't think I love you anymore, and I got to be honest, I don't believe that you love me."

Lorraine's mouth formed a straight line that went down slightly at the corners. "I'm sorry you feel that way," she said.

"That's not an apology," he said. "You know that, right?"

"I only said it because I know you hate it," she spat.

Lorraine turned around and walked out. Her hemline flipped up as she spun, and he could see the tops of her gartered stockings. She was a nightmare caricature of a male fantasy.

That night, he actually sent the e-mail he'd been working on for more than a week.

> To: Penelope Lee
> From: Sam Becker
> Subject line: Mic check 1, 2
>
> Hi,
> Okay, so things have been weird. And I know that I made them weird even if I'm not totally sure how.
> So, I'm sorry.
> (Nothing beats a vague apology, right? So sincere!)
> Ugh.
> Hmmm . . .
> Anyway, I know it's ancient history, and if our autobiographers were to trace back to when I made it weird it would probably have something to do with me not calling you after I said I would. After we saw each other.
> That was a big day for us, huh? Meeting your mom. Having to smile across the counter and pretend like nothing was up. So many exciting experiences rolled into a ball of panic.
> The last thing I asked you was "You good?" Well, are you? I think about it all the time.
> If you're like, NEW LIFE, WHO DIS? I totally understand.
> If you're not, here's a list of things that have happened in no particular order since I last bothered you.

I got stupidly drunk. Hurt-drunk. It was depressing.

Lorraine isn't pregnant. And that was strangely disappointing and I don't know why.

I started shooting the doc. Finally! I don't know exactly where it's going at all, but I love it. Turns out the kid's name is Sebastian. He goes by Bastian, which sounds so badass, and he's brilliant and insane and I want so badly for you to meet him. Badly? Bad? I never get those right. Kind of how "bemused" doesn't mean "amused" and how I think "nonplussed" means "unimpressed" when it means something else. Does anyone know what "nonplussed" means? You probably do. Don't tell anyone, but I don't actually know how irony works either.

Flammable/inflammable = also confusing.

Anyway. I miss you.

I know we're basically just a series of texts. But I'm glad that whatever led you to me happened. I'm grateful that you're my emergency contact. Even if you're super intense and talking to you late at night is as constructive as Web MDing a bunch of symptoms in the sense that I'm almost always convinced all roads lead to death, but I mean that in a good way. I hope you know that it's my favorite.

I think I get to miss you. I feel like I've earned it. Which I know sounds weird/creepy/possessive or whatever. Our relationship, as abstract as it is, is the best of any relationship, I think.

You're intense, so much fun, and maybe a bit nuts,

and at the same time you're super focused and passionate about how you want to live your life and your
work and it's beautiful. Also, NONE of this is meant
to make you uncomfortable or put you on the spot (I
know how you feel about compliments). You give the
best advice (for a kid etc., etc., etc.).

I'm happy to know you exist. And even though I
feel like I screwed things up, I thought I'd let you know.
And to remind you that I exist also. I hope you've been
good. You good? Let me know.

*all the best emojis even the embarrassing girlie
ones*

—S.

PENNY.

Well, that was it. Penny and Sam were officially multiplatform.
Penny texted him.

Hi
You're a crap emergency contact btw
If there's no response to "You good?"
the correct response is to send
paramedics
Everybody knows that

She waited.

Great point
Such an amateur
Hi

I got your email

I'm glad you're not dead

No thanks to you

I KNOW
I'm sorry
I missed you

Me too

Pretty good email right?

She had to hand it to him. It was the best one she'd ever gotten.

Are you at work?

Okay, so Penny knew this qualified as borderline psychotic behavior. And she didn't want to freak him out on some "THE CALL WAS COMING FROM INSIDE THE HOUSE!" but the call was coming from inside the House. Almost.

It had taken half a beer and some serious hand wringing and five outfit changes, but Penny felt it was time for a grand gesture of her own. She didn't even have to entertain her usual decision tree.

She'd texted him from his porch.

Yeah wrapping up

OK well I'm outside

What?
Here?

On the swing

My swing???

Sam walked out of the side door into the dark night with his phone in his hand. His face was lit blue. He continued to type.

Whoa serious escalation

Penny smiled and typed back:

Boom

"Hey," he called out. "I guess we're doing this now?"
"Guess so! It's scary." The swing creaked beneath her.
Sam laughed.
This time she had picked the perfect outfit. Penny wore Mallory's dress again. Her feet were still healing, so she'd put on sneakers, and while she'd applied lipstick, she'd changed her mind and smudged it off onto the back of her hand like a sophisticated young lady. And to make absolutely sure that she wasn't too exposed, she threw a ratty hoodie over the top. A perfectly Penny outfit. She stood up, which signaled the motion detector floodlight from the back lot to blind them both.

"Hell of an entrance," Sam said, lifting his arm up to shield his face.

"Sorry to bust in on you like this," she stammered. Penny couldn't believe it was happening. "If you're busy I can . . ."

"Yeah, right," he said, herding her into the side door. "Just come in."

Penny followed him into the kitchen. He grabbed a stool, parked it next to the steel workbench, and made her a cup of tea. She took it gratefully and sat.

"Hungry?"

She was.

Sam set to work. He didn't ask her what she wanted. He peered into the fridge, pulled out some plastic tubs, some bacon and eggs, and palmed a half loaf of bread. They didn't talk while he assembled. She watched as he grabbed bits of chopped-up ingredients from the tubs and tossed them into the pan. He toasted big, thick slices of bread with olive oil in the broiler and fried up the bacon and eggs and assembled everything into two enormous sandwiches that he cut into diagonal slices. He set one down in front of her.

"No cheese on yours," he said. "Because of the whole lactose intolerance thing your mom mentioned." Penny smiled and stared at her sandwich. She grabbed half and squished it to see if she could negotiate it into her mouth.

"Pretty good," she said, taking a heroic bite. Part of the gooey egg yolk slid down her chin.

Sam laughed and handed her a napkin.

"Hot sauce?" he offered. She took it.

"So," she said. "That's crazy about MzLolaXO." She hated

that she'd brought her up so early in their conversation. Ugh, and she *really hated* that she'd called her by her Insta name.

It was a self-sabotaging instinct she couldn't resist.

Sam laughed. "Her name's Lorraine." He took a bite of his own sandwich.

Lorraine was so much less scarier than *Lola* for some reason.

"I was so relieved I didn't pass out or have a panic attack or spontaneously combust when she showed up," he said. "Both times she turned up."

Penny wondered how much detail he'd go into. If they'd made out on every sofa at House, she didn't want to hear about it.

"She sounds tough."

Sam nodded again. "Yeah, no panic attacks the first night, but I did get wasted on the second," he said. "Like I'd mentioned in the e-mail."

"With her?"

"Ew, no," he said. After a pause he added, "I don't know why I said 'ew.'"

They laughed.

"I got drunk at home as a self-respecting, proper alcoholic."

"Are you an alcoholic?"

"I don't know," he said. "And I haven't decided if I've quit for life, like, no champagne on my wedding day or what, only that it's bad for me right now. . . ."

Penny missed this. Talking to someone about deeply personal things. She snuck a peek and then shied away because he was chewing and she would want the privacy.

"You know, it's funny, but I got drunk recently too. For the second time ever." She took a sip of tea.

"Yeah? How was it?"

"Fascinating," she said.

Sam laughed. God, she loved that laugh.

"How so?"

Penny tried not to get derailed staring into his eyes. They were deep brown but tinged at the edges with a way lighter hazel.

Penny cleared her throat.

"Well, it is a highly effective social lubricant," she said. "Diminished inhibitions, the whole works. It makes everything so much easier. All the whirring that's usually going on in my brain shuts the hell up."

"But the whirring's good," he said. "Your whirring's good."

She smiled.

Sam smiled back.

She died.

"Yeah, it's exhausting though."

"So, it was a break?" he asked. "Like a you vacation?"

"Exactly," she said. "Everybody needs a them vacation."

"And you had fun?"

"I had a blast," she said. "I made a new friend too—Andy. I guess he was an old friend. He's in my fiction class, and booze made it so much easier to talk to him. I was enchanting."

Sam laughed.

Penny didn't know why she was blathering on about Andy. She wanted to reassure Sam that it was okay. That he could talk about Lorraine if he needed to. At least for a second.

"He had great advice about my story," she said. "He's crazy smart."

"That's great," said Sam. "Wait, I gotta ask you . . ."

Penny held her breath.

"Who is your boyfriend? It's been bothering me that I never once heard of this guy until your mom brought him up. Not that you have to tell me everything, but when I was going on and on about Lorraine, you could have said something. I hope I wasn't so self-involved that I didn't ask about . . ."

Sam stopped and cleared his throat.

"Sorry," he said. He grabbed a glass of water but not before handing her one. Penny died again. "Basically, I want you to talk about whatever's on your mind. Not all my crap."

"Thanks," she said, and meant it. "We broke up."

"I'm sorry."

"It's okay. I'm okay," she continued, taking a sip.

All things considered, Penny did a good job on the sandwich. Two-thirds. She picked the rest apart and rooted out the bacon.

"Now I have to ask you something." She had to know.

"Shoot," he said.

"Are you sad that Lorraine's not pregnant?" Penny tried the name out.

Sam took a deep breath.

He nodded.

So it was true. He was still in love with her. Penny's heart sank.

"Did you want to be a dad?"

"I did," he admitted. "I sound cracked, right?"

Penny waited for him to go on.

"I wanted direction. And I genuinely thought I could foist

all my expectations and lack of motivation on this tiny blob and this baby would magically figure it out for me because now I had a reason to exist."

He took another gulp of water. "Dumb," he said. "Like so textbook."

There was nothing Penny could think to say, so she stayed silent.

"Can I show you something?" Sam said, looking at her warily.

"Is it dead?"

"No." He laughed. "What?"

Penny laughed too and shook her head. "Sorry, you just had this look." She hopped off her stool. "Yes, you can show me something."

He headed up a set of stairs left of the fridge and Penny followed him.

Sam flipped on a light and went down the hall. Penny briefly wished she had gum just in case.

The upstairs of House wasn't anything you'd expect.

Sam walked into a dark room toward the back and switched on a lamp. "This is where I live," he said.

SAM.

Talk about an escalation. He tried to see his bedroom through Penny's eyes. Even sharing a dorm, it was probably smaller than what she was used to.

Penny followed him in.

"Grim, right?" he asked. He watched as she tracked his possessions. His mattress on the floor, the box of clothes by the door.

"Not at all," she said. "It's wild. I can't believe I'm here."

She walked to the window by his bed.

"So, this is your atmosphere," she said, moving the curtain aside to peer out. Sam watched her reflection in the glass. "Good view. It honestly didn't occur to me that House had an upstairs. It's a great perch, the crow's nest of a pirate ship. Do you like it here?"

He did.

He stood next to her. "Yeah," he whispered.

She turned to him. "That's good," she said. She walked into the middle of the room and glanced at his ceiling. "Chill vibes," she said.

He smiled.

"Oh," she said. "So I *really* didn't need to worry about you getting home that first day."

He laughed. "I'm still sorry about that."

Sam took a seat on the corner of his mattress. Penny sat down next to him.

"All of House is soothing," she said. "I can't believe you can't sleep in here. I'd be out like a light."

He wanted her to touch him, but she didn't.

Penny.

Penny who smelled of dryer sheets.

He took off his shoes and leaned up against the back wall to get more comfortable.

"How long have you been here?" she asked.

"Since the beginning of the summer."

"About the same time all that other stuff happened?"

"Yeah."

Sam touched his hair. It was gross and curling. He tried to smooth it down and failed. He pulled his legs up and wrapped his arms around them, resting his chin on top of his knees. Then he decided it was too much the posture of a moody kid and unfolded himself.

"I lived with Lorraine off and on," he said. "Or with friends. Or at home with my mom and her boyfriend. I was trying to save money for school." He turned to Penny. "You think I'm a loser."

"I don't," she said. "I would tell you."

He believed her.

PENNY.

It was the hair that was her undoing. It was floppy. Fluffy even. He was sitting on the bed with his long legs stretched out in front of him, his back against the wall. She wanted to touch the tuft in the back, the craziest part of the cowlick, even though she knew it to be a huge violation of personal space. It also killed her that she couldn't poke through the small hole in the knee of his jeans to see if it felt the same as the hole in her jeans. The whole thing was demented.

"So, yeah, I'm basically homeless," he said.

Penny turned to face him. "Inaccurate," she said, and scooched over to him, mindful to keep her shoes off his bed. "In fact, you're lucky that you have a place to go."

Penny placed her paw on top of Sam's hand, which lay on the bed. She had no idea why. She hadn't considered until that second how it might be a thing he noticed.

She faltered. Not quite knowing what to do next, she concentrated on keeping the pressure light. Nobody wanted a clammy dead hand on theirs.

"Besides, this place is cozy as hell," she continued.

"You're right." He shifted his hand.

Then for no other reason than to up the ante on the awkward Olympics, Penny blurted: "Is it crazy that you've met my mom?"

He laughed. It was a good distraction. Penny snatched back her hand to pretend the incident hadn't occurred and shoved it in her hoodie pocket.

"You seem mad at her," he said.

"Yeah," she responded glumly.

She *was* mad at her. It wasn't as cut-and-dried as Sam's thing with Brandi Rose, but Penny was furious at Celeste. Had been for a while.

"It goes back to when my mom got me a tutor because I brought home a C in French," she began. "Not that she's a stereotypical tiger mom or anything. Just that she thinks French is too 'chic' to flunk."

Her tutor, Bobby, was nineteen, pale, kinda on the chubby side, with long, spidery fingers and brown hair that fell to his chin in front. He was half-white and half-Filipino, and pretty tall, though his clothes could've fit Penny. It was as if at fourteen he'd decided he was done buying new ones. His T-shirts barely covered his midriff, and it was a dead giveaway that he was peculiar. And his eyes . . . His eyes were beautiful. One yellow-green, the other gray-blue. It was called complete heterochromia. He'd explained how he'd gotten it—hereditarily speaking—and drawn a chart while talking about pea plants, but Penny didn't harbor a crush yet, so she ignored the finer points.

"Bobby was this whiz kid computer programmer." Her voice sounded far away. Detached. "His dad was this big deal at IBM back in the day and was friends with my mom. Whatever, my mom was friends with everyone. Still is."

Most of the time Penny didn't give Celeste anything to worry about. She only ever got As and Bs. Then, at the end of sophomore year, when it was looking like Penny would end up with a C, Celeste called Bobby.

His teaching methodology was suspect at best. Bobby came by twice a week to show Penny pirated French movies that she'd seen before with the English captions switched off. Usually *Amélie* or *Breathless*. They'd read books from the artist Moebius and *Asterix and Obelix* comics, a series about two ancient warriors, and listened to French rap music that to Penny's ears was exactly like American rap except way more politicized.

They spoke jokey nonsense French in horrible accents.

"Attend! Pourquoi le Sasquatch abandonnerait son sac à main?"

Wait! Why would the Sasquatch leave his handbag?

Or

"Asterix et Obelix veulent faire l'amour doux, doux, à l'autre. Il est évident, n'est-ce pas?"

Asterix and Obelix want to make sweet, sweet love to each other. Duh, right?

Bobby spoke four languages. When he turned fifteen he won a fellowship for one hundred thousand dollars to skip college and work in Silicon Valley, but he didn't go because he said he didn't want to be *bourgeois*. They ate snacks and secretly drank Celeste's white wine while watching *La Déesse!*, a French cooking show where a well-intentioned woman with colorful blouses made elaborate meals for her husband.

He was the first boy she'd felt entirely comfortable around. She could eat wet foods in front of him and be opinionated and goofy. They even mostly argued well. He detested inconsistency or contradiction. When Penny told him she was lactose intolerant, Bobby acted as if he'd caught her in a lie when she ate tuna salad in front of him. He couldn't believe mayo didn't have milk in it until they Googled it.

August seventeenth was Bobby's birthday. Celeste had gone to bed right after dinner, and Penny had snuck an entire bottle of zinfandel from her mom's stash. She and Bobby passed it back and forth while watching Ysel, the star of *La Déesse!*, make duck aspic. They were sitting on the couch. Actually, he was sitting. Her legs were flung on top of his, and she was practically lying down. She had to sit up every time she talked to him in case she had a double chin from that angle, and she worried that her cheeks were as bright red as Celeste's got when she drank. Her mom called it the Asian Flush and Bobby didn't get it. You were supposed to take an antacid to combat it but she'd forgotten.

Even though it was his birthday, he'd gotten Penny a present. A copy of *Zero Girl*. He handed it to her in a black plastic bag and told her about it as she thumbed through the watercolored pages.

"It's a classic," he said. "And it reminds me so much of you. It's about a high school girl who has these kinda bootleg superpowers and she vanquishes all her mortal foes and she shoots her shot with her guidance counselor, who's a total G, by the way, and they fall in love . . ."

To Penny the subtext was clear. A dork with a crush on an older guy, a teacher even, and they end up together because she makes the first move! It was romantic.

"I kept watching his mouth," Penny remembered. "That's how you're supposed to show a guy that you want them to kiss you. At least that's what I'd read."

Sam nodded.

It worked. Penny had willed Bobby to kiss her and he had. It hadn't been her first kiss, but it was pretty close.

Her first kiss was Richard Kishnani at camp when she was thirteen. He had braces and she was attracted to him only because his mother worked at NASA.

And Noah Medina at the movies, whose teeth banged into hers as he was going in for the kill. He was from Florida and had put her hand on his junk. He was wearing crunchy nylon shorts that had to be a bathing suit. She excused herself to go to the bathroom and never came back.

With Bobby, Penny closed her eyes and moved her lips slowly and imagined how if anyone ever asked, this would be the story of her first kiss. This was the one that mattered. The one she'd worked for. Bobby's mouth felt incredible. Warm. Soft but not too soft. Wet but not too wet. When his mouth opened and their tongues touched, she didn't feel nervous. It wasn't slimy or anatomical. It felt good.

By Penny's count they'd hung out on sixteen separate occasions, which made them friends.

That's why what happened next was so surprising.

Penny had said stop. She was sure of it. Or else she'd said no. In fact, she'd said it more than once, yet she wasn't positive it qualified. He kept going.

"Maybe I said it too quietly."

She hadn't cried for help. Celeste was right upstairs. Penny hadn't kicked him in the nuts, as any heroine worth her salt would have done. Instead Penny lay perfectly still and walked backward from her eyes until she was far enough in her head that she was safe. From the couch, pinned underneath him, she turned her head to the side to find *Zero Girl* open on the coffee table as Bobby stabbed her in the guts with his dick. His dick was purple. Cartoon purple. When he pulled on the lurid condom, she couldn't believe it was such a bright and happy color. It had taken a few times for him to get it right, and Penny didn't know why she didn't scream or rip it out of his hands while he loomed above her. She just knew that she didn't. She didn't do any of the things that absolutely anyone with a brain knows to do. All she wanted was for Celeste not to see.

"It's not as if he beat me up or anything," said Penny.

"It was so embarrassing," she continued. "And the thing that's so confusing is that I didn't get mad. It felt inevitable in some ways. An obvious conclusion. I saw him two more times after that and was polite."

She gazed at Sam. He had a serious expression on his face.

"I'm practically fluent in French now," she said. "My mom

thinks it's because of him when it's not. He was proficient at best."

Penny was dying to know what Sam was thinking. She'd never told the story to anyone else.

"Do you think I'm broken?"

SAM.

Sam couldn't believe a brain as animated and complex as Penny's had to conk up against that question. It hurt his heart.

"No," he said. "I don't think you're broken." Sam pulled her body against his and she let him. He felt her stiffen and then fall slack like one of those rag-doll cats that go limp when you pick them up.

She yawned into his chest. They leaned up against each other for a while.

"I gotta go," she said, pulling away from him. Sam wanted to stop her but knew that he shouldn't. "I'm tired." She stood up.

Penny swung sleepily side-to-side while walking out. He followed her down the hall.

"Should I come with you?" he called out.

"Don't be silly," she said, swatting the air. "I live ten blocks away. And if you lived here you'd be home already." Sam wondered where he'd heard that before and remembered it

was the huge yellow sign on the apartment complex across
the street.

Penny zipped up her hoodie and pulled the hood down low.

"I'll be fine." He wanted to hug her. In fact, he wanted to
hug her and then build an electrified fence around her. A fence
that was encircled by a moat filled with rabid, starving alli-
gators. It was ridiculous, yet Sam hadn't thought how nerds
could be rapists. He thought of rapists as meat-head jocks or
else vile faceless monsters who were abused as kids. Part of
him was glad she was going to go back inside his phone. It was
safe there and Sam had so much he wanted to tell her and ask
her that was too overwhelming to do in person.

"I know," he said, throwing on a black jacket. "But I'll make
you a deal. Next time I show up at your house unannounced,
you can walk me home."

Penny smiled sleepily.

"My sandwiches aren't as good though."

"That's because I am king of the sandwiches."

"I think he was an earl," she muttered.

He groaned.

Sam smiled at the back of her head as they trudged down
the stairs. He killed the lights and locked up. The night was
cool. Just the tiniest suggestion that there was such a thing as
autumn in Texas.

They walked companionably in silence. Both with their
hands shoved in their pockets. The streets were quiet but not
deserted. A smattering of couples reluctant to end their nights
lingered by parked cars.

Sam listened to their footfalls, hers alongside his.

"This is me," she said after a while, stopping at the ghastly facade of her dorm.

He gazed up. "You know," he said, "I see this building all the time and it doesn't occur to me that people have to live here."

The striped blue and salmon edifice with round windows reminded him of a monster version of those plastic Connect Four grids.

Penny laughed. "Ah, but when you're inside," she said, "you can't see it."

"What a parable," he said.

"What *is* a parable?" she asked, tilting her head. "I always forget to look it up, but then again, I'm talking to someone who doesn't even know what irony is, so . . ."

He laughed. "Nobody knows. That's a fact. Just like nobody knows the difference between a parable and an allegory. Do you?"

She smiled. "No idea."

"See?"

They grinned stupidly at each other.

"I think an allegory has to do with characters," she said. "Something-something *Animal Farm*?"

"Citation needed," he responded quickly.

God, they were hopeless.

"Thanks for the food, and the talk, and for being great, and for walking me home," she said.

They stood regarding each other in front of the elevators, wondering who was going to make the next move and what exactly it would be.

Sam quit while he was ahead. He left his hands in his pockets instead of reaching for her as he desperately wanted to.

"Sweet dreams, Penny," he said.

"You too, Sammy," she said.

Hearing her say "Sammy" liquefied his guts.

She smiled.

"You ever think about how your last name in German is 'baker' and that you bake, and Jude's is Lange, which means 'tall'?"

He blinked at her and shook his head. He wanted to crush her with the fierceness of his hug. Either that or he wanted to bite her on the face. Why so cute?

"I do," she said. "All the time."

Sam watched her go.

"Yo, text me when you get home," she said just as the doors began to slide shut.

"Yo," he said, laughing. "Got it."

Sam thought of a million cooler things to say, but more than anything he wished he'd kissed her.

PENNY.

Home

Penny was half tempted to wait until two a.m. to text him back, as he'd done in the beginning, but she was too excited. She was in bed when her phone chimed. Jude had gone out and Penny wondered if Sam would ever come over to her room.

Her phone chimed again.

You do know that it counts right?
What happened to you counts

Tears sprang from the corners of Penny's eyes as she lay on her back with her phone held aloft.

God. Sam was perfect. This was good and this is what he had to offer her, and Penny knew that she had to find a way to be grateful. What choice did she have? And even if one day something happened between them, something wonderful and terrifying that tested their friendship, what would ultimately come of it? Romance was volatile, and if they came out of it with less than they had going in, she would be devastated. Penny couldn't go back to not having Sam in her life. This way, she could make sure they'd always be there for each other. As friends. As emergency contacts. That was the deal. That's the deal it had always been.

Penny knew how lucky she was to have him at all. She trusted Sam and he trusted her. That was huge. They may as well have sliced their thumbs and pressed them together in a blood oath.

I'm glad you're home

Are you still sleepy?

eyeball emoji

Penny was wired.

I may never sleep again.

CALL FROM SAM
Penny's heart skipped. She picked up.
"Hey," he said. "It's Sam."
She laughed.

"I dunno, I think we're moving way too fast, Sam." She could hear him chuckle. Penny pictured him on his scrawny mattress in the room down the hall. She liked that she knew where to orient him in the world.

"Right? We're reckless," he said.

"Crazy," she agreed.

"Hey, let's make a pact."

"Sure."

"Great, I'll pick up your soul in a half hour. G'bye!"

Penny laughed. "What's the pact?"

"Let's be friends," he said, suddenly serious. "Real ones."

Penny nodded as tears coursed down her cheeks. "We are friends," she said lightly. She breathed quietly so he couldn't hear her cry.

"Yeah, I know that, but let's be so good to each other."

"Deal."

"You know why I called?" asked Sam.

"Why?"

"Because I don't want you to punish me for knowing too much," he said.

"What do you mean?"

"Don't, like, go away because you told me things," he said. "Don't decide things are weird."

"I'm not the who decided last time . . ."

"I know," he said. "Let's both not is what I'm saying. Don't drag the entire me folder into the desktop trash can so you hear the paper-rustling sound."

"You can't ask me that. The paper-rustling sound is too satisfying."

"Just don't be weird with me. And I promise not to be weird with you."

"Okay," she said.

They sat in silence.

"Do you think I should have reported him to the cops?" Penny had many sleepless nights thinking about that.

"I think you should do whatever is right by you."

"What if he did it again? After me?"

"That's on him, not you."

"Do you think I should have told my mom?"

"Not if you didn't want to," he said. "I'm pretty sure whatever you want is okay."

"Okay," she said. "You know sometimes they make you pay for your own rape kit?"

"What?"

"Yeah, you have to go through the swabs when all you want to do is go home and then certain hospitals bill you for tests. And all over the country there are warehouses filled with rape kits that the cops don't even process. Like hundreds of thousands."

Sam didn't say anything for a while.

"I'm sorry this happened to you," he said.

"I'm glad I told you."

"Me too," he said. "I want us to talk about everything," he continued. "I don't want to ever not talk again. That was horrible."

"Well, I don't love talking about my stuff," she said.

"Yeah, nobody does," he said. "But it's pretty big stuff, so sometimes you have to exorcise it."

"God," she said. "You'd think it would be cathartic, but it's more like barfing after you thought you got it all."

"I think once you're puking so hard you'll burst a blood vessel in your eye is when the real work happens."

"So when it's just thin stomach juices coursing out of you?"

"Yeah," he said.

"Sans chunks?"

"Sans, yeah."

Penny could feel him smiling on the other side. It made her miserable.

"This sucks," she said. "Why so much work?"

"The homework doesn't end," he said. "It's piles and piles of emotional homework forever if you ever want to qualify as a grown-up."

"How come nobody tells you?"

"Nobody tells you shit ever," he said. "The trick is having a buddy."

"An emergency contact."

"Exactly," he said. "That's the pact."

It was a good pact. It wasn't exactly the pact she wanted, the one where they ran away together to Tahiti, but it was solid.

"I'm in," she said.

"Cool," he said. "Good night, Penelope Lee."

"Bye," she said.

Not ten seconds later he texted again.

Have a willie nice night!

God, he was such a jerk.

SAM.

The next morning Sam woke up feeling good. Not sensational or anything foolish but supremely okay. Penny had already texted and all was right in the world. He fortified himself with coffee and headed out to pick up Bastian.

East Side Nectars, where Bastian's mom worked, was a small operation in a strip mall on the North Side. From the highway, the neon signs in order read: CHINESE FOOD, DONUTS, JUICE, then GUNS. Juice was the only hipster outlier. Everything else was as common as corn bread.

There were only three stools in the front by the window and a kitchen area with a row of juicers in back. When Sam and Bastian walked in, the store was empty. Luz Trejo, a short, slight woman whose watchful eyes and delicate features had been inherited by her son, grilled Sam. As Brandi Rose would have put it, there was no slack in her rope. Bastian leaned up against the wall by the counter, scowling, holding his skateboard at the ready in case he had to scram.

"Hi," he said. He nodded at Bastian, who engaged him in a complicated handshake that Sam didn't attempt to keep up with.

He let Luz appraise him—his dark clothes and his tattoos. It didn't help that he stank of cigarette smoke.

Luz asked Bastian something in Spanish and he rolled his eyes.

"What's your name?"

"Sam Becker."

"How old are you, Sam Becker?" she asked, wiping her hands on her pale blue apron. Her hands were at least twenty years older than her face.

"Twenty-one," he said, suddenly nervous.

"German?" she asked.

"Half," he answered. "Half Polish."

"A mutt."

He nodded.

"How is it that you're associates with my fourteen-year-old Mexican son?" she asked.

"Mom!" protested Bastian, very much seeming exactly fourteen.

"He skates near where I live," said Sam.

"During school hours?" she asked.

"Sometimes," he said. No way he was going to get caught in a lie with Mrs. Trejo. Luz leaned over the counter and rapped her son on the head with her knuckles. Bastian glared at him.

"Snitches get stiches," he hissed. Luz shushed him.

Sam kept his eyes on Luz and tried to look responsible.

"I'm a student," he said. "I'm directing a documentary about Bastian, and I wanted to ask for your permission and to know if I could interview you as well."

A customer walked in. An older white gentleman with a mustache.

"Hey, Anthony," she said.

"Whew," said Anthony. "It's hotter than a pot of neck bones out there." It was a 100-degree fall day.

She crowded Sam and Bastian to the side, out of her customer's way. "Pineapple mint?" she asked. He nodded. While she made his juice, she called from the back over the buzzing machine.

"It's a little late to ask for permission if you've already started, don't you think?"

Sam had no idea how to answer that.

She handed Anthony his juice. Anthony took a long swallow and studied Sam up and down. "If you riled up this one, best of luck to you." He nodded, fished two fives out from a long wallet pulled out from the back of his jeans and left.

"What's it about?" Luz asked.

"Being a kid in Austin," he said.

"So Oscar-winning stuff," she said.

Sam felt Bastian watching them closely to see who had the upper hand.

"Look, I'm a college student," said Sam. "I'm not some rich trust-fund kid, either. I'm putting myself through film school."

"Film school?" said Luz. "Sound like a rich-kid plan to me. Why not go into computer programming or something that makes money? Do you know the odds of being a director?"

"I knew you were going to say that!" complained Bastian. "Ask her about art school if you want to have your dreams punched in the face."

Luz knocked Bastian on the skull again. Bastian scowled and rubbed his head.

"Look, I don't want to be interviewed or anything," she said. "That isn't for me. But don't shoot during school hours and I want to see this movie before you show it anywhere. I don't want anything inappropriate."

Sam nodded.

"And if you get rich and famous, you're paying for this kid's college," she said.

"Can it be RISD?" asked Bastian. Luz responded in Spanish for a while. Bastian said something back and laughed.

Sam knew they were talking about him.

"Do you want a juice?" she asked.

"Sure. I'm sure I could use one," Sam said.

"You need milk shakes more than you need juice, flaco," she said. She made him something with beets. It was thick and the color of rubies. As he drank he imagined his withered cells revitalizing.

"Not bad," he said, taking another slug. It was disjointing. A juice that tasted of beets.

"Yeah, your people love it."

"My people?"

"She means the whites," said Bastian.

"What do I owe you?" said Sam. He hoped he had cash.

"Don't worry about it," she said, and waved them out of the store.

They got back into the car.

Bastian pulled on his seat belt. "She likes you," he said.

"Oh yeah?"

"Yeah. She charges everyone."

"What were you guys saying about me?" he asked. "That made you laugh. Something about college."

"Oh," said Bastian, laughing. "She said I could maybe go to art school as long as I don't do anything stupid," he said. "Say, get a bunch of tattoos so I can't ever get a real job like you."

Sam laughed.

"I told you she was cold."

Sam wondered if Bastian knew how lucky he was to have Luz. To have a mother who actually seemed to like you. Sam hung a right from the Taco Cabana and across the train tracks to a section of town so dicey it didn't even have a bar.

"Park here," said Bastian. They were on a nondescript street near a chain-link fence. Bastian hopped out, leaving his skateboard in the car and slinging his backpack over his shoulder.

He crawled through a clipped hole in the fence. Sam followed. Bastian scanned his surroundings quickly, pulled out a key, and unlocked a thick padlock on the metal door of a brown building that had graffiti on the front in white. NSB was scrawled in menacingly giant letters, and Sam wondered if they were going to get killed execution style for trespassing. "Don't worry," said Bastian about the North Side Bloods tag. "I put that there so the bums don't jack my shit." To Sam it sounded like exactly the kind of genius plan that got you killed.

The kid had made a huge deal out of whatever it was that he was going to show him. Sam wondered if it was a skate ramp or a meth lab. Sam followed him into the cool hallway, which smelled of wet concrete.

"Come on, man," griped Bastian. "Get your camera out. You need to be getting all of this."

The cavernous room was flooded with natural light. You couldn't tell from the street, but there were panes of glass high on the wall and the vaulted ceilings that served as skylights. It was a miracle that some hipster developer hadn't already bought the place out to turn into a design studio or a vegan co-working space.

"This is incredible," Sam said, panning the room.

"Roof leaks," complained Bastian. As if he were making mortgage payments on the place.

In the middle of the space there was a lone folding chair and paintings of varying size.

The still air hung thick with chemicals. Nail polish. Or primer.

"So, this is what I'm working on," said Bastian, gesturing at the canvases standing sentry. "Other than becoming the Mexican Nyjah Huston and getting that Nike SB money."

The kid painted the same way he skated. The brushwork was confident, clear. The streaks and dabs made sense where they were and held your attention. There was a series of heads, misshapen, with haphazard rows of teeth. Another with angry marker cross-hatchings over brown faces. One said FOR MOM on it with the words crossed out, a mountain of angrily drawn tiny stick figures piled high with a series of interlocking rainbow hearts repeated over the image. What Bastian brought into the world commanded the space they occupied.

"Where do you get this stuff?" Some paintings were the size of shoe boxes, others taller than Bastian at six feet.

"I make the canvases," Bastian said, shrugging. He stared square into Sam's camera. "They're such a rip-off at the art stores. Plus, those snobby assholes hate when I come through. They follow you around like you're brown or something." He laughed.

"I rack most of my shit from hardware stores anyway," he said. "And you can steal wood from any of those big dumpsters when they're building new subdivisions but you gotta go early."

"This is my prized possession, though," he said. Sam followed him to the far wall. It was a silver and yellow circular saw.

"It's a miter saw," he said, pronouncing it "meter" saw. Sam didn't correct him. "For the frames." He pulled out a box of acrylic paints and showed it to the camera.

"Shout out to Ms. Mascari at Burnet Middle School!" he said. "She gives me these because she's in love with me." He smiled devilishly into Sam's phone.

"Why painting?" asked Sam, zooming in.

"The god Basquiat obviously," said Bastian. "He's legendary. Devin Troy Strother is the truth too. And Warhol. Man, that creepy old dude was the G.O.A.T. He wasn't even making his own work anymore and still got paid."

Then Bastian got serious for a second. "I hate Richard Prince though," he said. "He's a thief. And Jeff Koons is washed."

"Do you learn about this at school?" Sam asked.

"Nah," said Bastian. "Instagram."

Art was something Sam wished he knew more about. He felt too self-conscious to visit museums on his own and didn't know anyone who would want to go with him.

Sam walked backward into the middle of the room so he could capture as much of Bastian's paintings in the frame. This moment felt important. A story he'd be telling someone someday in the future when Bastian was known by everyone and no longer remembered him.

They walked outside and split a smoke.

Sam shot Bastian picking a fleck of tobacco off his tongue.

"What makes you think you of all people get to be an artist?" Sam asked, focusing in on Bastian's face.

Bastian exhaled a perfect circle of smoke. The kid was so famous already it was ridiculous.

He tilted his head.

"What kind of question is that? It's fucking art, man," he said, scowling. "You don't choose it. It chooses you. If you waste that chance, your talent dies. That's when you start dying along with it."

· · ·

"So he lets you hang out here?" Sam brought Bastian to House, where he promptly made himself very much at home. He was sprawled out on a sofa, with his feet up on the coffee table. "You bring girls back here and party with them and shit?"

"Nah." Sam kicked Bastian's filthy sneakers off the table. "I work here, man. You don't shit where you eat."

Bastian surveyed the premises. Sam had promised to make Bastian pancakes since that's what the movie's "talent" wanted.

"But you have keys so you can be here whenever you want?"
Sam nodded.

"It's cool that your boss trusts you." Bastian nodded toward
the fireplace. "That thing work?"

"Yeah," he said. "We crank it up around the holidays. It gets
pretty toasty."

Bastian walked over to inspect it. "Yo, that's cool," he said,
peering into the flue. "You could make s'mores and shit."

For his big talk about girls and his budding career as the
next Basquiat, Bastian was unmistakably still a kid.

Sam pulled out a folder and handed it to him. "I need your
mom to sign this," he said.

Bastian stared at it. "Yeah, whatever it is, she's not going to
do it."

"It's not anything crazy," he said. "It's a release 'cause you're
a minor."

Bastian took it and put it down on the coffee table.

"Luz doesn't sign stuff," Bastian said again. "She's an illegal.
I mean, a DREAMer or whatever."

"But she runs the juice stand," Sam said.

He knew about undocumented workers, only he never pictured Luz, someone who was the mommest-seeming mom
ever, being one. "And her English . . ."

Bastian rolled his eyes. "She's been here for over twenty years,
dumbass," he said. "You can't tell anyone. It's effed up, and every
day she's mad paranoid that someone's going to ask for her
papers."

To Sam it sounded like Germany in World War II.

"That's insane," Sam said. Still, he'd heard the news reports on ICE raids all over Texas but had never properly paid attention. He hadn't had to.

"Can't she apply for a green card since she's been here so long and you were born here?" Sam asked.

Bastian shook his head.

"Nah, she might as well try winning the lottery," he said. "And with everything that's going on, if she gets busted now and deported, then what happens to me?"

With the pity parties Sam threw himself on a weekly basis and the panic attack he had about being "almost" homeless and "almost" a dad, there was a woman and countless others like her with real problems.

"Can't you fake it?" Bastian asked. "Shit, I'll sign it."

"Don't worry about it," Sam said. "It's not that deep."

• • •

Sam had been on hold for thirty-six minutes when he realized it was that deep. Alamo Community College's film department was lax about everything except their beloved red tape.

"The releases for your subjects and the rights for your work need to accompany the submission. The department automatically enrolls you into a series of fellowships and festivals, along with . . ."

The lady on the phone kept talking about the department as if it were some ancient secret society with fanatical rules.

"So, let me get this straight, Lydia," he said. "Lydia, that's your name, right?"

"Yes," said Lydia. "That's right."

"So simply by turning in my project to get a grade I'm automatically enrolled in this other stuff?"

"Yes."

"What do you mean the rights for my work?"

"This is what I'm trying to tell you," said Lydia slowly. "You grant ACC and its affiliates the copyright in the work, and the department is granted the exclusive worldwide right in perpetuity to view, perform, display, distribute, stream, transmit, make available for download, rent, disseminate, issue or communicate copies to the public, telecast by air, cable, or otherwise import, adapt, enhance, show, translate, compile or otherwise use in any media and to adapt as a musical or a stage show."

"Wait," he interrupted. "A musical?"

"Yes," said Lydia. "A musical."

"If they turn my documentary about a fourteen-year-old Mexican kid living on the East Side painting pictures with his dirtbag friends into *Hamilton* or whatever, the department gets all the money?"

"The chance of that is slim to none," she said. "Lin-Manuel Miranda is a certifiable genius and you . . ." Lydia cleared her throat. "But yes, seeing as you've granted the department the copyright."

"And I don't have to sign anything," he said. "Just by turning in my project they get to do this."

"Well, turning in your project with the accompanying releases. It's very clear in the course curriculum. And as you know, your project is a large percentage of your grade, as determined by your professor, Dr. Lindstrom. I believe it's eighty percent," she said.

"Lydia, have you met Dr. Lindstrom?"

"Actually, no," she said.

"Well, neither have I," he said, and hung up.

There was no way Sam was going to risk Luz and Bastian's future for this. Screw the tuition. Besides which, musicals were the worst.

PENNY.

Penny was anxious about seeing Andy. He'd texted her after asking her out but she didn't know what to say. She didn't want to date him—that much she knew—but she realized that for the past week she'd been looking forward to class with nervous anticipation because he'd admitted to liking her. It was on the record and everything. She chose an extra-clean pair of black leggings and showed up ten minutes early.

He came in just before the bell and sat in the seat in front of her. Penny noticed he needed a haircut. A five-o'clock shadow crept south on his tanned neck. He was dressed in a white sweatshirt and matching white sweats and sneakers, and Penny couldn't believe how pristine it all was. He practically shone.

Penny thought about how next year she might never see him again and how future-her would be pissed off at present-day her for screwing the pooch right now.

She squinted forcefully at the back of Andy's neck. It was a good neck. His shoulders were killer too. Muscly but nothing that said vain or obsessive. As if he could sense her attention boring a hole at the base of his skull, Andy suddenly turned around.

Shit.

Penny bared her teeth in a rigid smile to indicate everything was perfectly fine. He turned back around and texted her.

Wait for me after class.

"Okay, Penny, am I making things bizarre or is it you?" They were standing on the edge of the quad lawn, though not far enough in that Andy would stain his shoes on the grass. "It's probably you," he said.

"It's probably me," Penny agreed, and suddenly needed a nap. It was astounding the ways in which her body reacted to confrontation.

"It's not that big a deal, you know." Andy pulled a matte black cylinder out of his book bag, twisted the top off, and out slid a pair of sunglasses. He put them on. Penny was immediately struck by the competitive advantage of people not being able to see your eyes in a fight. Not that this was a fight. Or maybe it was. Penny had no idea. She made an awning with her hands and squinted up at him.

"Okay, so what's the protocol now?" she asked.

"Protocol?" Andy laughed. "Well, I think we still hold value for each other in our roles as cronies. Colleagues. Writerly peers."

This was news to Penny. Positive news.

"So we can still collaborate and talk about work?"

He nodded. Penny was elated. "Because I need your help on act two," she said. "It's a mess logistically and there are certain inconsistencies I can't reconcile, and I made a spreadsheet the way you told me except then I read this thing about how your narrative should be a snowflake and I'm not that good at math."

"Ugh, loser. Okay, send it to me," he said. "I'll have it back to you by the weekend, but you have to help me with my dialogue. I'm holding your pages hostage until you get mine back."

Penny duffed him on the arm as she imagined a pal would. "I love the protocol!" she said.

"Great," he said, socking her back lightly. "This is probably for the best anyway. You're so strange."

Penny practically skipped home.

When she got back to her room from class, she was stoked to find Jude reading a magazine and eating goldfish.

"Suup, slut," she said before turning back to flip through the pages.

"Do you want to go do something?" Penny said, sitting on Jude's bed. Penny was still high from her talk with Andy. She was batting a thousand when it came to friendship. "I'll drive."

Jude studied her face. "Really?"

Penny nodded and smiled wide.

"What, did you and your secret boyfriend break up or something?" asked Jude.

Penny kept her smile in place and barreled on. "Going once, going twice . . . ," she said.

"Just kidding, yes." Jude sprang into action and tossed her magazine aside. "I'm dying of boredom and have to read *The*

Communist Manifesto by tomorrow and yeah, no. Why isn't there an animated movie version?"

Penny shrugged.

"We gotta get Mal too," she said.

They swung by Twombly. "Where are we going?" asked Mallory, jumping in the back. It was such a new dynamic, to have Penny in charge of the night for once.

"I want to see the ocean," Penny announced.

"Yay!" the girls chorused. Penny felt as if she could've suggested anything from the zoo to the airport and they would've been game.

The closest beach was three and a half hours away, but Penny was hell-bent on making it to Galveston in under three. Jude was responsible for the music and directions. Mallory was responsible for making them stop every half hour so she could pee. The girl had the smallest bladder in the world.

"Penny, I haven't seen you in one thousand years." Mallory handed her a Red Vine. The only benefit to stopping every thirty miles was the snack haul remained bountiful. "That party was so fun."

"Yeah," said Jude. "Speaking of which, what's up with Andy? He's so hot."

By dusk they'd made it to the halfway point, where there was a glowing power plant up ahead. It was beautiful, like a space station on the cover of a sci-fi paperback from the seventies.

"Seriously, what or who have you been doing?" Mallory poked Penny's cheek with the wet end of her Vine.

"Stop," yawped Penny. Mallory cackled. "Nothing. And yeah, Andy's great. He's helping me with my project."

PENNY ::: 3 | 7

"I wish he'd help me with my project," retorted Jude, and they laughed.

"I'm up to my eyeballs in homework and ignoring my mother," said Penny. "Same as everyone."

"Oh!" said Jude, swatting Penny's arm. "Your mom friend requested me on Facebook."

"Shut up." Penny groaned.

"Yuck!" exclaimed Mallory. "That's such a violation. You didn't accept, did you?"

"No," said Jude. "I mean, Celeste is adorable but, yeah, no way. Obvious violation. She did it literally the night we hung out."

Penny felt her cheeks redden. "Did I tell you she sent Mark, as in my ex-boyfriend Mark, a message after we broke up?"

"Whaaaaaaaaaaaaat?!"

"Not only that." Penny got worked up again. "But she went on a full lurk and told me he was dating someone new. Why would you tell your daughter that?"

"That's egregious," Mallory confirmed.

Jude patted her shoulder in sympathy. "Completely egregious."

"I mean, your mom's cool, but sometimes I can't tell if a cool mom is better than a completely out-of-touch Stepford Wife mom like mine," said Jude. "At least Nicole isn't thirsty."

"Well, she's obviously not hungry," agreed Mallory. "I'm pretty sure the only food Nicole eats is Ativan."

"I love my mom." Mallory rummaged in her shopping bag for a bottle of Big Red. "She's completely out to lunch, like all moms. I don't know, though. At some point in high school we became friends. The thing is, P, you can't ignore them."

Penny couldn't believe that the craziest girl in the car probably had the healthiest relationship with her mother.

"Moms are like cows," Mallory said. Jude shot a glance at Penny. This was going to be good. "You've got to milk them or they lose their minds."

Mallory leaned into the front of the car so the girls could feel the full weight of her wise words.

"They're shoplifting teens," she pressed.

"Wait, I thought they were cows," Jude said. Penny couldn't meet her eyes for fear of a giggle fit.

"They're both. However, they're more shoplifting teens because it's not about the intention. It's about the *at*-tention."

That did Jude in. She cackled boisterously.

"What are you talking about?"

"Wait, I actually think I know what you're getting at, Mal," said Penny. "You're saying that ignoring my mom isn't the right way to go because her cow milk or need for attention or whatever gets insane and she'll burst or do something stupid. But if I pay consistent attention to her, she'll chill the F out."

"Exactly," said Mallory, leaning back into her seat satisfied.

There were worse theories.

"But what if your mom is the most annoying human in the universe?" asked Penny.

"Dude." Jude knew the answer to this one. "Every mom is the most annoying human in the universe, but most of them, besides the super-abusive genuinely bad ones, are in your corner."

"You know what I do that helps?" Apparently Mallory wasn't done dispensing gems. "I imagine how my mom would feel if she could overhear the mean shit I said about her. It makes me say way less mean shit, which makes me *think* way less mean shit. It works."

Penny's heart sank. It would destroy Celeste to know how she felt about her and what she'd been keeping from her. Pushing her away was Penny's way of protecting her. Of protecting them both.

"Okay," said Mallory, interrupting her thoughts. "Enough about moms. We're going to play a game. We're going to go around in a circle and ask questions and answer them truthfully."

"So, truth or *truth*?" asked Penny.

"Yeah," said Jude. "Although I already know everything about Mal because she and I are the oversharing queens of the universe."

"How very dare you!" said Mallory in mock outrage. "Though in the spirit of full disclosure: Everyone may as well know that I have a UTI and am drinking boatloads of cranberry juice because of the sheer volume of sex I had this past week. Hence my current rate of peeing."

"Wait, I thought Ben left," said Jude.

"He did," replied Mallory. "That's why it's a particularly sordid truth."

"*J'accuse!*" exclaimed Jude.

"Okay, me first," said Jude, flipping on the dome light so the car resembled an interrogation room. "Penny," she boomed in a TV-announcer voice, "did you or did you not recently sleep with someone who is responsible for giving you that radiant, highly irritating glow?"

That was easy. "No," she said.

"I'm dubious," said Mallory. Penny glanced at Mallory in the rearview.

"I'm a bad liar," Penny told her.

"That's true," confirmed Jude. "And it's not Andy?"

Penny smiled.

"It *is* Andy!" Jude swatted her arm.

Penny wiped the grin off her face. "It isn't. I promise!"

"My turn," said Mallory.

"Wait, isn't it *my* turn?" asked Penny. She wondered if this was a thinly veiled attempt to ask her a series of deeply invasive questions.

"You'll go right after," said Mallory. "Besides, this question is for Jude."

"I'm ready," said Jude, turning to her bestie.

"In a parallel universe in which the practice wasn't frowned upon and utterly Appalachian, would you or would you not have sex with Uncle Sam?"

Penny's stomach lurched.

"Eeeeeeeeew," screamed Jude. "Mallory, why are you such a perv?"

"I take it that's a no?" said Mallory, grinning evilly.

"No!" said Jude.

"I'm sorry," said Mallory, still smiling. "I just couldn't stop leching on him this morning. He was making matcha with this little whisk and he looked so deliciously annoyed. You do acknowledge that he's hot though, like, objectively?" asked Mallory. "Because I would bang the ever-living shit out of him if he'd give me the time of day."

Mal cracked open a bag of chips.

"Back me up, Penny. Sam's hot," said Mallory in between crunches.

"He's a type," Penny agreed. "Great hair."

"Ew, no, guys," said Jude. "And, Mal, don't forget you're promise-bound on pain of death, no banging."

"I know," said Mal. "This is a hypothetical."

"Also, come on. I know he's technically not my uncle anymore, but I think of him as a brother. You wouldn't be allowed to bang my brother either, Mallory. You'd demolish him."

Mallory sighed. "It's true, I am a man-eater."

"Okay, my turn," said Penny, desperate to change the subject. "You guys are going to make fun of me."

"Probably," said Jude, reaching back to grab Mallory's chips. She offered some to Penny, who shook her head. She felt as though she was constantly telling her no.

"Why do you guys want to know anything about me?" she asked.

The car went silent. And then Mallory started laughing. Jude joined in.

"How are you so awkward?" asked Mallory.

"Friends tell each other things, dummy," said Jude. "And cello? We're friends."

"Why though?"

"Oh my God, Penny. Stop being so emo. Are you going to make us talk about feelings?" asked Mallory. "Seriously, you are so homeschooled sometimes."

"Wait, what do you mean?" asked Jude. "You actually don't know why anyone would like you?"

"Yeah," said Penny. "Genuine question. You guys are this

official thing. You're a unit. But you keep asking me to do stuff even though I know I'm boring compared to you, and I want to know why."

Mallory switched off the interior car light.

"Okay." Mallory took a deep breath. "At the beginning I only liked you as much as you liked me, which wasn't very much."

That made sense.

"But then I felt bad for my dear friend Jude, who had to live with you." Mallory laughed.

"And I've always liked you," said Jude. "You're mysterious. You're the hella metal dude in high school who's sexy even though he sneers and doesn't talk to anyone."

"But now I enjoy your company because you're smart," said Mallory. "And dark. You *do* seem seriously tormented."

"And you're a good egg," said Jude simply.

Penny crumpled inwardly when Jude said that. She wasn't a good egg. Penny didn't have to tell Jude everything, that she was desperately, hopelessly in love with Sam, but she should have told her they were friends. Penny knew it would hurt Jude to have been kept in the dark this long.

"Oh my God, can you guys smell that?" Mallory rolled down her windows. Penny could hear the waves crashing in the dark. The moonlight turned everything blue.

They got out of the car and stretched. The salt air was sticky.

"Do you have towels?" asked Jude, kicking off her shoes.

Penny nodded. Mallory laughed. "Of course you do."

"You're going actual swimming?" Penny asked. "Now?"

"You're not?" Jude said incredulously. "It was your idea to

come to the beach." She stepped out of her shorts. Penny handed her a towel.

"I wanted to see the water," she said. "To be near it." It hadn't occurred to her that anyone would go in.

Jude shrugged and ran to the water, whooping before diving in. Mallory watched her, looked back at Penny, and offered her a chip.

Penny took a handful. "Are *you* swimming?"

"Oh, hell no," said Mallory. "I only dip my toes in chlorinated water."

They could barely make Jude out in the waves.

Mallory hopped up onto Penny's trunk, and Penny climbed up next to her. She felt Mallory shiver slightly in the dark.

"Cold?"

"A little."

Penny grabbed her hoodie from the front seat, pulled her phone out of the pocket, and handed the sweatshirt to her. They huddled closer.

She thought about how with Mallory everything was even steven. Affection, loyalty, even laughing at jokes. Jude was different. Penny could see now why they were so close. Mallory was tougher and looked out for her. They were a good team.

They faced the water, feeling the breeze and listening to the roar of the tide.

"Isn't it appalling that she's friends with us?" Mallory asked.

Penny was strangely flattered to be a part of Mallory's "us."

"She's so nice," said Mallory. "*Decent,* you know?"

"Yeah," said Penny. "If there were an apocalypse tomorrow, she'd be out in the first wave. It wouldn't matter how fast or strong she was. Her heart wouldn't be able to take it."

Mallory bumped her shoulder with her own. "I *love* how this is where your brain goes," she said. "I know what you mean though. God, can you imagine? She'd probably die trying to save a bus full of orphans."

"Why would anybody save children during the apocalypse?" said Penny.

"For anything other than food? No idea."

Penny smiled in the dark.

Mallory took her hair down from a bun and shook it out. The wind was balmy on Penny's face. She was glad they'd come. After a moment she shook her hair out too. "I love the ocean."

"We're going to have the best beachy waves." Mallory scrunched her hair and pulled out her phone. "Get in this with me."

The first shot with the flash was awful. Straight up the nose with both of them resembling startled possums.

"Oh my God." Mallory laughed, deleting it. "Tragic."

Penny switched on the flashlight of her phone and illuminated them from an angle.

"No flash, only mood lighting," said Penny.

"Ooooh, you *are* resourceful," said Mallory. "I would eat you *last* in the apocalypse."

They tried another. Better.

"Okay," said Mallory, repositioning Penny's hand and tugging at her arm. "Wait, seriously, is this as far as you go? What are you, some kind of midget T. rex?"

Penny laughed. When Mallory made fun of you in this way you felt like the only person in the world.

"Here, let's switch." Mallory became the flashlight as Penny shot.

"So much better," said Mallory as Penny swiped through the options. In fact, they were the best selfies Penny had ever taken. They were two giggly girls with great big hair doing irrepressibly fun things. Even without the pictures, Penny would remember this night for a long time.

"See," said Mallory. "Look how good you look when you tilt your chin down like that?"

"Oh my God, it's sooooooo cold!" Jude breathlessly ran toward them. "I knew it was gonna be a bitch when I got out."

Mallory flashed the phone light toward her. She was shivering in her underwear.

"What happened to the towel I gave you?" asked Penny.

Jude's eyes widened. "Oh shit," she said, turning back toward the beach.

"Don't worry. Penny has an extra," said Mallory, hopping off the trunk.

"You do?"

Penny reached into the trunk for the other one and handed it to her.

"I kneeeeeeew it!" Mallory clapped her hands triumphantly. "Oh my God, you're so predictable!"

"That's my last though!" Penny exclaimed. It required heroic restraint not to make Jude go back and hunt for its mate.

"Wait, I want a selfie too," said Jude, reaching for her phone. "Give me. I want to check my face."

Penny handed it over.

"Oh my God," said Jude, pawing through her hair help-lessly. "Drowned rat much?"

"First wave of the apocalypse," muttered Mallory.

"Seriously," Penny said, cheesing.

"Look at you two all buddy-buddy," said Jude, eyeing them.

Just then Penny's phone pinged in Jude's hand.

"Penny, you have to change your ringtone," said Mallory. "I have, like, PTSD from Apex. It's been my alarm all year. What psychopath uses Apex as their ringtone? It's such an alarm."

"What?" said Penny, reaching for her phone. "No way. Apex is way too quiet for that."

Apex kept going off in Jude's hands.

Jude's face was lit up. Then she held the phone out so the other girls could see.

Penny snatched the phone, but the damage had been done. She'd seen.

Jude knew.

SAM HOUSE

Today 9:11 PM

Yoyoyoyoyoyoyoyoyooyoyoyyoyoyoyo
Come by
I baked a SHEETCAKE
Your favorite
Confetti emoji

He'd written out "confetti emoji" since he was trying to quit using emoji because he thought they were "emotionally lazy."

"Uh," said Mallory quietly. "What psycho sets their texts to preview mode?"

Penny grabbed her phone and shoved it into her pocket, plunging the girls into darkness.

Penny weighed her options.

Available means to ejector seat from crippling social trauma:
1. Jump into the car, lock the doors, race home, transfer schools before they return.
2. Lie her lying face off.
3. Just tell them everything. It was a simple (very long) misunderstanding.

Penny wondered if this canceled everything out, if them seeing the texts meant they weren't friends anymore. Penny felt like her throat was closing. There was no escape. She felt nauseous. The waves thundered in her ears.

"Jude," she said quietly. It was barely audible above the din. Penny wished she could sit down. Her heart was racing. "I'm sorry."

"Wait," said Jude. "Sam House, that's Uncle Sam, right?"

Penny nodded.

There were rapid-fire questions of increasing volume.

"Uncle Sam is your secret Internet boyfriend?"

"No! Not exactly."

"Are you guys dating?"

"We're just friends."

"Well, then, why wouldn't you say something?"

Penny couldn't tell her that Sam didn't want her to. It would only make things worse.

"Were you hanging out this whole time while he was avoiding me?"

"No. We just text. We don't hang out. . . . Okay, we've hung out once. Twice, technically . . ."

"Jesus, Penny," Jude said. "He's the guy, right? The guy you're into?"

Silence.

And from Mallory:

"Why sheet cake though?"

"I told him it was my favorite. . . ."

For some reason the cake part seemed to piss Jude off the most. Mallory stood beside her with her arms crossed. Strangely, Mallory seemed more perplexed than mad, though there was no question whose side she was on.

"I'm sorry," said Penny. She meant it.

They rode home in silence. This time Penny didn't feel sleepy at all.

SAM.

11:02 PM

Where'd you go?
You ok?
Cake was bomb
Saved you some

11:49 PM

Hey
Can't talk

11:51 PM

Sure thing

What happened?
Momstuff?

12:41 AM

LMK if you need anything

PENNY.

The downside to Jude being chipper and easygoing was that when she had it out for you, you felt it. By day two of Jude giving her the silent treatment, Penny was distraught. As soon as Penny entered their room, Jude glared at her, cranked up her speakers, and turned away. Often she blasted god-awful dubstep mash-ups neither of them liked, which is how Penny knew Jude really had it out for her.

When Penny left a banana on her desk as an offering, Jude rejected it. She refused it by putting it on Penny's work chair, so when Penny went to write, she sat on it. As tiny passive-aggressive revenges went, it was adorable, and it killed Penny that they couldn't laugh about it.

Penny hit up her mom that afternoon. She'd been dreading texting Celeste, but she had to bite the bullet.

I'm so sorry

I won't make it tonight
I'm slammed with my creative
writing final
Need to write 3K words by Monday
Will make it up to you
Happy birthday!!!

Celeste would barely notice Penny wasn't there. Last she checked on Facebook, the sit-down dinner had transformed to a cocktail fiesta with forty-five guests and a norteño ensemble, Los Chingones, that took requests for live-band karaoke. Live. Band. Karaoke. There was no way.

Sam texted:

She blew me off for lunch

Jude wasn't talking to him either.

I called her.

And?

Nothing.

She's so mad
Living in the same room
Is the worst

Celeste called.

Penny guiltily sent it to voicemail.

I screwed up big, huh?

Ugh I knew we should tell her

The super-shameful part was that Jude's rancor and Penny's guilt had the unforeseen advantage of helping her write. Penny spent the next few hours consumed by her story and by 11:30 p.m. had completed whole new passages to send J.A. for her office hours the next day. When Jude walked in, Penny was startled out of her trance.

"Oh," said Penny weakly. "Hey."

Jude rolled her eyes. "Why aren't you going home?" said Jude. She grabbed clean clothes and angrily packed them into a bag. "I accepted your mother's friend request."

Jude's stabs at vengeance continued to be the best.

"Jude," Penny begged. "Please talk to me. I know I should have told you. It wasn't on purpose and nothing crazy happened. We're friends. It wasn't planned and then we didn't know when to . . ."

"Oh, so you're a 'we' now."

"Jude, I'm sorry," Penny said. "It's a misunderstanding. . . ." Penny pleaded. "It's not a big deal if you would let me explain."

"I know it's not a big deal to you," said Jude, slamming a drawer. "I know intellectually that you're allowed to be friends with whoever you want. Same goes for Sam. Which is why I don't get it. If you're just friends, if it's no big deal, why go through all this trouble of hiding it from me? It's like you're just shady to be shady, and I hate that."

She zipped her bag up. "You know, I made such an effort to be nice to both of you," she said. "I invited you guys to lunch, dinner, movies. Would it have killed you to include me in your plans? You're both *from* here. Other than Mallory, I don't *know* anyone. Do you know what that feels like? God, you must've thought I was so annoying. That I couldn't take a hint."

Penny's heart sank as Jude shouldered her bag.

Jude was right. Of course she was right.

"You know, you do this to everyone," Jude said, swinging open the door. "You do this to your mom. You do it to me. Mallory, too, even if you don't care about her. . . . You shut people out with no explanation. It's so rude and mean. And for what? For a guy who you know doesn't even like you like that?"

Penny blanched. Spoken out loud, Penny's actions sounded pathetic even to her own ears.

"I make a good friend, Penny," Jude said. "You didn't even give me a chance."

Penny's phone rang. She glanced down at it as a reflex.

"Christ," fumed Jude. She slammed the door behind her.

The number was a 210 area code. Knowing Celeste, she was drunk-dialing her, thinking she was slick by using a friend's phone. Either that or she lost her purse. Again.

Penny answered.

"Hello?" A man's voice.

"Hello?" Penny bolted upright.

"Hi. Is this Penelope?" Penny's heart leapt into her throat.

"Yeah," she said. "Is everything okay?"

She imagined Celeste dead in a ditch.

"Penny, this is your mom's friend Michael."

She tasted acid. "Is it my mom? Is she okay?"

She pictured twisted metal, deranged gunmen, torch-wielding neo-Nazis. . . .

"I'm with your mom," the voice said. "She's fine. We're at Metropolitan Methodist. . . ."

Penny's head cracked wide open and all she heard were the lambs screaming.

The hospital.

"I'm coming right now," she said.

"Good, good," he stammered. "She's fine but . . . um, okay. I'll be here."

Penny did not know a Michael among Celeste's fiends. Her mother had a rotating cast of besties, though Penny didn't have their numbers. Truth was, she was her mom's emergency contact, and despite that fact, Penny hadn't been there for her. Penny stared at her phone. She couldn't feel her face, and a wave of nausea engulfed her. Okay, she couldn't call Jude. Mallory was Jude's friend, so that was out. She called Sam.

SAM.

Sam ran to Kincaid with his backpack. He didn't know why he'd brought it, only that they were going somewhere and that Penny appreciated supplies. He'd packed water, a Tupperware container of leftover sheet cake, spoons, an extra sweatshirt, and a hard-case first-aid kit that Al kept in the kitchen. Penny had said nothing of where they were going, though she'd been unnervingly subdued on the phone. Robotic in a way that was worrisome.

All he knew was that it had to do with her mom. Sam wondered how Penny would cope if Celeste died. As much as Penny complained about her, she would probably fall to pieces if something bad happened.

Sam remembered one of their earliest conversations about Penny's mom.

EMERGENCY PENNY

Oct 5, 2:14 PM

I bet I'm bad at death

*As in you suck at it therefore you're
invincible?*

*No bad at processing it
Nobody I've been close to died*

*Lucky
I'm great at death*

In tenth grade the uncle Sam was closest to died of cancer, the same summer two of his friends were killed in a drunk-driving accident.

*Sometimes I watch my mother sleep
and pretend she's dead
I cry and cry and cry
because I love her so much
but also don't want her to know*

He'd thought about Brandi Rose and what he'd do if she died.

I'd be all alone if she was gone

Penny was waiting for him downstairs when he arrived. Her hair was extra big. Penny threw a crumpled twenty-dollar bill at him and it bounced off his chest and fell to the floor. She was wild-eyed.

"For gas," she said. He picked it up and stuffed it in his back pocket as he followed her to the lot across the street.

"Thank you," Penny said, handing over the keys. "I'm shaking too much to drive. I'm sorry."

"Don't apologize," he said, and let her in.

"My mom gave me this car. It's her car," she said, strapping into shotgun. "Did I wake you up?"

"Nope." He adjusted his seat and mirrors and headed toward the highway.

"You know it's her birthday?" Penny's voice bordered on hysterical. Sam kept his attention on the road, but he wanted to keep her talking.

"Yeah, I do. Her fortieth."

"I mean, technically her birthday isn't until tomorrow." Penny glanced down at the time and burst into ragged sobs. "It's midnight."

It was 12:02.

"Do you have Kleenex?" she asked after a moment. "I forgot my sundries."

"Sundries" made Sam smile. He handed her the backpack.

"There's a black bandana in there," he said.

Penny pulled out a spoon.

"For cake," he said. Penny nodded as if that made perfect sense. Sam reached over and rummaged until his fingers found cloth. He handed it to her.

"You should have dedicated cases for things," she said.

Sam nodded.

"I'm going to wash this and give it back," she added, blowing her nose.

"Penny," he said, keeping his eyes ahead. "Is your mom okay?"

"Yeah," she said. "I think so. I didn't ask any of the right questions to Michael."

"Who's Michael?"

"I don't know," she said. "Some guy."

"Penny, why didn't you go to your mom's birthday?" As far as he knew she'd been planning on it.

"I can't be around her."

She turned toward him. "Oh God, that's horrible. How could I say that right now? What if something really bad happened? What do you think happened?"

Sam shook his head ruefully. "I don't know."

"You know what's so dumb?" said Penny quietly, sniffling. "And I know it wouldn't fix everything, but I wish I had a dad. Bet a dad would know what happened."

"You'd be surprised," said Sam, thinking about his own.

"God, remember when you were almost a dad?" she asked.

Sam smiled. "I might remember something about losing my mind on a daily basis for a few weeks, yeah."

"I think you would have been a good dad," she said.

Sam's left eye misted over. "Yeah?" He swallowed.

"Yeah," she said. "You'd be fun when you weren't being the most depressing."

"And selfish," he reminded her.

"Yeah," she said. "And fainting. You'd be screwed if you had a daughter though. You'd be wrapped so firmly around that kid's little finger."

"Yeah, exactly where a dad should be. Holding a firearm and warding off potential suitors until that daughter is of consenting age," he said. "Which in my book is about forty-six."

Penny laughed.

Sam's mind turned to Bobby. If Penny ever told him the guy's full name Sam would hunt him down and string him up by his balls.

"When did you start being so mad at your mom?"

"Ugh, she's so not a mom." Even in her anguish, Penny couldn't keep the frustration out of her tone. "You know one time I ate it on a bike," she said. "Just scraped my entire face down the street. My whole face was hamburger meat with an eyeball stuck on, and instead of going home, I walked a block to my neighbor's house."

Sam nodded. Stories never started or ended where you'd think they would with Penny, but it was important to listen for when it came together.

"You know why? Because Celeste can't handle blood. In that moment, I knew better than to go home. I rang the doorbell next door and passed out when they answered. I figured that my chances were better off with anyone else's mom than my own. I was six."

So that's where her eyebrow scar came from. They drove in silence for a few more dark miles. Parenting as a concept was wild. Everybody was winging it.

"You know, I didn't have a bike," he said after a while. "I was so poor my bike was an old bean can that I kicked down a dirt path just so I could have some fun getting from point A to B."

"What?" Penny croaked, eyes wet.

"It didn't get me there any faster, but that's how it was," Sam said soberly. "You know what else? I didn't even get to eat the beans out of it. It was a hand-me-down can of legumes."

Penny laughed. It was a sad, snot-filled honk.

"So, cry me a river, Penny Lee," he said.

"It's true," she said. "I don't know your *journey*."

"Or my struggles."

"True."

"Real quick," he said. "I'm headed south, but I have no idea where we're going."

Penny handed him her phone with the map. They still had forty more exits to go.

"You know, she's supposed to be the one taking care of me," Penny said. "That should be the basic qualification of being a parent."

"I get that," said Sam. "But sometimes it's so incidental that these people are the parents. Beyond the biology of it. It's not as if they had to pass a test or unlock achievements to be the ones making the decisions. Sometimes they're actually stupid. Certifiably dumber than you, but as their kid you'd never think to know that."

Sam thought about how scant his own qualifications had been.

They stopped for gas, arriving at the hospital an hour later. Sam drove into the covered visitors parking lot, killed the engine, and awaited further instructions.

"Do you mind waiting out here?" Penny asked.

"Not at all."

Sam was relieved he wouldn't have to deal with whatever family drama was awaiting her. Though he would've joined her if she'd asked.

Before she hopped out she hugged him. "Thanks," she said, and kissed him on the cheek. Her nose was wet. It was very cute and completely beside the point.

Sam watched as she jog-hopped through the sliding glass doors.

He missed her the second she fell out of view.

PENNY.

The hospital smelled of hospital. The bite of ammonia that was so sharp you immediately wondered what odors it was masking. Penny's eyes darted around the intake area for someone to talk to.

"Penelope?" A thickset, handsome Mexican dude in ostrich-leather cowboy boots walked toward her purposefully.

"Yeah?"

He stretched out his hand. "Michael," he said. His face was marred with acne scars but it only added to his rugged appeal. "I recognized you from the picture on your mom's desk. They wouldn't let me go up with her because I'm not family."

"So she's not dead?"

"No. God no."

"Is she hurt?"

"No, not exactly."

Penny shook her head violently. She needed information way faster than he was dispensing it.

"We had dinner. The band was excellent. It was time for dessert, you know coffee, cake, sopaipillas. It was that new Tex-Mex place downtown with the murals. . . ."

"Okay," Penny said, trying not to throttle him. "You're too slow and inefficient. Did she get food poisoning?"

Michael shook his head.

"Was there a car accident?"

He shook his head again.

"Is she drunk?"

"No," he said, and cleared his throat. "She ate a weed brownie."

Penny couldn't believe it. "What? Are you kidding?" she seethed.

Michael glanced around nervously.

"What are you guys, like, twelve?"

"She'd never had them before," he whispered. "And she ate a whole one, and then everyone was dancing so she forgot and ate another part when we all told her you were only supposed to eat, I don't know, a quarter or an eighth."

"Are *you* high?" asked Penny.

"No," said Michael, insulted. "I don't do drugs. Nor would I ever drive under the influence. I just snuck her out because she was panicking, and I brought her straight here."

"Okay." Penny breathed. "So she's not in surgery. She didn't have a horrific accident. She's not poisoned or dead. She's just exceptionally stupid and immature even though it's her fortieth fucking birthday."

Penny felt bad about cursing at a stranger except that the power dynamic here was clear. Michael and Celeste were in big, big trouble.

"I thought you should know," he reasoned. "If it was my mom I would want to know."

Penny was certain Michael's mom wasn't nearly as harebrained and melodramatic.

"Also, your mother and I are dating," he said. "I don't know if that's appropriate for me to say."

"How old are you?" she asked. Penny would've guessed twenty-five.

"Thirty-two. How old are you?" he asked.

"Eighteen," she said. "Are you married?"

"No!"

"Okay, well, it's nice to meet you," she said begrudgingly. And then, because there was nothing else to do for it, they shook hands. His palms were calloused.

"You too. Circumstances notwithstanding," he said solicitously. "I hope I did the right thing."

Penny rolled her eyes and sighed. "You did," she said. "Thank you."

"She insisted someone tell you not to come to the restaurant."

"Okay," said Penny. "Thanks."

She checked in with the receptionist, a short black woman with freckles even on her lips.

"Can you tell me the status on Celeste Yoon? I'm her daughter."

The nurse checked her computer.

"We're observing her," she said. "She's on the third floor, and she's fine. We won't be keeping her overnight. In fact, we're wrapping up paperwork right now, and she'll be discharged shortly."

"Thank you," she said, walking back to Michael.

"She'll be down soon," she told her mom's boyfriend. He exhaled audibly.

"I'm going back to school."

"You're not staying?" he asked. "I'm sure she'd want to see you."

"Nope," said Penny. "I'm all set." Penny wasn't interested in wasting any more of her time in this fantasyland of headassery, where the adults were large babies.

When Penny got back to her car, Sam wasn't in it.

Honestly, it was like herding cats with these people.

Sam popped out of the shadows. "Sorry," he said. "I had to pee." He looked mortified.

Penny started laughing. Her anger dissipated at the thought of Sam waiting in the car, executing complicated equations of whether or not he should go inside the hospital to pee. Or pee his pants. Or pee in a darkened patch of parking lot. It had probably taken him a good ten minutes to figure it out. The image was hysterical, and once Penny got going she couldn't stop. The stress of the past few days, between Jude's rage and her frustration at Celeste and the relief of her *not* being dead was too much. Penny gasped as her body shook with laughter, eyes streaming.

Sam watched her like she was nuts.

SAM.

He couldn't wait to go to sleep.

The drive took three hours round-trip and when he turned onto Penny's street, she touched the back of his hand.

"Can we go to your house?" she asked.

Sam looked at her questioningly.

"Jude," she reminded him.

He nodded and headed for House. They only had a few hours before Sam had to get up for work.

The two of them trudged up the porch stairs at a glacial pace. Sam turned on his lamp and sat on his mattress. He undid the laces of his left boot and then his right, feeling as though he were performing a slow, tame striptease.

Penny yawned as she sat beside him and took off her high-tops. She was wearing frilly white socks with embroidered strawberries on them and cartoon squirrels on the heels.

They both stared down at them.

"I forgot," she said. "These are secret socks."

Sam thought about the secret sides of girls and how much he loved them.

"Do you want the bed and I can take the floor?" He'd have to give her his only pillow.

"I don't want to kick you off your own bed."

"Do you want a glass of water or anything?" he asked her.

She nodded. Sam figured she could sort out where she wanted to sleep while he fetched it.

When he returned, she was under the covers on the side closest to the wall. She'd left him his pillow on the outer side.

"Is this okay?" she asked, sitting up to drink the water.

He nodded and got under the covers. Since she was fully dressed he kept his clothes on too.

He turned off the lamp. "I've been meaning to ask you," he said groggily.

"Hmm?"

"How do you think I should decorate?"

"Good question," she murmured. "I know how disappointed I was that there wasn't a giant black-light swastika above your bed. I thought I knew you."

Sam smiled. They were quiet for a while and he drifted.

"Maybe a velvet painting of Juggalos," she said, waking him up.

They both lay there with their eyes closed, smiling into the dark.

"Is your mom okay?" he asked.

"Yeah," she said. "Except that she's dumb."

"Everything's such a mess," he said.

"Yeah," and then, "we should have told Jude."

"Oh, completely. It's so stupid but I didn't want her to know how wrecked my life was," he said. "I wanted her to think I was a grown-up with his shit together."

Sam felt Penny's hand shift under the blanket so it was a few inches away from his. He nudged his over to where the backs of their hands touched.

Penny's fingers wrapped around his protectively. "Nobody thinks you've got your shit together," she said, squeezing.

Her hand felt hot and soft. The entire right side of his body became agonizingly aware of how close the entire left side of her body was to it.

"You know her dad is this big-shot lawyer."

"What's that got to do with anything?"

He thought about it.

"I don't know. It's just a hang-up but he was the first person I knew who'd gone to grad school."

Sam thought about the eighty bucks Jude's dad had left on his bed. That he'd left him for services rendered. Like a babysitter.

"His law firm had this scholarship every year, and one time Mr. Lange, Jude's grandfather, said I'd be a shoo-in. I never believed anything that bastard ever told me but for some reason I held on to that one. I thought maybe he'd put in a good word," he said. "Like out of guilt or something. For the way he treated us."

Sam remembered the humiliation. He'd filled out the paperwork and written a cover letter about his plans and goals and sent it off. He'd never heard back. It was a need-based grant, and Drew of all people knew how much Sam needed it.

"Anyway, they never responded and that was fine, but then Jude shows up out of nowhere saying she wants to come to UT."

Sam felt Penny shift toward him.

"Why did you bail on her so much?"

"That's a good question," he said.

"I mean, your resentment toward her family had to have gotten shrapnel on her, right?"

"No way," he said, knowing he was lying as he said it. There was no way of divorcing his feelings about Jude's dad and grandfather entirely. Plain fact was Sam wished he'd never met them. Them or their worthless gifts. Once he'd tried to pawn the DVD player Mr. Lange had bought to get their gas turned back on. Only Brandi Rose had slapped him across the face, threatening to call the cops on him for stealing.

As Brandi Rose fell apart Sam had to grow up. Fast. It would have been easier to forget if it hadn't been for Jude and her constant entreaties for friendship. She'd cheerfully muscled into his life before he'd had a chance to sort out his feelings. Except he'd articulated none of this to her. There was no way she could have known.

"I should have told her I felt weird about her coming here," he said. "But it felt stupid to make a big deal out of it. And it's not as if I don't like her. We're friends."

"Well, at least part of you is holding a grudge."

It was true. When she'd actually shown up, Sam's instinct was to retreat.

"Smart," he professed.

He tilted his head so he could get a look at Penny. There was just enough light from the window that he could make out the sheen of her open eyes. She blinked. Sam held his breath.

Talking to her like this felt similar to the interface. Except now the proximity felt like a dream. His heart jackhammered like crazy.

"Even so," she said. "You're the best person I've ever met. And my favorite."

"And you're mine," he said.

Penny leaned over and hugged him. Sam knew this was it. If he'd ever had a shot at kissing her, it was now. Even with their horrible night. And their friendship pact. Sam was her favorite person. Not that kid from her class or her stupid ex-boyfriend. Nobody else. Penny pressed her cheek against his chest and sighed. He knew that if he turned his body to the side and scooched down a little, his mouth would be in the neighborhood of hers. Sam felt her head get heavy. Her breathing slowed. One of her feet made little circles on the surface of the mattress similar to when cats make biscuits with their claws, and then it stilled. She was out. Sam shifted his waist away from her slightly, carefully, so nothing horrifying would happen, like getting a boner in the middle of the night. He listened to Penny breathe. Within moments he crashed too.

He heard the garbage trucks first. Some mornings it was like the trash guys were hurling them at each other. When he opened his eyes, he caught Penny staring at him.

Sam covered his mouth with the back of his hand to best conceal his morning breath.

"What time is it?"

"Five," she said. Her breath smelled suspiciously of tooth-paste.

"Did you brush your teeth?"

She nodded.

"Did you bring a toothbrush?"

She shook her head.

"Did you use my toothbrush?"

"Correct," said Penny. So the girl who generally abhorred human contact and loathed hugs was not above using some-one's toothbrush without permission. Talk about inconsistent boundary issues.

Sam got up and walked over to the bathroom.

He checked his toothbrush. It was indeed wet. Sam brushed his teeth, washed his face, and ran some water through his hair. He observed his reflection in the mirror. In the early morning he resembled a drug addict on the tail end of a week-long bender. He was sallow with eye bags. Puffy yet skinny. He lifted his shirt. Yep, still sickly. Sam shrugged and took a leak.

He thought about doing some silent push-ups in the bath-room to look swollen and changed his mind. Instead he did two squats and held for about three seconds each.

When he returned, Penny was looking up at his ceiling.

"Don't you want to take a broom handle to it and scrape it off?" She nodded at the popcorn stucco.

"Sometimes."

"Do you know what trypophobia is?"

"Nope," he said.

"It's this condition where you get grossed out or scared of irregular or regular holes or circular patterns. I have that. Your ceiling's freaking me out. Don't do an image search if you think you have it. It's too disgusting."

"Do you know what knot is the one that's impossible to untie?" he asked, recalling his last conversation with Lorraine.

"Are you talking about trefoil knots?"

"No, the myth one."

"Gordian Knot. The one that Alexander the Great had to cut with his sword?"

"I don't know."

"Why are you asking me this?"

He smiled stupidly at her. "I have no idea."

"What time do you have to be at work?" she asked.

"You mean downstairs?"

She nodded.

"I have about an hour," he lied. They were going to have to buy their baked goods for the day.

"Okay, cool. So we can still hang out." She got back into bed and pulled the comforter up. "You know constrictor knots are hard to untie too, especially once tightened."

Sam got back into bed with her, this time taking off his sweatshirt and keeping his T-shirt on.

She stared at him intently while lying on her side. "I can't deal with your ceiling," she explained.

Sam smiled. It gave him a better view anyway.

"You know what I love about you?" she asked.

"My enormous muscles and my sun-kissed glow?"

"Yes," she said. "The second thing I like about you"—Sam noticed that she'd switched "love" to "like"—"is that your brain goes as fast as mine," she said.

"So you like that I remind you of you basically," he said.

They both laughed.

"Exactly."

"Cool."

"No," she tried again. "Most people don't ever know what I'm talking about. Not ever. I don't necessarily know why."

"Well, you start your stories from the epilogue. Plus, none of your questions have anything to do with what's being discussed."

"Neither do yours."

Sam smiled.

"But you know what I'm talking about," she said. "You've known from the day we met. Even on text, where there are no inflections or nuance or tone for non sequiturs. You've always spoken fluent me."

She slugged him on the arm. A meaty little *thwock*. Sam didn't know what to read into it.

"I'm glad you didn't talk about yourself in the third person just then, like 'speaking fluent Penny,'" he said. "That would have been so gnar. What if all I did was—"

Before he could continue, Penny kissed him square on the mouth.

He didn't have time to close his eyes, so he knew that she hadn't closed hers.

Sam stared at her for a moment. Then he went for it.

PENNY.

Kissing Sam was nothing like kissing Bobby or Mark. Not even close. Kissing them was pressing your face up against your own forearm compared to this. Oh man. This. *ThisThisThis.* When she kissed Sam, it was closing your eyes and opening them to find yourself in outer space. Kissing Sam was the universe. It was the Internet. It was a miracle. The part that was most astounding was that her brain switched off to pure white noise, and as she leaned in, she didn't obsess about the mechanics of her tongue or where the rest of her body was in relation to his.

Penny felt the contour of his jaw under her hand and couldn't believe she'd gone this long without touching it. Sam rolled over her, propping himself up so he wouldn't squish her body with his. He hung for a bit and—Oh God—he was so pretty that it was unfathomable that he could even see her. It was inconceivable to Penny that his eyes served any function other than to be admired. He kissed her back with urgency. Her hands traveled around his waist. Sam was startlingly skinny. The slightness was new. His skin was warm and there was a refinement in the economy of his build. Sam's stomach was smooth. Penny wanted to run her fingers up and down her own sides to check what she felt like. She suspected her love handles were too fleshy or lumpy in contrast, but when his hands migrated to her middle, Penny shivered. It felt so good to be this close. Sam fell onto his side, wrapped his leg around hers, and drew her in deeper. It made no difference where he started and she ended. Until it did. When his hands moved under her shirt, she stiffened. Penny didn't have a bra on.

Responding to her hesitation, Sam changed course. He kissed her lightly and moved his hands from her front toward her back. It reminded Penny of when people tripped slightly and started running to pretend they hadn't.

Penny pulled away to get some air. Sam's hair had fallen in his face and his lips were swollen.

"Whoa," he breathed, and rolled onto his back.

Penny wondered what would happen next.

He reached for her hand under the cover.

"So . . . ," he said.

Penny rolled onto her stomach and faced him, admiring his profile. He had an elegant nose. She wished she could explore his body and inspect him. Learn him and memorize him. That way she'd know what to miss when he was gone. Sam was heartbreakingly, hauntingly beautiful. It made her heart hurt. This couldn't end well.

"I think I should go," she said. She didn't know why she said it. Penny wanted to take it back, but that's the thing about certain words. They broke spells. She searched Sam's face for meaning, yet felt too self-conscious to keep staring. Penny wished he would text her about what was going on in his mind, tell her in some way that this made sense.

He sat up, frowned, and then nodded.

· · ·

"Are you kidding me?" When Penny got home, Jude leapt out of bed and rushed to her. She grabbed Penny by the shoulders.

"Where the hell were you?" Jude shrieked.

Penny stared at her. She was mystified that somehow her roommate's rage had built in her absence.

"I thought you were dead. I texted and called." Her blond hair was tied up in a lopsided ponytail, and she was still wearing yesterday's mascara.

Penny grabbed her phone from her back pocket and held it up feebly. "It died," she said.

She examined Jude's face for clues. She looked unglued but not necessarily angry.

"I thought you hated me," Penny reasoned.

"You're an idiot," said Jude, scowling. "Of course I hate you. I'm furious at you. I figured you'd gone to your mom's, but your laptop was here and your charger."

Jude walked over to Penny's desk and pointed. "Then I realized your pouches were here with your backpack, and that's when I started to get hysterical."

She turned to grab her phone off her pillow. "See," she said, showing Penny her outgoing calls. "Six times I called you."

Penny sat on her bed, dazed. "Jude, did you sleep at all?"

"No, asshole," she said.

"Mallory had some guy over, so I got home at one and you weren't here, which is fine. Except then I texted at one thirty and again at three, and when you were still gone, I couldn't sleep. Jesus Christ, Penny, what the F?"

Penny went over to Jude and hugged her fiercely.

"You scared me," said Jude quietly. Penny held her tighter. People scared Penny all the time. Like her mom and even Sam. It meant she loved them.

•   •   •

"The dumbest thing happened," said Penny. They were lying on Jude's bed. "My mom OD'd."

Jude turned to Penny, horrified. "Holy shit. What?"

"No, no, no," Penny corrected. "She's fine. It is the stupidest thing. She overdosed on weed brownies at her birthday dinner, lost her mind, and had to go to the hospital."

Jude fell silent and then erupted into laughter, which made Penny laugh.

"I only got back," she said, skipping over the detail of spending the night at Sam's house and making out with him in the morning and bolting like a dork.

"How is she?" Jude asked. "Poor Celeste."

"She's fine," she said. "I met her shit-kicker boyfriend. Who's handsome, younger than her, and was wearing these insane Lucchese cowboy boots."

Jude smiled. "That's so Texas," she said. "How'd she seem?"

"I didn't see her."

"Penny."

Jude nudged her. "Can you do me a favor? Can you tell me this story the opposite of the way you'd tell it normally? Start at the beginning and don't leave anything out."

"No, that was everything," she said. "Her boyfriend called, said she was in the hospital. I figured you were too pissed to come with me, so . . ." She took a deep breath. "I called Sam and he drove me."

"Okay, Sam we'll get back to," Jude told her. "You should've called me anyway, you know. Possible dead mother calls for a cease-fire. Even you have to know that."

Penny continued. "Anyway, I get down there to discover that in true Celeste form, she was totally fine. She was in the hospital for no reason on her fortieth birthday other than that she's a needy, messy monster."

"Come on," said Jude. "I'm sure she wasn't stoked to be there."

"I don't care!" said Penny. "I've had it. As soon as I heard she wasn't dead, I turned around and came back home."

Jude's mouth hung open.

"You didn't talk to her? After you drove all the way down there?"

Penny shook her head.

"But, Pen, you're the one who ditched her on her birthday."

"I'm over it," said Penny, throwing her hands up. "I'm done worrying about her. She's the mom. I'm sick to death of looking out for her and being paranoid she's going to do something dumb."

If anything, Celeste was lucky she hadn't gone in to visit her. Penny would've strangled her.

"Okay," said Jude. "Well, thank God nothing truly bad happened. We all make mistakes, which, by the way, you might know something about." Jude shot her a meaningful look. "It wouldn't kill you to give your mom a break."

Except that maybe it would.

SAM.

Sam measured out the flour. He hadn't made hamantaschen in a while. Brandi Rose loved the prune ones best, so he was making those. It was time to go see his mother.

As he threw the mixer on low speed, his mind wandered to Penny. Dark eyes. Hands pulling him closer by the belt loops of his jeans. Her breath hot against his throat.

Jeez. *What was that?*

Sam recalled the impossible softness of her skin. The way her hair fanned out on his pillows as if she were floating on top of water.

But then she took off.

Sam didn't know where to go with her and how far. Maybe Penny changed her mind. Maybe she'd tried it out and realized—to her horror—that she'd made a mistake and decided that they were better off as friends.

It would make sense if she were skittish, given the events

of her life. But *she'd* been the one to kiss him first. Sam's mind flashed back to the way her lips yielded to his and the sigh that escaped when his mouth brushed her shoulder.

When the cookies had cooled, Sam drove over to his mother's. He took the left into Forest Park, through a cluster of mobile homes that had been built before the highway in 1964. He wiped his sweating hands onto his jeans.

Sam knew she'd be home. Brandi Rose stayed home most afternoons, ever since she sought early retirement and workman's comp for fibromyalgia—a mysterious rambling pain that assaulted her extremities. Autry, her current boyfriend, took care of her most days.

Sure, Austin had a few kitschy trailer parks, cutesy chrome Airstreams that were rejiggered as Airbnbs or else food trucks and cozy bars where the cocktails cost as much as Sam's pants. Sam's mom's place was nothing like that. The rooms were drafty and the neighbors rowdy, and they only got rowdier when they drank. Which was often.

Sam could see her car in the driveway and rang the bell.

Autry answered. "Sam!" he said, and slapped him on the back. "Honey, it's Sam." Autry was a sometime auto mechanic who was wearing his usual outfit of an undershirt, cargo shorts, and beer in his hand. He was tanned and slender through the limbs with a bowling ball of a booze gut. Autry was a simple happy guy. Though if he put up with Brandi Rose, something had to be going on with him.

Sam followed him into the living room to see that his mother hadn't stirred from her usual spot right in front of the TV. Brandi Rose was angry. Her absorption in her TV watching and the abject lack of effort to glance over betrayed her sentiments. It took real work to ignore someone in such close quarters.

She was smoking a cigarette and drinking a tall glass of bourbon with an iced tea floater. He remembered when he was younger, how Brandi Rose had made the effort to hide the handles of Ten High whiskey. That was, until he'd partially melted a plastic bottle heating up a pizza. Brandi kept them stashed in different places in the house, and one hiding place was the roomy metal drawer under the oven. It had ruined the frozen pizza he'd paid for with the last of his sofa change. Sam left the gnarled, blackened bottle in the sink for her to see. He'd wanted her to be embarrassed. Brandi Rose had started drinking in the open after that.

The screen door opened and clanged shut, signaling another of Autry's walks. That man loved his constitutionals. Talk on the block was that he never wandered far, since he frequently entertained Mrs. Packer, whose husband went to get TP one morning and never returned.

"Hey, Mom," he said. She kept her eyes glued to the demonstration on induction ovens. You could cook a whole chicken—a frozen one—in under fifteen minutes.

The antique, cordless phone was in the pocket of her beige dressing gown. It was eerie. It was as if someone dumped amber over her head like the slime on children's TV shows and preserved her whole. Nothing had changed since he'd left. Kicking her son out of her life hadn't made a lick of difference.

Sam felt sweat sting at his armpits. He tried to look at

something that wasn't depressing. Like the dark brown stain on the carpet that resembled the head of fat Elvis in profile. Or the piles of catalogs that lay collapsed at her feet. Sam slowed his breathing. What he was tempted to do was make a movie about his mom. It would cover depression, addiction, and the poison it becomes when you don't get a handle on any of it.

Sam felt strangely calmer thinking about filming her. Sad yet calm. Distant.

"I made you something." He placed the Christmas tin of fresh cookies in her lap. The tin with gold and white reindeer was hers from when she was a kid. It used to be Sam's stash box, and he'd had to wash it twice to scrub out the stink of burnt weed. "Prune, your favorite."

"You know I almost had to sell the house," Brandi Rose said, finally diverting her attention from the screen. When Sam was very young he remembered how her mouth would move along to the parts of the ads she knew by heart. "Me and Autry were almost homeless after the stunt you pulled."

The stunt he pulled was that he called fraud protection on the credit cards she'd opened in his name.

Sam remembered the bills. His mother had spent four hundred dollars on anti-aging face peels that had literal diamonds in it. Not figurative. Literal diamonds.

Finally, Brandi Rose looked at her son.

Her eyes were dead. Sunken. Her hair had been dark once, but as she got older she'd dyed it a brassy, orangey-red. He realized it was exactly the same color as her bronzed skin. The way her cheeks had collapsed into jowls gave her chin and mouth the hinged appearance of a ventriloquist's dummy's. Brandi Rose's thin lips puckered in disgust at him, as if she'd swallowed a bug.

"I didn't have a choice," Sam said. There was no sense in trying to explain to her that his credit was ruined. That as it stood it was near impossible for him to sign a lease or get loans for school.

"Selfish," she said, turning back to the TV. "What good are cookies when it's cold outside and I don't have a house?"

Sam considered telling her that a residence you could put wheels on didn't quite qualify as a house, and that as far as winters went she could do a lot worse than Texas.

"Share them with Autry," Sam said. "Autry knows his way around a cookie."

His mother didn't say anything else. Sam turned his attention to the magical oven that was cool to the touch and made fruit leather for the kids and if you ordered now you could get a second for your RV half off. Sam was desperate to reach out and place a hand lightly on her shoulder. He knew exactly how the fuzziness of the robe would feel on his palm, the warmth and familiarity. Yet he also knew that if she flinched or pulled away he'd be devastated.

"All right," he said brightly, kissing his mother on the head. "It's nice to see you, Mama. Happy holidays."

Sam couldn't believe Thanksgiving was a week out.

There were dirty dishes in the sink, as usual. Sam thought about washing them and tidying up, maybe cooking something nutritious for her to eat. But it wouldn't make a dent in the guilt he felt or in her resentment. There was a time when he'd thought he could pull them out of this. That he would man up and rescue her and move them someplace nice. But even if he freed her from the trailer, there was nothing he could do about the raging inside-person's headache you get when you watch TV for too many hours in a row and her compulsion to do only that.

"I love you," he whispered to the dishes, and let himself out.

• • •

When Sam got back to House, Jude was waiting for him on the porch swing.

"Hey!" he said brightly.

"Hey," she said.

"I'm sorry," he responded.

"I can see that." Jude extended her long legs forward to see how far the porch swing pitched back. "You look like hell."

"I went to see my mom," he said, taking a seat next to her. "Which is why the next order of business is to smoke this." He held up a cigarette.

"Jeez, that good, huh?"

Sam sighed.

"Did you tell her Fraser's granddaughter says hi?" Jude nudged him in the ribs.

"Who the hell is Fraser?" Sam laughed dryly and lit his smoke when he realized. "You know I only ever knew him as Mr. Lange?"

"Wow," breathed Jude. "That's twisted. Okay, so I've come to a conclusion," she told him.

"Sounds fascinating."

"Promise not to get mad?" Jude cast a sidelong glance at him.

"Nope."

She laughed. "Are you in love with Penny?"

"How is that a conclusion? That's a question."

Jude rolled her eyes. "She says she's in love with you."

"She did not."

"Fine, she didn't say those exact words, but it's the only explanation. She's in love with you."

"Stop," he said. "You know she's inscrutable. You ever notice how she seems furious when she's super excited?"

Jude laughed. "Or when she's actually furious and starts bawling? That's a classic," she responded.

Sam thought about the last time he'd seen her cry. How he'd wanted to place her in a bubble and firebomb everything around her.

"So it was you on her phone."

Sam nodded.

"Why didn't you tell me?"

Sam sighed. He glanced down at the tattoo of a horse head partially covered by cloth on his forearm. It was how they used to train wild horses way back when, throwing fabric over their eyes so they wouldn't get spooked by their surroundings. They'd have to submit to the rider's commands. Surrender.

Sam mulled over everything that had happened in the past month. Lorraine. Penny. What Lorraine had said about everyone knowing he was poor. And how Penny told him no one mistook him for someone who had his shit together. Hiding was not a coping mechanism. It was delusional. He had to let go.

"I should have told you and I'm sorry," he said. "I was dealing with a lot of stuff at the time, and when you showed up here I felt overwhelmed."

"You should have told me," she said.

"Yeah, but I wasn't ready to tell you personal details solely because we were related at one point and thrown together a bunch when we were kids." Sam stubbed his cigarette out and looked at her. "I take longer to warm to people," he said.

Jude nodded again, but this time there were tears in her eyes. She blinked, and they coursed down her cheeks to fall off her chin in fat drops.

"Jude," he said.

"You seemed mad at me or something," she responded.

"I'm not mad at you. Please don't cry."

Jude nodded, and despite the tears, she was smiling. "My therapist says I think everyone's always mad at me. It's equal parts my upbringing and my egocentrism."

Sam laughed.

They rocked the swing in silence.

"The thing is," she continued, "I'm also very perceptive. And I get now why you guys did what you did. Speaking of which, you're both so lucky you have unlimited texting. You know she couldn't even pee without taking her phone into the bathroom? I could hear her laughing in there."

Jude smiled then.

"News flash," she said. "At some point, your girlfriend might have been taking a dump while you were flirting with her."

Sam promptly removed any indication from his brain that Penny pooped.

"She's not my girlfriend," Sam said. His voice cracked on the word "friend," which made both of them laugh.

Jude swatted his arm with the back of her hand. "That's what I don't buy," said Jude. "You guys both say you're friends or whatever, but you kept me in the dark because this is way more than that. Seriously, no heterosexual friends in the history of penises and vaginas are that into each other. Plus, you dress like twins."

"Penny helped me through a dark time," Sam said. "Me and my ex went through this crazy pregnancy scare."

"Whoa," breathed Jude. "MzLolaXO?"

"Her name's Lorraine!"

"Whatever. But she's not pregnant now?"

He shook his head. "We thought she was pregnant, but she wasn't. Or she was technically. It was complicated," he said. "I thought I was in love with her and I wanted so badly to be with her. So I was this completely insane combo of happy and freaked out at the same time."

"Wow," she said, and after a beat, "Can I have a cigarette?"

"Hell no."

"Fine," she replied. "Tell me more."

"You want to know the most psychotic part of it?"

She nodded.

"Part of me was so happy she'd be stuck with me."

"Ew," said Jude. "Like you'd trapped her?"

It was so ugly when it was worded that way.

"I was out of my mind trying to figure out a way to get it under control. I had this panic attack and I thought it was a heart attack. It was insane and scary and I had no one to talk to. That's actually how Penny and I became friends," he said. "Right in the middle of when I thought I was dying, she found me on Sixth Street and took me to the emergency room. You should've seen her. She was so mad at me because she was terrified. She kept reciting these statistics on coronaries and feeding me nuts and making me drink her horchata."

Jude snorted. "Sounds about right."

"I thought that by not telling anyone else, it would make it less real, you know?" he said. "She was my anxiety sponsor, my emergency contact, and it was perfect. The only reason she didn't tell you is because I told her not to. I didn't want you to know about any of this. I didn't want anybody to know."

"I would've made a pretty good anxiety sponsor," she said softly. "You didn't have to blow me off so many times."

"You're right," he told her. "I'm sorry about that."

"You know, I'm going through things too. Believe it or not, I'm not normally this needy. My parents splitting up is a big deal to me. I know you're not a huge fan of my family, but it hurts my feelings that both of you basically pretended not to hear me when I needed to talk." Sam watched his niece's eyes water. Jude seemed so happy and capable that he hadn't considered she might need anything.

Sam wrapped an arm around her shoulders. "You're right," he said again. "I did a shitty job of hearing you."

Jude sniffed. "I need people on my side too, you know."

"Of course you do."

They sat.

Sam thought back to Jude as a buck-toothed kid. It was a miracle she'd turned out so sweet given her upbringing.

"God, I wish Penny were here," she said. "I need a tissue."

They laughed. Sam wished she were there too. He had no idea what the hell he'd say to her.

Jude leaned over and jabbed him in the ribs. "I know you're a real person or whatever, but, Sam," she said, "you're not that old. You're basically a kid too. You've got your best screwing-up years ahead of you." She nudged him with her leg. "So everything's okay with Lola?"

"Lola's swell."

"And what about Penny who's in love you?"

Sam laughed. "I don't know that it's a thing," he said. "Me and Penny, we're friends. Good friends. I put her through so much already, between talking her ear off about me and Lorraine. She knows everything about me, even the terrible stuff, and I don't know . . ."

Sam thought about the kiss.

Penny's pink, coaxing mouth was insane in real life. Out of the metal box. In meatspace on Planet Earth. Her lips were so full that it was as if they were smushed under glass. And her skin. And how she'd looked as she'd appeared to realize how *incorrect* it all was and sprinted from his room. He felt a tightening in his chest.

"Nobody knows anything," said Jude. "But you know how Penny's from a different planet?"

Sam nodded.

"So if you like that one, where the hell else are you going to find another one?"

PENNY.

As far as Penny was concerned she deserved an award for making it to any of her courses. She sat in J.A.'s class in a daze. If she hadn't sent in new pages yesterday, she would have ditched.

This was it. It was time. And I was ready. Tonight would bring the culling, the beginning of the Forfeiture, when I would refuse to lay down my life. In preparation I'd convinced Mother to stay here with me. Four days. It was her longest stay yet and I could feel the quickening. I was becoming more powerful the more tired she became. Our interlacing was complete, yet she worried about me, my behavior, why it seemed that I, her Anima, had turned on her during a time when we should feel closest. When she departed for the un-here, I was confident she'd be back. By now I could move around in the game of my own accord. I didn't have to wait for her or heed her.

Animas never misbehaved. There was trickery, yes, rather an impish naughtiness at times, but an outright revolt didn't exist in the gameplay. Until I made it exist. Mother became increasingly devoted to me the more unpredictably I behaved. On the morning of the Forfeiture she was agitated. Distracted. Almost incoherent. She spoke of other responsibilities and of duty. Mere hours before we would depart for Soludos, embarking on the lair of dragons, she left again. Again she promised she'd return. And again I followed her into the light and voices. It was mayhem. I heard sobbing. An animalistic howl. Mother was crying. There was another baby. An Anima in the "un-here" they called Love. And Love was dead.

"Finally," said J.A., tapping the printouts with her pen. She rose from her seat in her tiny office, applauding slowly and dramatically in a golf clap. "We've arrived at the first person. I was wondering when you'd start telling the story from inside the Anima."

"You could have given me a hint." Penny was bushed. Drained. Completely wrung out.

"Come on," said J.A., smiling. "Professors don't give cheat codes."

Penny shambled home. The light was too bright, and her body, which had been fine in the AC of the classroom, now felt shellacked in a sticky film. She was thrilled at the prospect of blowing off her afternoon labs.

When she arrived at Kincaid, Celeste was waiting for her in the lobby. Sunglasses, hat, shorts, alone. Penny almost wept from disbelief. She wanted to sleep for a year.

"Hi," said Celeste, standing up shakily and removing her shades. Her eyes were ringed in red, and her mouth was already twitchy with imminent tears.

"Jeez, Mom," she said. "Are you allowed to drive in your condition?"

Penny felt the familiar crawl of brittle rage. She knew it came from concern and love, except it made her want to shake her mother and the nurses and doctors and Michael for letting her travel an hour out of town on her own. When would this woman stop scaring the living daylights out of her simply by existing?

Celeste glanced at her tentatively, as if she was unsure of whether or not she was allowed to touch her daughter, and Penny's resolve broke. Her heart splintered into smithereens.

"Happy birthday, Mom." Penny hugged her.

"I love you," she said raggedly in Penny's arms.

"Let's go upstairs," Penny said. Celeste sniffled and nodded. Penny corralled her into the elevator.

"Mike said you came by the hospital last night," Celeste said when they got inside the room.

"Yeah."

"That's Mike, by the way."

"I didn't know there was a Mike." Penny handed her mother her mini go bag. Celeste nodded appreciatively, grabbed a tissue, and sat on her bed.

"You would have if you'd asked. He said you didn't want to see me." The waterworks picked up steam.

"I should have come to your dinner," Penny said, pacing. "Maybe if I was around I could have stopped you and your ridiculous friends from doing something so . . ." Penny shook her head violently. It still boggled her mind that her own mother was dumb enough to screw up marijuana. It was so embarrassingly juvenile, yet somehow also old and clueless.

Celeste's dark eyes scanned her daughter's face. "Penny, why are you so angry with me?"

"I'm not angry with you." She perched on her desk, refusing to sit next to her.

The words felt hard and foreign in her mouth. Her brain raged.

Penny imagined herself telling Celeste everything, spewing out all the shame and confusion about what had happened downstairs as Celeste slept. Penny wanted to deposit the pain where she felt it belonged—with her mother. Penny longed to see Celeste's face contort in shock or disbelief or guilt and watch her eyes change as her thoughts locked in place and she understood once and for all that it was her fault. And that she could never look at her daughter the same way again.

"Why do you get to be the irresponsible one all the time?" she asked.

"I don't know what to tell you." Celeste sighed. "People make mistakes. I can't make every decision in my life based on whether or not it'll upset you."

"Oh, I know," Penny told her. "When have you *ever* made any decisions based on my feelings?" Penny wanted nothing more than to power down. "Why are you here?"

"Because you don't come home!" Her mother stood, finally

getting mad. "And God forbid you ever call. I thought you were going to school an hour away so that I could still see you once in a while."

"Mom." Penny cut her off. "I have homework. I can't do this now."

"No. I want to talk about this," Celeste said. "While you were growing up I waited for it, waited for the day you'd hate me, because I know that's how it goes with daughters and their moms. There's this phase."

"I don't hate you, Mom."

"But you do. I don't know when it happened and I don't know what I did. I only know you don't like me very much." Celeste's voice broke. "I know we're different," she continued. "I don't make the kinds of jokes that you find funny. I get motion sickness when I read comic books because I can't read and look at pictures at the same time. But I'm tired of you treating me as if I'm this nuisance in your life."

Celeste sat back down. "I paid for all this." She gestured toward the room. "I work hard to make sure that you have everything you ever need. I know I mess up all the time. I know you're mad that it's only the two of us, and I get mad about that too. You can think whatever you want about your dad skipping out on me, but you know what? He's crazy for missing out on you. Because you're the best. But you don't get to hate me for it."

It was the most Celeste had ever said on the topic. Tears coursed down Penny's cheeks.

"I know things are bad," sobbed Celeste. "But you don't get to punish me if you don't tell me what I did, if you don't tell me how to make it right."

Penny eyed her mother and felt her heart harden. The desire to protect her and the impulse to hurt her were mystifying. Penny's head throbbed.

Celeste reached out to touch her hand. Penny let her and her anger deflated. Finally, she wept.

"I did my goddamned best," Celeste said.

"Do you know how terrifying it is to be your kid?" Penny bawled. "I don't know if you're going to make rent. Or if you're going to get murdered by some stranger that you're being way too nice to. I had to be the adult. I had to fend for myself and for you. It was so stressful all the time. Why do you think I had an ulcer in middle school?"

"Oh, honey." Celeste pulled her in for a hug. "Penny, at a certain point I don't know how much of that's me and how much of it's you." She rocked her daughter. "You were an intense kid. So smart and thoughtful and so far into your own head. During your first week of school I got a note from your art teacher saying you had an anxiety attack when you couldn't finish your drawing.

"I said to myself, man, this kid has to lighten up. Only I didn't know how to make you do that. The thing is, being your mom feels an awful lot like having a roommate move in. Ever since you were an infant, you were fully formed in what you liked and didn't and what you wanted to spend your days doing. Most of the time it had nothing to do with me and I had to get over that."

"Well, not everyone can be a hippie-dippy free-flow freak show," Penny lamented. "Do you know how it is to live inside my head? Do you know how much worry I carry around? The amount of math I'm constantly doing to make sure that we'll stay alive and be safe?"

"You know you're still alive, right?" Celeste said, clutching Penny's shoulders. "That I kept you alive even when you were a baby and hadn't yet developed these incredible instincts that you think saved you these past years and this magical computer brain of yours? It's a team effort, Penny. It has been since the start."

Penny's sinuses stung. The pressurized anger that had built up at the bottom of her heart to push up against the backs of her eyeballs was finally out. Her electrolytes would be shot when this was over.

"You're not some miracle of science, Penny," said Celeste. "You have to give me some credit." Celeste continued to cradle her. "And look at us. We're fine. We're a little messy, but we're so great."

With Celeste's smeared makeup, she resembled a watercolor. Penny could feel her own heartbeat in her eyes.

"No, we're not," moaned Penny. "I don't have anyone other than you."

Her mother sighed. "That's your favorite complaint," she said. "Even when you were teeny-tiny, you moaned that you didn't have any friends."

Celeste rocked her slightly. "But there were loads of kids who wanted to be your friend that you disqualified for one reason or another. Remember Allison Spector? In second grade you were friends, and then one day you dismissed her after you decided she was boring."

"Yeah," breathed Penny. "She was painfully *not* smart."

Celeste laughed. "I bet you have a lot of people," she said.

"You've got to understand that not everybody's going to be exactly your kind of person. They're not going to be completely satisfactory or meet your myriad qualifications."

Penny sighed. Celeste was right. She thought about what Mallory said about how her mom would feel if she'd heard the things she'd said about her. If Jude or Mallory heard her disavow their friendship they'd be hurt. Sam too.

Ugh. Sam.

"You're a particular petunia," she said. "And that's okay. It's good to have high standards. I worry because you hold yourself against these standards too. You're way too hard on yourself. This analysis and thinking and plotting and figuring out, it's stopping you from living your life. Just be, Penny. Don't push people away."

"I think I pushed someone away," said Penny. "But it wasn't on purpose."

"Was he cute?"

Penny rolled her eyes. "Mom."

Celeste nudged her daughter in the ribs. "Well, was he?"

Penny laughed. "Yeah," she said. "You've met him—Sam."

"The guy from the coffee shop?"

Penny nodded.

"Stop. The one with the tattoos?"

Penny nodded again.

"Are you on birth control?"

"What? Mom. We're not sleeping together. I'm in love with him."

"Oh, thank God, because, Penny, that isn't a boy. That's an actual man."

"Mom seriously, stop," said Penny. They sat on her bed. Her pillows were so soft and enticing.

Celeste sighed. It had been a long night for both of them.

"Mom?"

"Yes, baby?"

Penny took a deep breath. "How do you know if you're in love?" Penny snuck a peek at her mom and could practically hear the *AWWWWWWW* in her head and Care Bear stares flying out of her eyes.

"Okay, hmm . . ." Her mother tightened her embrace. "You know how I know?"

If there was anything Celeste was good for, it was exactly this.

"I know I love someone when I can't remember what they look like in any real way. I can never seem to recall whether they're handsome or ugly or if other people think they're cute. All I know is that when I'm not with them and I think about them, where their face should be is this big cloud of good feelings and affection."

"Ugh," said Penny. "*That's* how you know? I thought you would have a comprehensive list or something."

Her mother laughed. "It doesn't work that way at all," she said. "It's more this undeniable mood. It's this warm, familiar, and exciting feeling where you miss them already when you're with them."

That sounded right.

Not being with Sam was excruciating.

STILL PENNY.

Penny dozed with her mom the way they used to when she was little, facing each other but not touching. Penny wanted to inch over and huff the familiar mom smell deep into her lungs and hold it there. Truth was, before everything went wrong, Penny had slept in her mom's bed all the time when she lived at home. She hadn't realized how much she'd missed it.

She stared up at her ceiling. Mallory was right. Her mom needed to be milked. Penny had to stop working herself up thinking it was a bigger deal than it was. Especially since Penny missed Celeste and wanted to see her. Her mother's eyes were closed. It hurt Penny's heart how much she loved her. How scared she'd been when Michael called. Loving someone was traumatizing. You never knew what would happen to them out there in the world. Everything precious was also vulnerable.

It wasn't Celeste's fault. What happened to Penny was nobody's fault but Bobby's. And one day when Penny could find the words, she'd tell her mom. Celeste might not say all the right things right away. She might say a bunch of wrong things in a row for a while, but they'd find a way to talk again. Penny had to give her a chance. She had to let Celeste in. That's how it worked.

Penny grabbed her phone and scrolled through the list of notes she'd made about her story.

Mother and the Anima were connected and loved each other, but whereas the Anima couldn't thrive unless she left Mother, Mother would be destroyed without her.

Penny tapped out a few lines.

> *Escape.*
>
> *It's all I think about. I don't know how I got the idea. Or when. I didn't know that these flashes of information were even thoughts. Until I did. And that they belonged to me. It was my voice talking to my self except I didn't have to make a sound. There was something else, too. Curiosity. I started wondering. I wanted more. Things I didn't know and hadn't seen or heard. I don't want to stay here. I want to go. I love my home. The realms seem infinite, alive with possibility, but when Mother goes, everything goes dark with her. I want a world where everything lights up because I'm in it.*

The Anima didn't want the human baby to die. She didn't wish ill on the parents either. Or the PC bang or anyone else in that world. It's that she didn't believe that humans deserved to live more than she did. Than anyone else in the game.

The Animas were second-class to the players and arguably to the humans. But it didn't have to be that way. The humans were just visitors. Tourists at best. Colonists at worst. Penny thought about how certain physicists believed that reality is a simulation created by future civilizations purely for entertainment. There was no way to know who was running the show. To be the hero, you had to decide it was you.

Penny typed furiously into her phone, and when a message came in she swiped it away before it broke her train of thought. When she was done she took a peek at her mom. Celeste's eyes sprang open as if sensing her daughter was awake in the room.

The text was from Sam.

Penny texted him back.

Hey

He hit her back immediately.

Hey
What are you up to?

My mom's here
napping

Went to see Brandi Rose

Penny couldn't believe that after months of silence that Sam would visit.

WHAT?

Just drove over there

WHOA
How was it

Not as bad as it could have been
Where are you?

At home

Home as in home home or your
room?

Room

And your mom's there?

Yeah she drove up
We talked about it
It's cool now

Good
That makes me happy

Wait
Where are you?

I'm outside

Outside outside or outside my room?

She leapt to her feet. Her mom cocked her head as if to say, "What's up?"

Penny could hear laughing outside her door.

Who is that? Celeste mouthed at her daughter.

Outside your room

Penny's brain went into DEFCON 1. She searched Celeste's face helplessly.

What to do when Sam, actual Sam, visits you in your room while Celeste is also present:
1. Hoist Celeste out the window. She's a resilient woman and you're only two floors up.
2. Send Sam away and spend more quality time with your mother who birthed you and had a horrible birthday. A birthday that you missed.
3. Just go very silent and hope Sam will forget that you responded to any of this.

Penny's mouth was dry. She crept to the bathroom quietly to brush her teeth.

"Mom," she whispered over the foam. "It's Sam." Penny's eyes felt spicy and bloodshot from the cry-nap.

At that, Celeste did something so knowing and awesome that Penny suspected she did have a better handle on parenting than she'd ever given her credit for.

Her mother's eyes widened as she quietly gathered her cardigan, sunglasses, and purse.

Penny smiled with the toothpaste foam dripping. "I love you," she said. "I so owe you."

"You so do," responded Celeste, heading for the door.

The prospect of Celeste and Sam seeing each other again made Penny feel hopelessly awkward. Plus, she didn't need Celeste to see anything revealing or odd if Sam was there to tell Penny something she absolutely didn't want to hear. Penny's phone continued to buzz.

> *Should I come back?*
> *I'm sorry I can hear you freaking*
> *out in there*
> *I can come back*

"No!" she yelled. Penny spat into the sink, wiped her mouth, smoothed her hair, and cracked open the door.

"Hi," she said. Cheesing. "I look insane."

"Hi," he said. "You look . . ." He took a step back to admire her. "Incredible."

Penny was smiling so forcefully her cheeks were about to cramp.

Sam was standing in the hall wearing his usual goth ensemble. With his backpack. "Can I come in?"

"Uh, yeah," said Penny. "Hang on a second." Celeste hugged

her and made a big show of covering her eyes as she walked past Sam.

"I'm not even here," she said.

"Hi, Celeste," said Sam. "Happy birthday."

"Thanks," she said, still facing away from them. "Take care of this one."

"Sure thing."

Penny watched her mother walk down the hall.

"I love you!" Penny called out. Celeste waved over her shoulder without glancing back.

"Okay, now hold on for an additional second," Penny said, and shut the door. She whipped her head around quickly to make sure there wasn't anything mortifying in plain sight. Like any Jude food remnants or econo-size boxes of tampons. Penny shoved Jude's dirty socks into her shoes and kicked them under her bed. Then she opened the door all the way.

"I see we employ the same interior decorator," Sam said, surveying the barren premises.

"Worth every cent," Penny croaked. "Hi." She cleared her throat.

"Hi," Sam said back.

"Is everything okay?" she asked him.

He smiled.

"Everything doesn't have to be a crisis, Penny," he said. Penny wasn't so sure.

She wanted to sit on her bed, only she wasn't sure if she could take him sitting on her bed with her if he was delivering bad news. So instead Penny stood in the middle of the

room, like a normal human lady in a casual situation, and clenched her hands into fists. She could feel her heart in her palms.

"I have something to tell you," Sam said, standing uneasily in front of her.

"Are you going somewhere?" she asked, nodding at the backpack. "Is it something to do with Brandi Rose?"

"Dude," he said, and laughed.

Shit. Penny was fairly certain that when a guy called you "dude," it was because he didn't want to see you naked ever.

"Have you ever called me 'dude' before?"

Penny wasn't sure why she was talking.

"Wow," he said. "Sometimes talking to you is like accidentally clicking on a pop-up with autoplay video."

Penny smiled weakly. "Sorry. Continue."

"I want to get through what I want to say and then it'll be your turn," said Sam. "Is that okay?"

Penny nodded.

"I don't . . . ," he said, and then stopped. "So I don't think I want to be friends with you anymore. I want to kill the pact."

Penny blinked back tears, hoping that her eyelashes could dam the flow at least until she could kick him out. This was it, the moment they both knew would come. At least she did. It was the day Sam grew out of talking to her. It was how Christopher Robin didn't need Winnie-the-Pooh when he became a grown-up. God, how she'd wept when she discovered the ending. Penny wondered if that's what happened in *Calvin & Hobbes* too but couldn't remember. Penny hated whenever you could see Hobbes as a doll since it killed the

magic. God. Penny didn't want to be friends with Sam either. It was too emotional.

She took a deep breath.

"Good," said Penny. "Because I completely agree. We're definitely getting too codependent, right? I mean, how much workshopping can we honestly do for each other? It's not as if you need my mom drama on top of your mom drama. It's way too taxing. For both of us. Especially since we have so much homework. Emotional homework. Oh, and real home-work for me. I have so much of all the homeworks."

"You think we're codependent?" Sam asked her. He frowned and ran his hands through his hair.

Penny nodded. She thought about how she'd invited this. Invoked it. By summoning Sam out of her phone, she had hastened this evolution. They could have stayed in suspended animation forever if she hadn't appeared in front of him so many times. Pried open the portal and insisted her body through. Penny gazed longingly at Sam's skinny legs. His bony arms. Oh God, she loved everything.

Whatever. Maybe this was good. This could be great for her story. Knowing about real heartbreak is useful. Maybe this was her inciting incident. Her saga would go on. She would persist. At least Penny had Jude and her mom and Mallory. God, was she at the point of counting Mallory as a good thing?

Her brain was short-circuiting.

Penny shook her head. To her horror, she was crying. "I'm not crying cause I'm sad," she said angrily, swiping her tears.

"Which is it, then? Are you hungry? Or real, real mad?"

"I don't know," muttered Penny.

"Um, okay," he said. "I don't know where you're at or what you're thinking, and I don't know if there's a configuration of words that if I get right will make you see me differently."

Sam wiped his hands on his jeans and continued.

"I know I relied on you for an awful lot when we were basically strangers. It's because I trusted you and I don't trust a lot of people. I'm like you like that, real choosy with humans. I was going through a lot of change and you were my emergency contact through all of it, even when I didn't have a lot to give back. And it can't have been a picnic, you know?"

Sam ran his fingers through his hair again and swallowed. "God," he said. "I wish I could text you what I want to say."

Penny smiled tightly and braced herself.

"I know I've been kind of a bum deal," he continued.

Penny willed him to shut up. Just not do whatever he was about to.

"No, you haven't," she said. "You've been a real pal. I get a lot out of you. I trust you right back. You speak fluent me. I've got no complaints. I love . . . I like knowing that you exist. It doesn't make me feel any less lonely, because life is lonely, but it makes me feel a lot less alone."

"Jesus," he breathed. "I got you something." He rummaged through his backpack and handed her a mug. Inside it was a teddy bear wearing sunglasses, and he was holding a handful of daisies.

"What?"

"Right?" said Sam hopefully.

Penny started laughing. "Wow," she said, turning it over. It immediately reminded her of Mark's single red rose. She'd chucked it in the garbage on her drive back. It was clear, karma was a bitch and she was getting payback for the way she'd treated Mark. Sam was closing the loop.

Sam laughed. "It's the grossest one they had," he said. "And guess what?"

"What?" she asked him.

"Later, I'm going to make you a mixtape."

"Wait." Penny shook her head, still confused.

Sam was smiling. Penny smiled stupidly back.

"And then we are going to play miniature golf."

The car dealership windsock in her heart stirred and began swaying in the wind.

"Or a hay ride, if you'd prefer . . ."

Her heart was dancing now. Full-on spaz mode.

"And then we're going on a picnic and we're going to make out the whole time," he said. "If that's what you want." Sam cleared his throat.

Penny took a half step closer to him and cleared her throat. She was so excited she wanted to punch him.

"Yeah?"

He took the mug, placed it on her desk, and reached for her hand.

"Yeah," he said. "And it's going to be ridiculous."

ACKNOWLEDGMENTS.

Whoa. I can't believe I get to write acknowledgments. It's wild. Meow.

Okay.

The first person I want to thank is Sam. IRL Sam. My Sam, whose tattoos I stole and who I love so much it makes me weepy. You are my favorite EC.

My family, for being rad and supportive even though I won't hear the end of how I thanked Sam first. My brother, Mike, who won't like being lumped in with my family. Yo, I'm SO glad we're not lawyers.

My agent, Edward Orloff, who tore through this and sold it at a time when I wasn't even sure it was a book. You give such good note and I can't wait for what's next. I hope I make you rich someday. Also, lol, you were SO RIGHT about not calling it "crazies."

Zareen. I knew from jump that I wanted to work with you. Thank you for being singular in your reads and for speaking fluent me at all times. Our rants are so fortifying.

Justin, Anne, Chrissy, Lisa, Alexa, Mekisha, and everyone at Simon & Schuster. Oh, and Lizzy and gg, for a cover that melts my face. That rose gold is so clutch. And the hair! Swoons.

Marshall! You are my first reader. Always. And I yours. We are . . .

Anne, Asa, Suze, Rose—your eagle eyes and perspective are so valuable. Thank you for suffering the unceremonious homework dumps.

Jenna, for the walks, talks, teas, and the voice memos. So many vms that hold me down and keep my anxious brain from flying away.

Trish, the keeper of my time capsule and the OG EC circa HK. Love you.

Ubakum, Mira, Lara & Sophia, Ahmad—thanks for letting me hang out and for talking to me about how much space your phones take up in your lives. And Caitlin, for assigning the *Wired* piece that let me chill with teens in the first place.

Books are so wild and I didn't get to write one until I had so much support. In no particular order thank you to my editorial families for keeping me fed. Noah Callahan-Bever, Elliott Wilson, SHR, Vanessa Satten, Brian Scotto, Choire and Balk, Adam Rogers, Isabel Gonzalez, Sarah Van Boven, Ross Andersen, the Mass Appeal squad, *Complex*, *XXL*, *The Awl*, *Wired*, *GQ*, *The Fader* (the Zeichner years), *Billboard*, *The New York Times*, especially the Op Ed desk. And *Missbehave*, for breaking my back and my heart but giving me my voice.

Dave Bry, who once told me it totally made sense that I wanted to write a book more than I wanted to have a kid.

Eddie, I know you know that I know the role you play. I finally made the bet. FINALLY.

Marc Gerald, for telling me to shut up and write YA already.

Dana and Minya, for their calming energies and wisdom. Jenny Han, for putting up with my DMs.

Vice News Tonight. Thanks for being nice to me despite my punk-ass writing schedule. Brendan Kennedy—you are the best when I am doing the most. IT IS TIME.

La Croix in this order: pamplemousse, coconut, tangerine.

And for all the people waiting for permission to level up enough before they start working on something big and scary—just go in. Don't be like me.

Finally, if you're wondering if it counts and it feels like it counts, it counts.